SATURNALIA
An Anthology of Bizarre Erotica

Paul Scott is an editor of erotic fiction.

SATURNALIA

An Anthology of Bizarre Erotica

Edited by Paul Scott

This book is a work of fiction.
In real life, make sure you practise safe sex.

First published in 2002 by
Nexus
Thames Wharf Studios
Rainville Road
London W6 9HA

Editorial Sections Copyright © Paul Scott 2002

Catullus Translation Copyright © John Porter 2002

The right of Paul Scott to be identified as the Author of this Work has been asserted by him in accordance with the Copyright, Designs and Patents Act 1988.

www.nexus-books.co.uk

Typeset by TW Typesetting, Plymouth, Devon

Printed and bound by
Mackays of Chatham PLC

ISBN 0 352 33717 6

All characters in this publication are fictitious and any resemblance to real persons, living or dead, is purely coincidental.

This book is sold subject to the condition that it shall not, by way of trade or otherwise, be lent, resold, hired out or otherwise circulated without the publisher's prior written consent in any form of binding or cover other than that in which it is published and without a similar condition including this condition being imposed on the subsequent purchaser.

To Jeannette,
for inspiration and perspiration

Contents

Introduction

Our Aim is to Satisfy

If you've picked up this strange beast of a book, you may be wondering exactly what the intention behind it is. Putting it broadly, it aims to present a sampler of erotic, surreal and mind-broadening writing about sex of a kind which has, for one reason or another, made it into mass-market bookshops only sporadically since its publication.

What follows by way of editorial by no means pretends to be academically rigorous, nor to offer a comprehensive social history, but should give a context to the choice of extracts presented here. When Nexus began publishing erotic fiction in 1988, it followed a tradition established by Star Books and the Olympia Press around two decades before. As the cultural stoicism engendered by the demands and domestic horrors of World War II began to dissipate in Britain and the US, successive groups, made up of the young and the independent-minded, questioned received notions of duty and sexual self-denial. They'd had sex for its own sake, and lived to tell the tale. The ban on *Lady Chatterley's Lover* had been lifted in 1963, and Star enjoyed unexpected commercial success, first with the works of writers such as Marco Vassi in the early 1970s, then with Anaïs Nin's *Delta of Venus* in 1977. It was apparent that there was a ready market for licentious, sensual writing which was more sexually direct than the florid and inexplicit prose of romance novels.

The purpose of the latter, then as now, is to offer the life-affirming feelgood factor that wish-fulfillment brings. The function of the former is to offer a far more focused experience. Whether erotic fiction is actually read with one hand, or much as one would read any other book, its aim is obviously to gratify, much as a thriller should thrill. But it can also play with the very notion of gratification while keeping sight of its primary purpose.

In the late 1960s, the sexual revolution was supposedly in full effect. TV documentaries are forever telling us, over stock footage of the human be-in in San Francisco's Golden Gate Park, or else the Rolling Stones' Hyde Park concert, how a new generation were rediscovering sex for its own sake, outside the context of marriage and procreation.

Never mind that the earliest high-dosage contraceptive pills allegedly piled on the pounds and arguably induced depression, or that many a lank-haired Lothario shamed a girl into bed with the thought that she wouldn't want to be seen as 'uptight'. For every epiphanic in-body, out-of-body experience of the beautiful kind there must have been an exponential number of unsatisfactory, stoned humps in bedsits, squats and VWs. It must have been a great time if you had a fetish for cheesecloth, BO and armpit hair.

And that was among the 'enlightened'. There's a revisionism that pervades cultural history, as it's popularly presented, which suggests that at any given time, a majority of people behaved in the fashion being documented, at least when dealing with the trends history has favoured. That a majority of white British youth, for example, was gobbing and pogoing to the Pistols in 1977 rather than, more accurately, wearing flares and listening to Kate Bush. Likewise with the 1960s. In fact, of course, Britain in particular was still a country of limited access to sexual material, where the closest one would get to pornography with moving images were the grainy stag films shown in private cinema clubs, where *Health and Efficiency* fulfilled the function of a pornographic magazine, and where acquiring contraception was a predominantly male pursuit which most likely required an unnecessary haircut.

In that context, it's easy to see why erotic fiction enjoyed success. Sex sold, and there was really little alternative to the printed word. Sex itself, whether good or bad, had a rebellious cachet for the sons and daughters of the hard-grafting, pleasure-deferring middle-classes, never mind that the horse-racing classes, upper and lower, had always known how to have fun. Those same sons and daughters maintained their parents' belief in the virtue of reading, though. After all, books, even in our technological age, remain the chief means of education, portable thought-packages for the material world, the promissory notes of a once-oral culture. Books are de facto respectable, and those who couldn't bring themselves to 'stoop' to visual pornography felt comfortable using them. By that happy concatenation erotic fiction, by the standards of the publishing industry of the time, boomed.

And it still thrives today. At the turn of a new century, Nexus publishes two wholly original novels per month, as well as reissuing a classic from the list that's out of print at the time. That's thirty-six books per year, distributed throughout the English-speaking world, and the question we face is not *if* each one will sell out its print run but *when*. And of course we're not the only publisher on the block with such an imprint, either.

So why, in this increasingly visual and technological age, does erotic fiction flourish more than ever? A quick internet search on any engine will reveal more porn sites than you can, well, shake a stick at, and there are enough with comprehensive free previews to offer a rewarding internet experience without even ever subscribing to one. In the UK, at the time of writing, most newsagents will sell you any number of well-produced – and quite specific – porn mags for around three pounds, and twenty pounds will buy you a video or DVD. In the latter media, an increasing number of sexual interests are catered for, from the playfully naughty 'splosh' genre to the most ritualised SM. Nonetheless, erotic writing not only survives but thrives, particularly in the US, where there are any number of websites and resources for the erotic author.

Its continued popularity is perhaps puzzling in a visual age such as our own, but there are a number of factors at work. Firstly, women have embraced the form both as consumers and writers more than ever in the last decade or so. The style to be found in a modern Black Lace novel, for example, is gutsy, hip and direct compared to the more florid and euphemistic style of old-school romance writing. The popularity of a comedy of sexual manners like *Sex and the City*, and the growth of women's sex shops, show just how much the debate has moved on, through the pioneering writings of feminists such as Pat Califia and Anita Philips, since the moralistic, Dworkinite stance espoused in many a students' union bar during the 1980s. That brand of anti-sex feminism, however much it was intended to liberate, made a number of women ashamed of their sexual instincts, and in effect – at least socially if not intellectually – played into the pre-existing distinction between inviolate Madonna and sluttish, fair-game whore that did and still does typify a less than evolved brand of straight male thinking. As the poet Fiona Pitt-Kethley puts it, it doesn't make you cheap if you are free. The difference in attitude between that of this millennium and twenty years or so ago is perhaps even as great as that between the Interregnum and the Restoration of the English monarchy in 1660.

Secondly, there's the pleasing way that erotic fiction allows the imagination to take flight. Watching a porn film, the viewer is given no escape from the location that's there on a perceptual plate before them, whether it's an LA motel room, an office space in the heartland of Germany, or wherever. Likewise with the studio or location shoots that typify porn magazines. Reading any genre of fiction, by contrast, involves the pleasurable process of bringing one's own imagination to bear on narrative. As readers, we all picture John Jarndyce's house in *Bleak House*, or the Congolese river of *Heart of Darkness*, differently, made up of composites of what we've experienced directly in our own lives. So it is with erotic fiction. It kick-starts the imagination, allows us to direct our own scenes, in a way that visual material can't, and permits us to indulge our personal visions of the erotic, perhaps our private visions of alternative beauty too. What could be more appropriate, for a masturbatory medium, than having to do half the work oneself!

Thirdly, erotic fiction, when well executed, is never bland, in contrast to much soft porn of the tits-and-ass variety. It's surely only the most intellectually challenged who can fail to feel patronised by what passes for copy in most top-shelf magazines, which, inadvertently perhaps, still subscribe to the implicit notion that you must be a social and mental inadequate to resort to having one off the wrist, and that masturbation is second best – rather than a qualitatively different experience that doesn't bear comparison with it – to having sex with another individual. Erotic fiction, by contrast, understands this: that much about sexual arousal is situational. It offers what visual pornography never can – access to a character's inner experience. And after all in the real world, it's the qualities of a partner's sexual response which endear them to us as much as whatever characteristics drew us to them in the first place.

As the mainstream porn industry continues to offer new and more affordable products and services, erotic fiction focuses ever more on the sadomasochistic, edgy and extreme, and it can without compunction. No one is exploited in its production, because no one in an erotic novel really exists. If this sounds facile and socially irresponsible, I should point out that we don't condone non-consensual behaviour in the books we commission, since they're written to arouse, nor anything that glorifies or encourages genuine hurt and suffering. Apart from the question of responsibility, it results in unchallenging, unsatisfying prose, since the challenge for the author is often to bring a character to a place of weirdness or extremity through their own volition, and to do so plausibly. Motivation and character are as important in this genre as in any other. Nonetheless, erotic fiction has found its niche catering for tastes which are popularly held to be marginal, even though the thriving fetish scene and the fetish influences which can be seen in advertising, fashion, film and TV, particularly in Europe, would suggest otherwise.

As such, it can cater for the outsider in all of us, the dark heart of the imagination which we fail to acknowledge at our peril. There's a pejorative quality about the word 'vanilla' when used to describe straightforward (as opposed to straight) sex, since it remains at the summit of most people's sexual experience after all, but I'll use it here as shorthand. It's hard to imagine now how in the 1960s vanilla sex itself could be seen as an act of rebellion. We live in an age when to be sexually active is part and parcel of being a good consumer, and almost mandatory. Not to be bothered with sex at all is now commonly seen more as weird than virtuous. We primp and preen ourselves with overpriced products and squeeze and shoehorn ourselves into fashionable gear, shoring ourselves against our insecurities and, in pursuit of sexual companionship, spending our way out of economic recession! It's all rather fun, of course, but occasionally bland. In this context, erotic fiction is a genre which accommodates the weird and perceivedly marginal, and can help reclaim the intimate as a place of originality and actual self-determination.

This collection acknowledges some of those who have influenced the craft of edgy, erotic writing, established its frame of reference and some of its 'stock' characters, and continue to provide inspiration for its writers today. I apologise unreservedly for the fact that every featured author is a man. That's a reflection of the social iniquities, in education and opportunity, of the periods during which these works were created. We're planning further volumes of *Saturnalia*, and so I hope to have the opportunity to redress the balance, at least partly, in the future. Enjoy!

Paul Scott
London 2002

I'll jam it up your ass and down your throat,
fairy Aurelius and queen Furius,
you who've deduced from my little poems,
because they're somewhat soft and sensual, that I'm not quite proper.
I'll admit that the godly poet ought to be modest of behaviour himself,
but there's no need for his *poems* to be –
those only have wit and charm
if they *are* somewhat soft and sensual and not quite proper
and have something in them that might arouse an itch,
not in boys, but in those shaggy greybeards
who can scarcely move their sluggish members.
You two, because of what you read about those
many thousands of kisses, do you think me less than a man?
I'll jam it up your ass and down your throat.

Catullus (1st century BC)

Giovanni Boccaccio (1313–1375)

Laughter in the Dark

I'll spare you the GCSE cribsheet, but Geoffrey Chaucer produced some of the finest writing one can ever read. Of any writer of the Early Modern period, Boccaccio was the one he was most influenced by. He based 'The Knight's Tale' on the Italian's *Il Teseida*, and 'The Monk's Tale' on another story. A number of the Canterbury Tales relate events that also appear in *The Decameron.* Chaucer is rightly a touchstone of bawdy literature as Sade is of fetish fiction, although there the comparison stops. It goes without saying that as writers they're in different leagues. So why mention Chaucer three times in the first paragraph of a brief introduction to Boccaccio, and why include either in a predominantly fetishistic collection at all?

To start with, if not fighting censorship, then both pushed the envelope of permissible themes as literature moved from the preserve of courtly lovers to the comparative realism of the Early Modern period. Both featured characters from a variety of social backgrounds, and dealt with sex within what passed for the literary mainstream, if not in terms of cunt and cock then thematically full-on, and intimately. In 'The Wife of Bath's Tale' (Bath then was hardly a gentrified spa town), for example, the spouse in question famously expounds in wonderful detail on her sexual history with a gusto that confirms The Smiths' lyric

'A double bed, and a stalwart lover for sure/These are the riches of the poor'. The social historian Ivan Bloch, writing in 1958, thought her frankness socially naïve, but it's a narrative device. Today we might think of her as having the frankness of the tart with the heart, straight out of central casting, or else a post-feminist insouciance. That she doesn't spare her own blushes hardly makes her naïve in our post millennial *Moulin Rouge* milieu.

Tel me also, to what conclusioun
Were membres made of generatioun,
And of so parfit wise, and why ywrought?
Trusteth right wel, they were nat made for nought.
Glose who-so wol, and say bothe up and doun,
That they were made for purgatioun,
Of urine, and oure bothe things smale,
Were eke to know a female from a male:
And for non other cause? say ye no?
The experience wot wel it is not so.
So that these clerkes be not with me wroth,
I say this, that they maked ben for both,
This is to sayn, for office and for ese
Of engendrure, ther we God not displese.
Why shuld men elles in hir bookes sette,
That man shall yelden to his wif his dette?
Now wherwith shuld he make his payment,
If he ne used his sely instrument?
Than were they made upon a creature
To purge urine and eke for engendrure.

As help me God, I was a lusty one
And faire, and riche, and yonge, and wel begone:
And trewely, as min husbondes tolden me,
I had the beste queint that mighte be.
For certes I am all fulli venerian
In feling, and my herte alle marcian:
Venus me yave my lust and licorousnesse,
And Mars yave me my sturdy hardinesse.
Myn ascent was Taur, and Mars therinne;

Allas, alas, that ever love was synne!
I folwed ay min inclination:
By vertue of my constellation:
That made me that I coude nat withdraw
My chambre of Venus from a good felaw.
Yet have I a marke of Mars upon my face,
And also in another privee place.
For God so wisly be my salvation,
I loved never by no discretion,
But ever folwed min owne appetite,
All were he shorte, longe, blake or white;
I toke no kepe, so that he liked me,
How poure he was, ne eke of what degree . . .

My fourthe housbonde was a revelour,
This is to say, he had a paramour,
And I was yonge and ful of ragerie,
Stibborne and strong, and joly as a pie.
Lord! how coude I dance to an harpe smale,
And sing ywis as any nightingale,
Whan I had dronke a draught of swete wine.
Metillius, the foule cherl, the swyn,
That with a staf by raft his wyf hir lyf
For sche drank wyn, though I hadde ben his wif,
Ne shuld he nat have daunted me fro drinke:
And after wine of Venus most I thinke.
For al so siker as cold engendreth hayl,
A likorous mouth most han a likorous tayl.
In woman vinolent is no defence,
This knowen lechours by experience.

But in our bed he was so fresh and gay,
And so well therewithal he coude me glose,
When that he wolde han my belle chose,
That, though he had me bet on every boon,
He coude win agen my love anoon.

With regard to Boccaccio himself, there's a further reason for inclusion in a collection such as this: the illegitimate son of a wealthy merchant who nonetheless educated him well, he flourished as a young literary figure and friend of Plutarch, was a member of the Neapolitan Court, and put in diplomatic service in Florence. In short, he was a high-flier, who would have ticked all the right boxes on a fourteenth-century dating agency application form – until the pivotal event of his life, the Black Death of the 1340s, which, unimaginably, took his whole family, many friends, and devastated the entire context of his life. *The Decameron* is his great secular work, a monumental response to these adversities, which focuses on a group of individuals who are hiding out from the plague. Their stories are told, like the Canterbury pilgrims', of necessity and for their own entertainment, and many of the tales are about sex – and death. Boccaccio was grief-stricken, and Eros and Thanatos were writ large for him. The storytellers are themselves the light against the dark, as if in a Eugene Delacroix painting, with the cheerful stoicism of those blown on the winds of fate. Like Voltaire's Cunegonde in *Candide*, who continually slips off her donkey thanks to having only one buttock, the other having been cooked in a past effort to stave off starvation, the scurrilousness and irreverence of some of the tales is born of their being freed by the suffering they've seen to feel that nothing much matters.

Story six is a good example, and excerpted here. The heroine is an accidental *femme fatale*, if you like, though an off-the-peg courtly moppet rather than a *noir* vixen, of course. Like Helen of Troy, she can't help that trouble follows in her wake. She's no Ophelia though, given the ingeniousness of her explanation of events – namely having passed through the hands and beds of eight different murderous men – to her patrician father, by which she preserves her stock in the marriage market society compelled her to play. In story eight, a roguish cad finds copious sex to be materially redemptive. As in all these tales, vice and sin are shown to bring in one case, survival, and in the other, amoral benefit. Free from religious baggage despite coming from a religious man, these tales were a literary tipping-point to which even the boozy bawdy of Bukowski owes a debt.

The Decameron

6

There was of yore a Soldan of Babylon, by name of Beminedab, who in his day had cause enough to be well content with his luck. Many children male and female had he, and among them a daughter, Alatiel by name, who by common consent of all that saw her was the most beautiful woman then to be found in the world. Now the Soldan, having been signally aided by the King of Algarve[1] in inflicting a great defeat upon a host of Arabs that had attacked him, had at his instance and by way of special favour given Alatiel to the King to wife; wherefore, with an honourable escort of gentlemen and ladies most nobly and richly equipped, he placed her aboard a well-armed, well-furnished ship, and, commending her to God, sped her on her journey. The mariners, as soon as the weather was favourable, hoisted sail, and for some days after their departure from Alexandria had a prosperous voyage; but when they had passed Sardinia, and were beginning to think that they were nearing their journey's end, they were caught one day between divers cross winds, each blowing with extreme fury, whereby the ship laboured so sorely that not only the lady but the seamen from time to time gave themselves up for lost. But still, most manfully and skilfully they struggled might and main with the tempest, which, ever waxing rather than waning, buffeted them for two days with immense unintermittent surges; and being not far from the island of Majorca, as the third night began to close in, wrapped in clouds and mist and thick darkness, so that they saw neither the sky nor aught else, nor by any nautical skill might conjecture where they were, they felt

---

[1] Garbo, the coast of Africa opposite Andalusia and Granada.

the ship's timbers part. Wherefore, seeing no way to save the ship, each thought only how best to save himself, and, a boat being thrown out, the masters first, and then the men, one by one, though the first-comers sought with knives in their hands to bar the passage of the rest, all, rather than remain in the leaky ship, crowded into it, and there found the death which they hoped to escape. For the boat, being in such stress of weather and with such a burden quite unmanageable, went under, and all aboard her perished; whereas the ship, leaky though she was, and all but full of water, yet, driven by the fury of the tempest, was hurled with prodigious velocity upon the shore of the island of Majorca, and struck it with such force as to embed herself in the sand, perhaps a stone's throw from *terra firma*, where she remained all night beaten and washed by the sea, but no more to be moved by the utmost violence of the gale. None had remained aboard her but the lady and her women, whom the malice of the elements and their fears had brought to the verge of death. When it was broad day and the storm was somewhat abated, the lady, half-dead, raised her head, and in faltering accents began to call first one and then another of her servants. She called in vain, however; for those whom she called were too far off to hear. Great indeed was her wonder and fear to find herself thus without sight of human face or sound of other voice than her own; but, struggling to her feet as best she might, she looked about her, and saw the ladies that were of her escort, and the other women, all prostrate on the deck; so, after calling them one by one, she began at length to touch them, and finding few that showed sign of life, for indeed, between grievous sea-sickness and fear, they had little life left, she grew more terrified than before. However, being in sore need of counsel, all alone as she was, and without knowledge or means of learning where she was, she at last induced such as had life in them to get upon their feet, with whom, as none knew where the men were gone, and the ship was now full of water and visibly breaking up, she abandoned herself to piteous lamentations.

It was already noon before they descried anyone on the shore or elsewhere to whom they could make appeal for help; but shortly after noon it so chanced that a gentleman, Pericone da Visalgo by name, being on his return from one of his estates, passed that way with some mounted servants. Catching sight of the ship, he apprehended the circumstances at a glance, and bade one of his servants try to get aboard her, and let him know the result. The servant with some difficulty succeeded in boarding the vessel, and found the gentle lady with her few companions ensconced under shelter of the prow, and shrinking timidly from observation. At the first sight of him they wept, and again and again implored him to have pity on them; but finding that he did not understand them, nor they him, they sought by gestures to make him apprehend their forlorn condition.

With these tidings the servant, after making such survey of the ship as he could, returned to Pericone, who forthwith caused the ladies, and all articles of value which were in the ship and could be removed, to be brought off her, and took them with him to one of his castles. The ladies' powers were soon in a measure restored by food and rest, and by the honour which was paid to Alatiel, and Alatiel alone by all the rest, as well as by the richness of her dress, Pericone perceived that she must be some great lady. Nor, though she was still pale, and her person bore evident marks of the sea's rough usage, did he fail to note that it was cast in a mould of extraordinary beauty. Wherefore his mind was soon made up that, if she lacked a husband, he would take her to wife, and that, if he could not have her to wife, then he would make her his mistress. So this ardent lover, who was a man of powerful frame and haughty mien, devoted himself for several days to the service of the lady with excellent effect, for the lady completely recovered her strength and spirits, so that her beauty far exceeded Pericone's most sanguine conjectures. Great therefore beyond measure was his sorrow that he understood not her speech, nor she his, so that neither could know who the other was; but being inordinately enamoured of her beauty, he sought by such mute blandishments as he could devise to declare his love, and bring her of her own accord to gratify his desire. All in vain, however; she repulsed his advances point blank; whereby his passion only grew the stronger. So some days passed; and the lady perceiving Pericone's constancy, and bethinking her that sooner or later she must yield either to force or to love, and gratify his passion, and judging by what she observed of the customs of the people that she was amongst Christians, and in a part where, were she able to speak their language, she would gain little by making herself known, determined with a lofty courage to stand firm and immovable in this extremity of her misfortunes. Wherefore she bade the three women, who were all that were left to her, on no account to let any know who they were, unless they were so circumstanced that they might safely count on assistance in effecting their escape: she also exhorted them most earnestly to preserve their chastity, averring that she was firmly resolved that none but her husband should enjoy her. The women heartily assented, and promised that her injunctions should be obeyed to the utmost of their power.

Day by day Pericone's passion waxed more ardent, being fomented by the proximity and contrariety of its object. Wherefore seeing that blandishment availed nothing, he was minded to have recourse to wiles and stratagems, and in the last resort to force. The lady, debarred by her law from the use of wine, found it, perhaps, on that account all the more palatable; which Pericone observing determined to enlist Bacchus in the service of Venus. So, ignoring her coyness, he provided one evening a supper which was ordered with all possible pomp and beauty, and graced by the presence of the lady. No lack was there of incentives to hilarity; and Pericone directed the servant who waited on Alatiel to ply her with divers sorts of blended wines; which command the man faithfully executed. She, suspecting nothing, and seduced by the delicious flavour of the liquor, drank somewhat more freely than was seemly, and forgetting her past woes, became frolicsome, and incited by some women who trod some measures in the Majorcan style, she showed the company how they footed it in Alexandria. This novel demeanour was by no means lost on Pericone, who saw in it a good omen of his speedy success; so, with profuse relays of food and wine he prolonged the supper far into the night.

When the guests were at length gone, he attended the lady alone to her chamber, where, the heat of the wine overpowering the cold counsels of modesty, she made no more account of Pericone's presence than if he had been one of her women, and forthwith undressed and went to bed. Pericone was not slow to follow her, and as soon as the light was out lay down by her side, and taking her in his arms, without the least demur on her part, began to solace himself with her after the manner of lovers; which experience – she knew not till then with what horn men butt – caused her to repent that she had not yielded to his blandishments; nor did she thereafter wait to be invited to such nights of delight, but many a time declared her readiness, not by words, for she had none to convey her meaning, but by gestures.

But this great felicity which she now shared with Pericone was not to last: for not content with making her, instead of the consort of a king, the mistress of a castellan, Fortune had now in store for her a harsher experience, though of an amorous character. Pericone had a brother, twenty-five years of age, fair and fresh as a rose, his name Marato. On sight of Alatiel Marato had been mightily taken with her; he inferred from her bearing that he stood high in her good graces; he believed that nothing stood between him and the gratification of his passion but the jealous vigilance with which Pericone guarded her. So musing, he hit upon a ruthless expedient, which had effect in action as hasty as heinous.

It so chanced that there then lay in the port of the city a ship commanded by two Genoese, bound with a cargo of merchandise for Klarenza in the Morea: her sails were already hoist; and she tarried only for a favourable breeze. Marato approached the masters and arranged with them to take himself and the lady aboard on the following night. This done he concerted further action with some of his most trusty friends, who readily lent him their aid to carry his design into execution. So on the following evening towards nightfall, the conspirators stole unobserved into Pericone's house, which was entirely unguarded, and there hid themselves, as pre-arranged. Then, as the night wore on, Marato showed them where Pericone and the lady slept, and they entered the room, and slew Pericone. The lady thus rudely roused wept; but silencing her by menaces of death they carried her off with the best part of Pericone's treasure, and hied them unobserved to the coast, where Marato parted from his companions, and forthwith took the lady aboard the ship. The wind was now fair and fresh, the mariners spread the canvas, and the vessel sped on her course.

This new misadventure, following so hard upon the former, caused the lady no small chagrin; but Marato, with the aid of the good St Crescent-in-hand that God has given us, found means to afford her such consolation that she was already grown so familiar with him as entirely to forget Pericone, when Fortune, not content with her former caprices, added a new dispensation of woe; for what with the beauty of her person, which, as we have often said, was extraordinary, and the exquisite charm of her manners, the two young men who commanded the ship fell so desperately in love with her that they thought of nothing but how they might best serve and please her, so only that Marato should not discover the reason of their assiduous attentions. And neither being ignorant of the other's love, they held secret counsel together, and resolved to make conquest of the lady on joint account: as if love admitted of being held in partnership like merchandise or money. Which design being thwarted by the jealousy with which Alatiel was guarded by Marato, they chose a day and hour when the ship was speeding amain under canvas and Marato was on the poop looking out over the sea and quite off his guard; and going stealthily up behind him, they suddenly laid hands on him, and threw him into the sea, and were already more than a mile on their course before any perceived that Marato was overboard. Which when the lady learned, and knew that he was irretrievably lost, she relapsed into her former plaintive mood. But the twain were forthwith by her side with soft speeches and profuse promises, which, however ill she understood them, were not altogether inapt to allay a grief which had in it more of concern for her own hapless self than of sorrow for her lost lover. So, in course of time, the lady beginning visibly to recover heart, they began privily to debate which of them should first take her to bed with him; and neither being willing to give way to the other, and no compromise being discoverable, high words passed between them, and the dispute grew so hot, that they both waxed very wroth, drew their knives, and rushed madly at one another, and before they could be parted by their men, several stabs had been given and received on either side, whereby the one fell dead on the spot, and the other was severely wounded in divers parts of the body. The lady was much disconcerted to find herself thus alone with none to afford her either succour or counsel, and was mightily afraid lest the wrath of the kinsfolk and friends of the twain should vent itself upon her. From this mortal peril she was, however, delivered by the intercessions of the wounded man and their speedy arrival at Klarenza.

As there she tarried at the same inn with her wounded lover, the fame of her great beauty was speedily bruited abroad, and reached the ears of the Prince of the Morea, who was then staying there. The Prince was curious to see her, and having so done, pronounced her even more beautiful than rumour had reported her; nay, he fell in love with her in such a degree that he could think of nought else; and having heard in what guise she had come thither, he deemed that he might have her. While he was casting about how to compass his end, the kinsfolk of the wounded man, being apprised of the fact, forthwith sent her to him to the boundless delight as well of the lady, who saw therein her deliverance from a great peril, as of the Prince. The royal bearing, which enhanced the lady's charms, did not escape the Prince, who, being unable to discover her true rank, set her down as at any rate of noble lineage; wherefore he loved her as much again as before, and showed her no small honour, treating her not as his mistress but as his wife. So the lady, contrasting her present happy estate with her past woes, was comforted; and, as her gaiety revived, her beauty waxed in such a degree that all the Morea talked of it and of little else: insomuch that the Prince's friend and kinsman, the young, handsome and gallant Duke of Athens, was smitten with a desire to see her, and taking occasion to pay the Prince a visit, as he was now and again wont to do, came to Klarenza with a goodly company of honourable gentlemen. The Prince received him with all distinction and made him heartily welcome, but did not at first show him the lady. By and by, however, their conversation began to turn upon her and her charms, and the Duke asked if she were really so marvellous a creature as folk said. The Prince replied – 'Nay, but even more so; and thereof thou shalt have better assurance than my words, to wit, the witness of thine own eyes.' So, without delay, for the Duke was now all impatience, they waited on the lady, who was prepared for their visit, and received them very courteously and graciously. They seated her between them, and being debarred from the pleasure of conversing with her, for of their speech she understood little or nothing, they both, and especially the Duke, who was scarce able to believe that she was of mortal mould, gazed upon her in mute admiration; whereby the Duke, cheating himself with the idea that he was but gratifying his curiosity, drank with his eyes, unawares, deep draughts of the poisoned chalice of love, and, to his own lamentable hurt, fell a prey to a most ardent passion. His first thought, when they had left her and he had time for reflection, was that the Prince was the luckiest man in the world to have a creature so fair to solace him; and swayed by his passion, his mind soon inclined to divers other and less honourable meditations, whereof the issue was that, come what might, he would despoil the Prince of his felicity, and, if possible, make it his own. This resolution was no sooner taken than, being of a hasty temperament, he cast to the winds all considerations of honour and justice, and studied only how to compass his end by craft. So one day, as the first step towards the accomplishment of his evil purpose, he arranged with the Prince's most trusted chamberlain, one Ciuriaci, that his horses and all his other personal effects should, with the utmost secrecy, be got ready against a possible sudden departure: and then at nightfall, attended by a single comrade (both carrying arms), he was privily admitted by Ciuriaci into the Prince's chamber. It was a hot night, and the Prince had risen without disturbing the lady, and was standing bare to the skin at an open window fronting the sea, to enjoy a light breeze that blew thence. So, by preconcert with his comrade, the Duke stole up to the window, and in a trice ran the Prince through the body, and caught him up, and threw him out of the window. The palace was close by the sea, but at a considerable altitude above it, and the window through which the Prince's body was thrown looked over some houses, which, being sapped by the sea, had become ruinous, and were rarely or never visited by a soul; whereby, as the Duke had foreseen, the fall of the Prince's body passed, as indeed it could not but pass, unobserved. Thereupon the Duke's accomplice whipped out a halter, which he had brought with him for the purpose, and, making as if he were but in play, threw it round Ciuriaci's neck, drew it so tight that he could not utter a sound, and then, with the Duke's aid, strangled him, and sent him after his master. All this was accomplished, as the Duke knew full well, without awakening any in the palace, not even the lady, whom he now approached with a light, and holding it over the bed gently uncovered her person, as she lay fast asleep, and surveyed her from head to foot to his no small satisfaction; for fair as she had seemed to him dressed, he found her unadorned charms incomparably greater. As he gazed, his passion waxed beyond measure, and, reckless of his recent crime, and of the blood which still stained his hands, he got forthwith into the bed; and she, being too sound asleep to distinguish between him and the Prince, suffered him to lie with her.

But, boundless as was his delight, it brooked no long continuance; so, rising, he called to him some of his comrades, by whom he had the lady secured in such manner that she could utter no sound, and borne out of the palace by the same secret door by which he had gained entrance; he then set her on horseback and in dead silence put his troop in motion, taking the road to Athens. He did not, however, venture to take the lady to Athens, where she would have encountered his Duchess – for he was married – but lodged her in a very beautiful villa which he had hard by the city overlooking the sea, where, most forlorn of ladies, she lived secluded, but with no lack of meet and respectful service.

On the following morning the Prince's courtiers awaited his rising until noon, but perceiving no sign of it, opened the doors, which had not been secured, and entered his bedroom. Finding it vacant, they supposed that the Prince was gone off privily somewhere to have a few days of unbroken delight with his fair lady; and so they gave themselves no further trouble. But the next day it so chanced that an idiot, roaming about the ruins where lay the corpses of the Prince and Ciuriaci, drew the latter out by the halter and went off dragging it after him. The corpse was soon recognised by not a few, who, at first struck dumb with amazement, soon recovered sense enough to cajole the idiot into retracing his steps and showing them the spot where he had found it; and having thus, to the immeasurable grief of all the citizens, discovered the Prince's body, they buried it with all honour. Needless to say that no pains were spared to trace the perpetrators of so heinous a crime, and that the absence and evidently furtive departure of the Duke of Athens caused him to be suspected both of the murder and of the abduction of the lady. So the citizens were instant with one accord that the Prince's brother, whom they chose as his successor, should exact the debt of vengeance; and he, having satisfied himself by further investigation that their suspicion was well founded, summoned to his aid his kinsfolk, friends and divers vassals, and speedily gathered a large, powerful and well-equipped army, with intent to make war upon the Duke of Athens. The Duke, being informed of his movements, made ready likewise to defend himself with all his power; nor had he any lack of allies, among whom the Emperor of Constantinople sent his son, Constantine, and his nephew, Manuel, with a great and goodly force. The two young men were honourably received by the Duke, and still more so by the Duchess, who was Constantine's sister.

Day by day war grew more imminent; and at last the Duchess took occasion to call Constantine and Manuel into her private chamber, and with many tears told them the whole story at large, explaining the *casus belli*, dilating on the indignity which she suffered at the hands of the Duke, if, as was believed, he really kept a mistress in secret, and beseeching them in most piteous accents to do the best they could to devise some expedient whereby the Duke's honour might be cleared, and her own peace of mind assured. The young men knew exactly how matters stood; and so, without wearying the Duchess with many questions, they did their best to console her, and succeeded in raising her hopes. Before taking their leave they learned from her where the lady was whose marvellous beauty they had heard lauded so often; and being eager to see her, they besought the Duke to afford them an opportunity. Forgetful of what a like complaisance had cost the Prince, he consented, and next morning brought them to the villa where the lady lived, and with her and a few of his boon companions regaled them with a lordly breakfast, which was served in a most lovely garden. Constantine had no sooner seated himself and surveyed the lady, than he was lost in admiration, inwardly affirming that he had never seen so beautiful a creature, and that for such a prize the Duke, or any other man, might well be pardoned treachery or any other crime: he scanned her again and again, and ever with more and more admiration; whereby it fared with him even as it had fared with the Duke. He went away hotly in love with her, and dismissing all thought of the war, cast about for some method by which, without betraying his passion to any, he might devise some means of wresting the lady from the Duke.

As he thus burned and brooded, the Prince drew dangerously near the Duke's dominions; wherefore order was given for an advance, and the Duke, with Constantine and the rest, marshalled his forces and led them forth from Athens to bar the Prince's passage of the frontier at certain points. Some days thus passed, during which Constantine, whose mind and soul were entirely absorbed by his passion for the lady, bethought him that as the Duke was no longer in her neighbourhood, he might readily compass his end. He therefore feigned to be seriously unwell, and, having by this pretext obtained the Duke's leave, he ceded his command to Manuel, and returned to his sister at Athens. He had not been there many days before the Duchess recurred to the dishonour which the Duke did her by keeping the lady; whereupon he said that of that, if she approved, he would certainly relieve her by seeing that the lady was removed from the villa to some distant place. The Duchess, supposing that Constantine was prompted not by jealousy of the Duke but by jealousy for her honour, gave her hearty consent to his plan, provided he so contrived that the Duke should never know that she had been privy to it; on which point Constantine gave her ample assurance. So, being authorised by the Duchess to act as he might deem best, he secretly equipped a light bark and manned her with some of his men, to whom he confided his plan, bidding them lie to off the garden of the lady's villa; and so, having sent the bark forward, he hied him with other of his men to the villa. He gained ready admission of the servants, and was made heartily welcome by the lady, who, at his desire, attended by some of her servants, walked with him and some of his comrades in the garden. By and by, feigning that he had a message for her from the Duke, he drew her aside towards a gate that led down to the sea, and which one of his confederates had already opened. A concerted signal brought the bark alongside, and to seize the lady and set her aboard the bark was but the work of an instant. Her retinue hung back as they heard Constantine menace with death whoso but stirred or spoke, and suffered him, protesting that what he did was done not to wrong the Duke but solely to vindicate the sister's honour, to embark with his men. The lady wept, of course, but Constantine was at her side, the rowers gave way, and the bark, speeding like a thing of life over the waves, made Egina shortly after dawn. There Constantine and the lady landed, she still lamenting her fatal beauty, and took a little rest and pleasure. Then, re-embarking, they continued their voyage, and in the course of a few days reached Chios, which Constantine, fearing paternal censure, and that he might be deprived of his fair booty, deemed a safe place of sojourn. So, after some days of repose the lady ceased to bewail her harsh destiny, and suffering Constantine to console her as his predecessors had done, began once more to enjoy the good gifts which Fortune sent her.

Now while they thus dallied, Osbech, King of the Turks, who was perennially at war with the Emperor, came by chance to Smyrna; and there learning that Constantine was wantoning in careless ease at Chios with a lady of whom he had made prize, he made a descent by night upon the island with an armed flotilla. Landing his men in dead silence, he made captives of not a few of the Chians whom he surprised in their beds; others, who took the alarm and rushed to arms, he slew; and having wasted the whole island with fire, he shipped the booty and the prisoners, and sailed back to Smyrna. As there he overhauled the booty, he lit upon the fair lady, and knew her for the same that had been taken in bed and fast asleep with Constantine: whereat, being a young man, he was delighted beyond measure, and made her his wife out of hand with all due form and ceremony. And so for several months he enjoyed her.

Now there had been for some time and still was a treaty pending between the Emperor and Basano, King of Cappadocia, whereby Basano with his forces was to fall on

Osbech on one side while the Emperor attacked him on the other. Some demands made by Basano, which the Emperor deemed unreasonable, had so far retarded the conclusion of the treaty; but no sooner had the Emperor learned the fate of his son than, distraught with grief, he forthwith conceded the King of Cappadocia's demands, and was instant with him to fall at once upon Osbech while he made ready to attack him on the other side. Getting wind of the Emperor's design, Osbech collected his forces, and, lest he should be caught and crushed between the convergent armies of two most mighty potentates, advanced against the King of Cappadocia. The fair lady he left at Smyrna in the care of a faithful dependant and friend, and after a while joined battle with the King of Cappadocia, in which battle he was slain, and his army defeated and dispersed. Wherefore Basano with his victorious host advanced, carrying everything before him, upon Smyrna, and receiving everywhere the submission due to a conqueror.

Meanwhile Osbech's dependant, by name Antioco, who had charge of the fair lady, was so smitten with her charms that, albeit he was somewhat advanced in years, he broke faith with his friend and lord, and allowed himself to become enamoured of her. He had the advantage of knowing her language, which counted for much with one who for some years had been, as it were, compelled to live the life of a deaf mute, finding none whom she could understand or by whom she might be understood; and goaded by passion, he in the course of a few days established such a degree of intimacy with her that in no long time it passed from friendship into love, so that their lord, far away amid the clash of arms and the tumult of the battle, was forgotten, and marvellous pleasure had they of one another between the sheets.

However, news came at last of Osbech's defeat and death, and the victorious and unchecked advance of Basano, whose advent they were by no means minded to await. Wherefore, taking with them the best part of the treasure that Osbech had left there, they hied them with all possible secrecy to Rhodes. There they had not long abode before Antioco fell ill of a mortal disease. He had then with him a Cypriot merchant, an intimate and very dear friend, to whom, as he felt his end approach, he resolved to leave all that he possessed, including his dear lady. So, when he felt death imminent, he called them to him and said – ' 'Tis now quite evident to me that my life is fast ebbing away; and sorely do I regret it, for never had I so much pleasure of life as now. Well content indeed I am in one respect, in that, as die I must, I at least die in the arms of the two persons whom I love more than any other in the world, to wit, in thine arms, dearest friend, and those of this lady, whom, since I have known her, I have loved more than myself. But yet 'tis grievous to me to know that I must leave her here in a strange land with none to afford her either protection or counsel; and but that I leave her with thee, who, I doubt not, wilt have for my sake no less care of her than thou wouldst have had of me, 'twould grieve me still more; wherefore with all my heart and soul I pray thee, that, if I die, thou take her with all else that belongs to me into thy charge, and so acquit thyself of thy trust as thou mayst deem conducive to the peace of my soul. And of thee, dearest lady, I entreat one favour, that I be not forgotten of thee, after my death, so that there whither I go it may still be my boast to be beloved here of the most beautiful lady that nature ever formed. Let me but die with these two hopes assured, and without doubt I shall depart in peace.'

Both the merchant and the lady wept to hear him thus speak, and, when he had done, comforted him, and promised faithfully, in the event of his death, to do even as he besought them. He died almost immediately afterwards, and was honourably buried by them. A few days sufficed the merchant to wind up all his affairs in Rhodes; and being minded to return to Cyprus aboard a Catalan boat that was there, he asked the fair lady what she purposed to do if he went back to Cyprus. The lady answered, that, if it were agreeable to him, she would glady accompany him, hoping that for love of Antioco he would treat and regard her as his sister. The merchant replied that it would afford him all the pleasure in the world; and, to protect her from insult and their arrival in Cyprus, he gave her out as his wife, and, suiting action to word, slept with her on the boat in an alcove in a little cabin in the poop. Whereby that happened which on neither side was intended when they left Rhodes, to wit, that the darkness and the comfort and the warmth of the bed, forces of no mean efficacy, did so prevail with them that dead Antioco was forgotten alike as lover and as friend, and by a common impulse they began to wanton together, insomuch that before they were arrived at Baffa, where the Cypriot resided, they were indeed man and wife. At Baffa the lady tarried with the merchant a good while, during which it so befell that a gentleman, Antigono by name, a man of ripe age and riper wisdom but no great wealth, being one that had had vast and various experience of affairs in the service of the King of Cyprus but had found fortune adverse to him, came to Baffa on business; and passing one day by the house where the fair lady was then living by herself, for the Cypriot merchant was gone to Armenia with some of his wares, he chanced to catch sight of the lady at one of the windows, and, being struck by her extraordinary beauty, regarded her attentively, and began to have some vague recollection of having seen her before, but could by no means remember where. The fair lady, however, so long the sport of Fortune, but now nearing the term of her woes, no sooner saw Antigono than she remembered to have seen him in her father's service, and in no mean capacity, at Alexandria. Wherefore she forthwith sent for him, hoping that by his counsel she might elude her merchant and be reinstated in her true character and dignity of princess. When he presented himself, she asked him with some embarrassment whether he were, as she took him to be, Antigono of Famagosta. He answered in the affirmative, adding – 'And of you, madam, I have a sort of recollection, though I cannot say where I have seen you; wherefore, so it irk you not, bring, I pray you, yourself to my remembrance.' Satisfied that it was Antigono himself, the lady in a flood of tears threw herself upon him to his no small amazement, and embraced his neck: then, after a little while, she asked him whether he had never seen her in Alexandria. The question awakened Antigono's memory; he at once recognised Alatiel, the Soldan's daughter, whom he had thought to have been drowned at sea, and would have paid her due homage; but she would not suffer it, and bade him be seated with her for a while. Being seated, he respectfully asked her, how, and when and whence she had come thither, seeing that all Egypt believed for certain that she had been drowned at sea some years before. 'And would that so it had been,' said the lady, 'rather than I should have led the life that I have led; and so doubtless will my father say, if he shall ever come to know of it.' And so saying, she burst into such a flood of tears that 'twas a wonder to see. Wherefore Antigono said to her – 'Nay but, madam, be not distressed before the occasion arises. I pray you, tell me the story of your adventures, and what has been the tenor of your life; perchance 'twill prove to be no such matter but, God helping us, we may set it all straight.' 'Antigono,' said the fair lady, 'when I saw thee, 'twas as if I saw my father, and 'twas the tender love I bear him that prompted me to make myself known to thee, though I might have kept my secret; and few indeed there are whom to have met would have afforded me such pleasure as this which I have in meeting and recognising thee before all others; wherefore I will now make known to thee as to a father that which in my evil fortune I have ever kept close. If, when thou hast heard my story, thou seest any means whereby I may be reinstated in my former honour, I pray thee use it. If not, disclose to none that thou hast seen me or heard aught of me.'

Then, weeping between every word, she told him her whole story from the day of the shipwreck at Majorca to that hour. Antigono wept in sympathy, and then said – 'Madam, as throughout this train of misfortunes you have happily escaped recognition, I undertake to restore you to your father in such sort that you shall be dearer to him than ever before, and be afterwards married to the King of Algarve.' 'How?' she asked. Whereupon he explained to her in detail how he meant to proceed; and, lest delay should give occasion to another to interfere, he went back at once to Famagosta, and having obtained audience of the King, thus he spoke – 'Sire, so please you, you have it in your power at little cost to yourself to do a thing which will at once redound most signally to your honour and confer a great boon on me, who have grown poor in your service.' 'How?' asked the King. Then said Antigono – 'At Baffa is of late arrived a fair damsel, daughter of the Soldan, long thought to be drowned, who to preserve her chastity has suffered long and severe hardship. She is now reduced to poverty, and is desirous of returning to her father. If you should be pleased to send her back to him under my escort, your honour and my interest would be served in high and equal measure; nor do I think that such a service would ever be forgotten by the Soldan.'

With true royal generosity the King forthwith signified his approval, and had Alatiel brought under honourable escort to Famagosta, where, attended by his Queen, he received her with every circumstance of festal pomp and courtly magnificence. Schooled by Antigono, she gave the King and Queen such a version of her adventures as satisfied their enquiries in every particular. So, after a few days, the King sent her back to the Soldan under escort of Antigono, attended by a goodly company of honourable men and women; and of the cheer which the Soldan made her, and not her only but Antigono and all his company, it boots not to ask. When she was somewhat rested, the Soldan enquired how it was that she was yet alive, and where she had been so long without letting him know how it fared with her. Whereupon the lady, who had got Antigono's lesson by heart, answered thus – 'My father, 'twas perhaps the twentieth night after my departure from you when our ship parted her timbers in a terrible storm and went ashore nigh a place called Aguamorta, away there in the West: what was the fate of the men that were aboard our ship I knew not, nor knew I ever; I remember only, that, when day came, and I returned, as it were, from death to life, the wreck, having been sighted, was boarded by folk from all the countryside, intent on plunder; and I and two of my women were taken ashore, where the women were forthwith parted from me by the young men, nor did I ever learn their fate. Now hear my own. Struggling might and main, I was seized by two young men, who dragged me, weeping bitterly, by the hair of the head, towards a great forest; but, on sight of four men who were then passing that way on horseback, they forthwith loosed me and took to flight. Whereupon the four men, who struck me as persons of great authority, ran up to me; and much they questioned me, and much I said to them; but neither did they understand me, nor I them. So, after long time conferring together, they set me on one of their horses and brought me to a house, where dwelt a community of ladies, religious according to their law; and what the men may have said I know not, but there I was kindly received and ever honourably treated by all; and with them I did afterwards most reverentially pay my devotions to St Crescent-in-Hollow, who is held in great honour by the women of that country. When I had been some time with them, and had learned something of their language, they asked me who and whence I was: whereto I, knowing that I was in a convent, and fearing to be cast out as a foe to their law if I told the truth, answered that I was the daughter of a great gentleman of Cyprus, who had intended to marry me to a gentleman of Crete; but that on the voyage we had been driven out of our course and wrecked at Aguamorta. And so I continued, as occasion required, observing their usages with much assiduity, lest worse should befall me; but being one day asked by their superior, whom they call abbess, whether I was minded to go back to Cyprus, I answered that there was nought that I desired so much. However, so solicitous for my honour was the abbess, that there was none going to Cyprus to whom she would entrust me, until, two months or so ago, there arrived some worthy men from France, of whom one was a kinsman of the abbess, with their wives. They were on their way to visit the sepulchre where He whom they hold to be God was buried after He had suffered death at the hands of the Jews; and the abbess, learning their destination, prayed them to take charge of me, and restore me to my father in Cyprus. With what cheer, with what honour, these gentlemen and their wives entertained me, 'twere long to tell. But, in brief, we embarked, and in the course of a few days arrived at Baffa, where it was so ordered by the providence of God, who perchance took pity on me, that in the very hour of our disembarkation I, not knowing a soul and being at a loss how to answer the gentlemen, who would fain have discharged the trust laid upon them by the reverend abbess and restored me to my father, fell in, on the shore, with Antigono, whom I forthwith called, and in our language, that I might be understood neither of the gentlemen nor of their wives, bade him acknowledge me as his daughter. He understood my case at once, made much of me, and to the utmost of his slender power honourably requited the gentlemen. He then brought me to the King of Cyprus, who accorded me welcome there and conduct hither so honourable as words of mine can never describe. If aught remains to tell, you may best learn it from the lips of Antigono, who has often heard my story.'

Then Antigono, addressing the Soldan, said – 'Sire, what she has told you accords with what she has often told me, and with what I have learned from the gentlemen and ladies who accompanied her. One thing, however, she has omitted, because, I suppose, it hardly becomes her to tell it; to wit, all that the gentlemen and ladies, who accompanied her, said of the virtuous and gracious and noble life which she led with the devout ladies, and of the tears and wailings of both the ladies and the gentlemen, when they parted with her to me. But were I to essay to repeat all that they said to me, the day that now is, and the night that is to follow, were all too short: suffice it to say so much as this, that by what I gathered from their words and have been able to see for myself, you may make it your boast that among all the daughters of all your peers that wear the crown none can be matched with yours for virtue and true worth.'

By all which the Soldan was so overjoyed that 'twas a wonder to see. Again and again he made supplication to God, that of His grace power might be vouchsafed him adequately to recompense all who had done honour to his daughter, and most especially the King of Cyprus, for the honourable escort under which he had sent her thither; for Antigono he provided a magnificent reward, and some days later gave him his *congé* to return to Cyprus, at the same time by a special messenger conveying to the King his grateful acknowledgements of the manner in which he had treated his daughter. Then, being minded that his first intent, to wit, that his daughter should be the bride of the King of Algarve, should not be frustrated, he wrote to the King telling him all, and adding that, if he were still minded to have her, he might send for her. The King was overjoyed by these tidings, and having sent for her with great pomp, gave her on her arrival a hearty welcome. So she, who had lain with eight men in all, perhaps ten thousand times, was bedded with him as a virgin, and made him believe that a virgin she was, and lived long and happily with him as his queen: wherefore 'twas said – 'Mouth, for kisses, was never the worse: like as the moon reneweth her course.'

8

In this very countryside of ours there was and yet is a convent of women of great repute for sanctity – name it I will not, lest I should in some measure diminish its repute – the nuns being at the time of which I speak but nine in number, including the abbess, and all young women. Their very beautiful garden was in charge of a foolish fellow, who, not being content with his wage, squared accounts with their steward and hied him back to Lamporecchio whence he came. Among others who welcomed him home was a young husbandman, Masetto by name, a stout and hardy fellow, and handsome for a contadino, who asked him where he had been so long. Nuto, as our good friend was called, told him. Masetto then asked how he had been employed at the convent, and Nuto answered – 'I kept their large and beautiful garden in good trim, and, besides, I sometimes went to the wood to fetch the faggots, I drew water, and did some other trifling services; but the ladies gave so little wage that it scarce kept me in shoes. And moreover they are all young, and I think they are one and all possessed of the devil, for 'tis impossible to do anything to their mind; indeed, when I would be at work in the kitchen-garden, "put this here," would say one, "put that here," would say another, and a third would snatch the hoe from my hand, and say, "that is not as it should be"; and so they would worry me until I would give up working and go out of the garden; so that, what with this thing and that, I was minded to stay there no more, and so I am come hither. The steward asked me before I left to send him anyone whom on my return I might find fit for the work, and I promised; but God bless his loins, I shall be at no pains to find out and send him anyone.'

As Nuto thus ran on, Masetto was seized by such a desire to be with these nuns that he had quite pined, as he gathered from what Nuto said that his desire must be gratified. And as that could not be, if he said nothing to Nuto, he remarked – 'Ah! 'twas well done of thee to come hither. A man to live with women! he might as well live with so many devils: six times out of seven they know not themselves what they want.' There the conversation ended; but Masetto began to cast about how he should proceed to get permission to live with them, He knew that he was quite competent for the services of which Nuto spoke, and had therefore no fear of failing on that score; but he doubted he should not be received, because he was too young and well-favoured. So, after much pondering, he fell into the following train of thought – The place is a long way off, and no one there knows me; if I make believe that I am dumb, doubtless I shall be admitted. Whereupon he made his mind up, laid a hatchet across his shoulder, and saying not a word to any of his destination, set forth, intending to present himself at the convent in the character of a destitute man. Arrived there, he had no sooner entered than he chanced to encounter the steward in the courtyard, and making signs to him as dumb folk do, he let him know that of his charity he craved something to eat, and that, if need were, he would split firewood. The steward promptly gave him to eat, and then set before him some logs which Nuto had not been able to split, all which Masetto, who was very strong, split in a very short time. The steward, having occasion to go to the wood, took him with him, and there set him at work on the lopping; which done he placed the ass in front of him, and by signs made him understand that he was to take the loppings back to the convent. This he did so well that the steward kept him for some days to do one or two odd jobs. Whereby it so befell that one day the abbess saw him, and asked the steward who he was. 'Madam,' replied the steward, ' 'tis a poor deaf mute that came here a day or two ago craving alms, so I have treated him kindly, and have let him make himself useful in many ways. If he knew how to do the work of the kitchen-garden and would stay with us, I doubt we should be well served; for we have need of him, and he is strong, and would be able for whatever he might turn his hand to; besides which you would have no cause to be apprehensive lest he should be cracking his jokes with your young women.' 'As I trust in God,' said the abbess, 'thou sayst sooth; find out if he can do the garden work, and if he can, do all thou canst to keep him with us; give him a pair of shoes, an old hood, and speak him well, make much of him, and let him be well fed.' All which the steward promised to do.

Masetto, meanwhile, was close at hand, making as if he were sweeping the courtyard, and heard all that passed between the abbess and the steward, whereat he gleefully communed with himself on this wise – Put me once within there, and you will see that I will do the work of the kitchen-garden as it never was done before. So the steward set him to work in the kitchen-garden, and finding that he knew his business excellently well, made signs to him to know whether he would stay, and he made answer by signs that he was ready to do whatever the steward wished. The steward then signified that he was engaged, told him to take charge of the kitchen-garden, and showed him what he had to do there. Then, having other matters to attend to, he went away, and left him there. Now, as Masetto worked there day by day, the nuns began to tease him, and make him their butt (as it commonly happens that folk serve the dumb) and used bad language to him, the worst they could think of, supposing that he could not understand them: all which passed scarce heeded by the abbess, who perhaps deemed him as destitute of virility as of speech. Now it so befell that after a hard day's work he was taking a little rest, when two young nuns, who were walking in the garden, approached the spot where he lay, and stopped to look at him, while he pretended to be asleep. And so the bolder of the two said to the other – 'If I thought thou wouldst keep the secret, I would tell thee what I have sometimes meditated, and which thou perhaps mightest also find agreeable.' The other replied – 'Speak thy mind freely and be sure that I will never tell a soul.' Whereupon the bold one began – 'I know not if thou hast ever considered how close we are kept here, and that within these precincts dare never enter any man, unless it be the old steward or this mute: and I have often heard from ladies that have come hither, that all the other sweets that the world has to offer signify not a jot in comparison of the pleasure that a woman has in connection with a man. Whereof I have more than once been minded to make experiment with this mute, no other man being available. Nor, indeed, could one find any man in the whole world so meet therefore; seeing that he could not blab if he would; thou seest that he is but a dull clownish lad, whose size has increased out of all proportion to his sense; wherefore I would fain hear what thou hast to say to it.' 'Alas!' said the other, 'what is 't thou sayst? Knowest thou not that we have vowed our virginity to God?' 'Oh,' rejoined the first, 'think but how many vows are made to Him all day long, and never a one performed: and so, for our vow, let Him find another or others to perform it.' 'But,' said her companion, 'suppose that we conceived, how then?' 'Nay but,' protested the first, 'thou goest about to imagine evil before it befalls thee: time enough to think of that when it comes to pass; there will be a thousand ways to prevent its ever being known, so only we do not publish it ourselves.' Thus reassured, the other was now the more eager of the two to test the quality of the male human animal. 'Well then,' she said, 'how shall we go about it?' and was answered – 'Thou seest 'tis past noon; I make no doubt but all the sisters are asleep, except ourselves; search we through the kitchen-garden, to see if there be any there, and if there be none, we have but to take him by the hand and lead him hither to the hut where he takes shelter from the rain; and then one shall mount guard while the other has him with her inside. He is such a simpleton that he will do just whatever we bid him.' No word of this conversation escaped Masetto, who, being disposed to obey, hoped for nothing so much as that one of them should take him by the hand. They, meanwhile, looked carefully all about them, and satisfied themselves that they were secure from observation: then she that had broached the subject came close up to Masetto, and shook him; whereupon he started to his feet. So she took him by the hand with a blandishing air, to which he replied with some clownish grins. And then she led him into the hut, where he needed no pressing to do what she desired of him. Which done, she changed places with the other, as loyal comradeship required; and Masetto, still keeping up the pretence of simplicity, did their pleasure. Wherefore before they left, each must needs make another assay of the mute's powers of riding; and afterwards, talking the matter over many times, they agreed that it was in truth not less but even more delightful than they had been given to understand; and so, as they found convenient opportunity, they continued to go and disport themselves with the mute.

Now it so chanced that one of their gossips, looking out of the window of her cell, saw what they did, and imparted it to two others. The three held counsel together whether they should not denounce the offenders to the abbess, but soon changed their mind, and came to an understanding with them, whereby they became partners in Masetto. And in course of time by divers chances the remaining three nuns also entered the partnership. Last of all the abbess, still witting nought of these doings, happened one very hot day, as she walked by herself through the garden, to find Masetto, who now rode so much by night that he could stand very little fatigue by day, stretched at full length asleep under the shade of an almond tree, his person quite exposed in front by reason that the wind had disarranged his clothes. Which the lady observing, and knowing that she was alone, fell a prey to the same appetite to which her nuns had yielded: she aroused Masetto, and took him with her to her chamber, where, for some days, though the nuns loudly complained that the gardener no longer came to work in the kitchen-garden, she kept him, tasting and re-tasting the sweetness of that indulgence which she was wont to be the first to censure in others. And when at last she had sent him back from her chamber to his room, she must needs send for him again and again, and made such exorbitant demands upon him, that Masetto, not being able to satisfy so many women, bethought him that his part of mute, should he persist in it, might entail disastrous consequences. So one night, when he was with the abbess, he cut the tongue-string, and thus broke silence – 'Madam, I have understood that a cock may very well serve ten hens, but that ten men are sorely tasked to satisfy a single woman; and here am I expected to serve nine, a burden quite beyond my power to bear; nay, by what I have already undergone I am now so reduced that my strength is quite spent; wherefore either bid me Godspeed, or find some means to make matters tolerable.' Wonder-struck to hear the supposed mute thus speak, the lady exclaimed – 'What means this? I took thee to be dumb.' 'And in sooth, Madam, so was I,' said Masetto, 'not indeed from my birth, but through an illness which took from me the power of speech, which only this very night have I recovered; and so I praise God with all my heart.' The lady believed him; and asked him what he meant by saying that he had nine to serve. Masetto told her how things stood; whereby she perceived that of all her nuns there was not any but was much wiser than she; and lest, if Masetto were sent away, he should give the convent a bad name, she discreetly determined to arrange matters with the nuns in such sort that he might remain there. So, the steward having died within the last few days, she assembled all the nuns; and their and her own past errors being fully avowed, they by common consent, and with Masetto's concurrence, resolved that the neighbours should be given to understand that by their prayers and the merits of their patron saint, Masetto, long mute, had recovered the power of speech; after which they made him steward, and so ordered matters among themselves that he was able to endure the burden of their service. In the course of which, though he procreated not a few little monastics, yet 'twas all managed so discreetly that no breath of scandal stirred, until after the abbess's death, by which time Masetto was advanced in years and minded to return home with the wealth that he had gotten; which he was suffered to do as soon as he made his desire known. And so Masetto, who had left Lamporecchio with a hatchet on his shoulder, returned thither in his old age rich and a father, having by the wisdom with which he employed his youth, spared himself the pains and expense of rearing children, and averring that such was the measure that Christ meted out to the man that set horns on his cap.

Li Yu
(early seventeenth century)

Sex and Zen

Li Yu's *The Carnal Prayer Mat* remains a classic of Chinese literature and of the erotic literature of the world. Most recently, it formed the basis of director Michael Mak's film *Sex and Zen* which, starring as it does the lustrous Amy Yip, will be known to many fans of Hong Kong cinema as a commendably bizarre, pornographic sex comedy. The film features the wince-inducing grafting of an equestrian penis onto its hero, played by Kent Cheng, automated whipping machines, and, at its denouement, the karmic payback in which the 'Before Midnight Scholar' is compelled to fuck the mare who has been deprived of sex thanks to the aforementioned surgery. Amazingly, although produced with surreal cinematic aplomb, the film is not that far removed from the book on which it's based, first published in 1634.

The book is written in the form a moral fable, by which means Li Yu justifies its sexual content. How much of this is the author's own moralism, and how much a matter of getting away with it, is lost to history, but it's a fair bet to assume he's playing the age-old literary game of having his moral cake and eating it, putting some distance between himself and the salaciousness of his work, and pandering to the prurience of his audience. Nonetheless, it's a marvellous tale that works on two counts. As a Buddhist fable, its relative explicitness is thematically justified, and as pornography it displays a high degree of sexual mind-games, power-play and perversity: its young hero Wei Yang Sheng has – this time – a lupine penis graft, and the way that the tables are turned – literally as well as figuratively – on the archly dominant Madam Cheng (in an episode extracted here) is worthy of a modern piece of situational sub-dom literature. The power-play of social position is exploited to the full. It's also playfully pervy in the consistently high degree of sexual anticipation it gets across.

Arrogant, indomitable and thinking himself god's gift to women, the hero is nicknamed the 'Before Midnight Scholar', and the novel opens when he visits an esteemed, ascetic Buddhist monk who, in his unworldliness, doesn't get the double-entendre, and takes it as a reference to the young student's level of hard work. When the irrepressible young stud finds the strictures the monk will impose on him if he is to enrol as a novice too self-denying, he goes on his way. For although he feels called to a spiritual life, he must first – if ever – get his sensual needs out of his system. As he works his way through a number of women like a magpie adding shiny things to his nest, he is sowing the seeds of his own destruction.

One cuckolded husband, Honest Ch'eng, presented here in a following extract as, it turns out, a man of fine penile dexterity himself, decides to avenge himself on the young scholar's own domestic situation, and runs off with his neglected first wife back home. The Before Midnight Scholar has a fine time of things until, visiting a brothel, he finds his first wife, the lovely Noble Scent, ensconced therein as the star attraction. She hangs herself before he can find out her shame, and in grief and mortification he returns to the monk, who accepts him into his monastery where he meets Honest Ch'eng, who in shame at the ruination of such a flower as Noble Scent has become a novice too. None of this karmic rapprochement occurs, however, until the Before Midnight Scholar has worked his way through – and strung along – a bevy of Asian beauties.

The book is both a morality tale of karmic redress, in which humankind is revealed as vain, flawed but redeemably loveable, much as for Boccaccio, and a sex manual, of sorts. Though very neatly plotted, it's rather a strange beast when functioning as the latter, as the author intended it to, if wonderfully arcane. Did you know, for example, that prolonged tongue-kissing is good for the liver? (One for us all to bear in mind down the *Dog and Duck* of a Friday night.) Of interest from a contemporary point of view is the attitude taken to female sexuality. *The Vagina Monologues* (inspired, by the way, by Diderot's *The Indiscreet Jewels,* which will be extracted in a future volume of *Saturnalia*) it is not. Li Yu labours under some 'blokey' misconceptions. Though au fait with the female orgasm – a 'cloud burst' – he doesn't treat it as a goal in itself, perhaps to spare his readers' chauvenistic sensibilities, and of all the men in the book, Honest Ch'eng is the only one who seems aware of the clit, even then tickling it purely for lubrication, so that his cock can finish the job. Evidently, a sexologist such as Betty Dodson wouldn't have got much of a look-in in seventeenth-century China. Even though the Before Midnight Scholar prides himself on his ability to please women, and is hardly selfish with the favours of his lupine cock, he could do better.

The Carnal Prayer Mat

'Dearest!' she whispered, fighting back her impulse to cry aloud. 'Oh, oh, however did you get in?'

'Over the rooftops.'

'Oh, what a wonderful man! Come, let's go to bed.'

They undressed. But though far from reluctant, he could not keep pace with her. She was lying stark naked on her back while he was still removing his clothes. At last he had finished. He climbed in, lay down on top of her, and groped for her legs, meaning to toss them over his shoulders as usual. But his hands met with the void. She had already raised her legs and spread them wide. She had prepared an eager welcome for him.

'She certainly comes straight to the point,' he said to himself. 'Well, so much the better. There will be no need to waste my time beating around the bush. I too shall come straight to the point.' And he poised his battle-axe for a frontal attack. But she had not been prepared for so violent an onslaught. What a vigorous warrior was storming at her gate and demanding admittance! And she began to squeak and struggle.

'*Hach . . . hh . . !* Take it easy. You are hurting me,' she pleaded, gasping for air.

Gentleman as he was, he granted her a respite which he utilised to finger her portal, gently parting the wings of her gateway and rubbing persistently this way and that. Then he attacked again. But again he failed to breach the fortress. The head of his 'tortoise' squeezed in an inch or so, while the van of his army was repulsed.

'There is nothing to be gained by pussyfooting,' he explained to her. 'The best strategy is an all-out offensive. It may hurt you at first, but if you can stand it, your pleasure will be all the greater afterward.'

And he attacked vigorously. But again she struggled and resisted.

'*Shih pu-te!* It won't work that way. Please, a little saliva would help.'

'Certainly not. That is contrary to all the rules of the game. That may be permissible when there's a maidenhead to be pierced, but not otherwise.' He attempted another assault, but her resistance was undiminished.

'*Shih pu-te!* It can't be done. If you are too proud to break the rules, I'll attend to it.'

She struggled loose, spat in the hollow of her hand, and used one half the saliva to lubricate her gate, the other half to anoint the head and neck of his tortoise.

'It will be better now. But gently please.'

He disregarded her plea. On the contrary, he wished to show her what he could do. Clutching her hind cheeks firmly and pulling her to him so brusquely that flesh met flesh with a loud report, he attacked with all his might. This time he broke through, successfully introducing his entire armament into the fortress.

She uttered a soft scream, this time less from pain than from admiration.

'Goodness! Who would have expected a young scholar like you, a stay-at-home bookworm, to be so mighty a warrior! He doesn't even care whether his victim lives or dies. He just pushes his way in and that's that. You've reached rock bottom, you can't get any further. So out with you, and make it quick!'

'Oho! We're just beginning. A fine how-do-you-do if I were to retire from business now,' he replied with a merry laugh and began to heave and thrash with all his might and main. At first each of his thrusts brought forth a moan; '*hach . . . hh*.' After fifty odd strokes she fell silent. After he had passed the hundred mark, she began to moan again, the same sounds of '*hach . . . hh . . .*' issued from her lips. At first her moaning had been from pain, but now it signified rapture. It is indeed a strange fact about women that they can express very different feelings with the same sound; first it is a sound of suffering and then it becomes a sound of pleasure. With her pleasure moan a woman makes it known that her ecstasy is approaching the peak, that the cloud over the magic mountain is close to bursting.

Now Aroma's neighbour exerted all her guile and cunning. Her cloud had already burst twice, but when our young man asked her if she had come to the point, she said no no and insisted that he persevere in his efforts. Why did she lie? Because she knew that she was only Aroma's substitute and that Aroma was listening. If she admitted that her joys had come to a head, Aroma would step in and take her place. She wished to enjoy the rare pleasures of this night to the full, to prolong them as much as possible. She observed the well-known practice of the substitute officials described in the popular saying:

These worthy gentlemen are substitutes in office:
Slowly does it, take your time.
The public may be good and sick of waiting their turn.
What matter! Meanwhile we draw our wages.

In this love battle there was a certain amount of cheating on both sides. She cheated in defence of her interests. He for his part cheated in defence of his prestige. When in answer to his question she kept saying no, she had not yet come to the point, he felt himself in honour bound to give the same untruthful answer to the same question, and to continue bravely in his efforts. He didn't want her to be disappointed in him, though by now he was hard pressed and would have welcomed a breathing spell. In this phase of the battle, he was very much like a drunken man riding a donkey, his head tottering alarmingly at every step.

She must have noticed the difference between the easy spontaneous vigour with which he had started out and his present convulsive effort. Taking pity on him, she asked:

'Dearest, have you come to the point?'

And still his pride would not let him give in. Her question produced the same effect as the scolding with which a master shakes up a sleepy pupil and spurs him to new wakefulness. He redoubled his exertions and struggled bravely on. But when he began to sweat and pant, she relented.

'*Wo tiu la!* I've done it. Stop. I can't go on. I am dying. Put your arms around me and let us go to sleep side by side.'

With these words she offered him the armistice for which he had been secretly longing. He was only too glad to accept.

Meanwhile Aroma had played the eavesdropper. The whole time she had lain motionless on the love seat at the foot end of the bed, listening intently.

In the beginning, when the neighbour woman had squeaked and struggled and his attack seemed to be making no progress, she had said to herself, well, his utensil can hardly be so insignificant; it must indeed be quite imposing and serviceable. Already half her doubts were dispelled. And as the battle progressed, when she saw, or rather heard, how perseveringly he held up his end and how, after a brief moment of weariness, he rallied his flagging troops and led them back into the fray with redoubled vigour, she was wholly reassured. 'He is a born conqueror of ladies' chambers, my chosen hero,' she said to herself. 'I shall belong to him with joy and without regrets.'

'Well,' said Aroma with an affectation of coldness, 'why are you still lying here? The other has settled accounts for me. We are quits. You have had your pleasure. Why don't you go home?'

He protested vigorously. 'Oho, we are far from being quits. Quite on the contrary. You owe me reparation for the injustice you have done me by defrauding me with so inferior a substitute. It is midnight already, soon it will be dawn. We have no time to lose. Quickly. Crawl in here beside me, and not another word!'

'Do you really mean it?'

'I certainly do.'

'Very well. In that case, will you kindly get up and dress? Before we go to bed, there is something important to be done.'

'What can be so important? As far as I can see, the one important thing is that we go to bed together.'

'Stop asking questions and come along.'

He jumped up and flung on his clothes. Taking him by the hand, she led him through several rooms and inner courtyards to the kitchen. There she pointed to the bathtub and the kettle full of boiling hot water on the hearth fire. Now he understood. He was to take a bath, and since it was far to the kitchen and the way led through open courtyards, she had bidden him dress, fearing that he might catch cold if exposed to the cool night air. How considerate of her! In his thoughts he performed a kowtow of thanks.

Meanwhile she plied the ladle and filled the tub half with cold, half with hot water. The result was a fine warm bath, not too hot and not too cold.

'There. Now you can get in. You will find soap and washcloths over there. Help yourself.'

And she continued:

'An unsavoury smell of strange woman still clings to you. I should not like you to pass it on to my sensitive body.'

'You are perfectly right,' he agreed. 'It is indeed of the utmost importance. I shall also wash my mouth out to obliterate every trace of kisses.'

And he reached for the water bowl and the toothbrush which had been placed in a rack affixed to the outside of the bathtub. He was very much impressed to note that despite the late romantic hour she was still the perfect housewife, attentive to every imaginable domestic detail. How carefully she had prepared his bath, complete with soap, washcloths and steaming warm towels! When he had finished drying himself, she had wiped off the wet bath mat with a rag, and later on in the bed chamber she had prepared a sweat cloth and placed it in readiness beside the pillow.

'What an excellent housekeeper!' he thought in silent admiration. 'She thinks of everything.'

She put out the lamp and sat down on the edge of the bed. Slowly she undressed, carefully smoothing out each garment and folding it over a chair.

Graciously she let her lover finish undressing her, loosen her silk brassière and remove her thin batiste panties. He embraced her and kissed her and sent out a hand to explore. He found her twin hills, so full and elastic that they slipped out of his hands when he tried to pull and pluck at them. Everywhere her flesh was firm, but at the same time it was soft and tender; nowhere did he find a hard place. Further down, on the vault of her fortress wall, he met with the same soft firmness, but here the skin seemed to be even smoother and more supple than elsewhere.

He moved her carefully into place, raised her legs over his shoulders, and opened the battle, employing the same tactics as with her ugly precursor; a frontal attack without introductory love play. His calculation was that though this approach might hurt her at first, her pleasure would be all the greater afterward. The offensive ran off without a hitch. But contrary to his expectations, she remained utterly apathetic as though she felt nothing at all, giving no sign either of pleasure or of pain. Then he remembered what his experienced friend, K'un-lun's Rival, had told him about the mighty calibre of her husband's last. No wonder his forces had been able to slip into the enemy fortress so easily, without encountering the least resistance. He had not been prepared for a shoe of such dimensions. In a shoe so deep and wide his last, though by no means unimpressive, seemed to shrivel into nothingness, to lose itself like a needle in a haystack.

Aware that he would get nowhere by the old methods, he decided on a change of tactics. Removing the pillow from under Aroma's head, he pushed it beneath her loins. In so doing, he intentionally neglected to provide her head with another support. This impressed her and inspired her with a secret admiration. Thus far she had experienced no pleasure at all, but she saw by his preparations that he knew a thing or two about bedchamber technique and was confident that everything would come out all right in the end.

Esteemed reader, the battle of the sexes is in many respects not unlike the art of warfare: before the opening of hostilities, the two contestants spy upon each other, feeling out one another's strengths and weaknesses. He tries to find out whether she is deep or not so deep, in order to plan his offensive and retreat accordingly. She tries to obtain accurate information about his armament, whether short or long, thick or thin, in order to meet it with suitable movements and adapt herself to it. Success in battle depends on knowledge of the enemy's strength or weakness. The length and thickness of men's utensils vary exceedingly, and the same applies to the depth and width of women's pleasure houses. If she is not particularly deep, an over-long utensil is out of place; there will not be room for it, at least not for all of it. If he should nevertheless attempt to force the whole of it in, he will give her not pleasure but pain. Ought he to get all the pleasure? That would be unfair. But if she possesses an extraordinarily deep pleasure grotto, she needs a mate with unusually long and powerful armament; otherwise she will get no satisfaction. But the length of the male organ is fixed by nature once and for all; it does not go on growing and there is no way of lengthening it artificially. Consequently a knowing lover resorts to a stratagem: he removes the pillow from beneath his lady's head and wedges it under her waist. Thus raised, her pelvis lies flatter and the lover's utensil is so enabled to reach the bottom. This should not be taken to mean that the pillow beneath the waist is indispensable or should be employed in every case. It is indicated only in cases when the lady's pleasure grotto is too deep for her lover's armament. We see then that this shortcoming can be remedied. But there is another discrepancy that cannot be made good: when the lady's shoe is too wide for her lover's last.

The itinerant surgeon's operation had considerably increased the thickness and stamina of our young man's equipment, but had not lengthened it. On his first attempt to penetrate Aroma's pleasure grotto, his utensil had proved too short and had failed to plumb the depths. By hitting on the above-mentioned stratagem of wedging the pillow under her waist, he had impressed her with his competence; she said nothing but secretly she was very pleased.

This use of a pillow is a simple and widely known trick, but few men are considerate enough to bother and still fewer know how to do the thing properly. In addition to supporting the waist, most men leave the pillow under their lady's head. This is a big mistake. For her body is then raised at both ends, with the result that she is bent in the middle. If, to make matters worse, her lover rests his whole weight upon her, it is easy to imagine how uncomfortable she must feel. In this unnatural position, a kiss requires the most painful contortions on both sides: *he* must hump his back in order to reach her mouth; *she* must stretch her neck and twist her head backward before her lips and tongue can meet his lips and tongue. All this because of the troublesome and superfluous pillow under her head. And so I say, away with it! Let the lady's cloud-coiffure lie directly on the sheet. Then the heads and limbs of both parties will fit harmoniously together; his noble yak whisk will penetrate her pleasure grotto without difficulty, her purple little tongue will find its way easily into his mouth, no inequalities of position will prevent them from merging and blending inwardly, no discomfort will mar their pleasure.

After this brief digression, let us get on with our story. Raising her nephrite thighs over his shoulders, planting both hands on the bed sheet, our scholar resumed the interrupted battle – this time with success. His valiant henchman did not bely his partly canine origins and nature. The longer the battle raged, the more imposing became his stature and with it his courage; no longer was her pleasure grotto a bottomless pit; both on the sides and in the depths the desired contact was established. Aroma's attitude changed accordingly. The first assault had left her totally apathetic and inert, no sound of pleasure or pain had escaped her; but now her body began to quiver and writhe voluptuously, and moans of '*hach . . . hh . . .*' issued from her lips.

'*Hsin-kan*, dearest. It's coming! I feel a pleasant sensation.'

'So soon? Why, I've hardly begun', he whispered back. 'Just wait until I get going, then you will really feel something, *wo-ti kuai jou*, my perverse little lump of flesh.' And he proceeded to heave and thrash until heaven and earth were stricken with terror and threatened to lose their balance. Her stifled cries of 'Dearest' and 'Oh, I'm dying' became more and more frequent and the grass and bushes round her gate grew moist with the dew of pleasure. He reached for the sweat cloth to wipe away the dew, but she restrained him. How so? It has already been stated that she was very passionate by nature. A battle of the sexes, she felt, should be a wild frenzy, an ecstatic temple dance with a rousing accompaniment of gongs and drums. Interrupt the temple dance with a prosaic sweat cloth? Out of the question. Even in her everyday dealings with her husband she had taken the same attitude. Let the dew of pleasure sprinkle her as it might, there would be no wiping until afterward, after the cloud had burst. This was a very personal eccentricity of hers. I mention it only in passing and – it goes without saying – only for the benefit of gourmets and connoisseurs!

Our young man was still going strong when she flung her arms round his neck, pressed him close, and groaned: '*Wo yao tiu la!* My cloud is bursting. Let us die of joy together.'

Actually it was too soon for him, He would have been glad to go on a little longer and impress her with his vigour and endurance. But she would not allow it.

'Stop. I am fully convinced of your strength and endurance. You've been battling all through the night, you've taken on two women and laid them low. Grant yourself a little rest, save your strength for tomorrow night; I shouldn't like you to get sick from overexertion; I want you to stay well for my sake.'

Ah, she was concerned for his health. How considerate! How touching! Deeply moved, he folded her in his arms, pressed her tight, and body to body, they shared the ineffable bliss of the bursting cloud.

Since her husband's more or less forced departure – his father-in-law had driven him out of the house with his quarrelsome, schoolmasterly ways – Noble Scent, abandoned when she had just grown accustomed to love, found herself in the condition of a drinker who has just been obliged to give up spirits or of a gourmet whose doctor has suddenly ordered him to forego all roasts and condiments and live on insipid vegetables.

Three nights, five nights of solitary sleeping were already a torment, but now the torture had been going on for six months. She felt like a widow. Deprived of bedtime pleasures, she took refuge in fantasy and tried, with the help of the thirty-six illustrations from the *Ch'un-kung*, or *The Vernal Palace*, the spicy volume the Before Midnight Scholar had purchased in the early days of their marriage, to arouse and satisfy her desires artificially. She made the same mistake as the fool who thought he could quench his thirst by looking at a still life of succulent fruit and appease his hunger by gazing at a still life of inviting pastries and incurred the same sort of disappointment; far from being appeased, her hunger and thirst for love only became more intense. She put the useless picture book back in the drawer and tried another way out; perhaps she could dispel her desperate *ennui* with light reading.

Esteemed readers, you may ask what sort of reading matter she selected to this end? In my humble opinion, she ought to have turned to the books which her father had recommended and given her as a young girl, innocent, virtuous books of an educational nature, such as the *Liehnü chuan*, *Biographies of Heroines*, or the *Nü Hsiao-king*, *Daughters' Guide to Childlike Piety*, and such like.

Reading matter of this kind might have distracted her, banished her boredom and discontent, and even made her forget her hunger and thirst. Grass widows and even real widows can derive consolation, forgetfulness, and peace of mind from the proper sort of reading matter. But what did Noble Scent do? Instead of the books recommended by her father, she selected the dissolute, salacious trash that her husband had brought home with him. Erotic novels of dubious quality, such as the *Ch'i p'o-tzu chuan*, *The Love-Crazy Women*, or the *Hsiu-t'a yeh-shih*, *The Romance of the Embroidered Couch*, or the *Ju-yi-chün chuan*, *Lovers Galore*, and so on. She eagerly devoured this spicy reading matter and never skipped a page.

In the course of her reading, she often ran into the most amazing passages in praise of the hero's equipment, vaunting its imposing thickness or incredible length. She encountered troubling similes such as 'like a snail crawling from its shell,' or 'comparable in dimensions and general appearance to a skinned rabbit'. As for the endurance and efficiency of these heroes, there wasn't a one of them who couldn't manage a thousand thrusts without stopping.

In reading such descriptions Noble Scent couldn't help thinking of her own connubial experience and drawing comparisons. 'Is it possible?' she wondered. 'Can such things be? My young husband's utensil was barely three inches long and no more than two fingers thick, and when we sported together, his outside limit was two hundred thrusts, then the cloud burst. He even used to boast of his vigour and endurance; and here I read about men capable of delivering at least ten times more than he. Seems hardly credible. Come come. You mustn't believe everything you read in books; the best thing you can do is to give up this sort of reading. Surely the miraculous items described in these pornographic books are pure invention, products of the author's imagination . . .'

She vacillated between doubt and belief, until at length belief won the upper hand. 'There are millions of men in the world; that leaves room for plenty of deviations from the norm and average – why should there not be men of unusual build such as those described in these novels? Just imagine! What ineffable bliss to get one of those for your husband! A demigoddess could ask no better. Oh, why has such happiness been denied me?'

From then on the thought left her no peace. She lost all interest in her needlework. Her only distraction was the reading matter in question and the more she read the more the sultry yearning of her senses curdled into storm clouds – oh, if only he would come home, she would . . . oh, then the clouds would burst and the saving rain would fall.

But the poor thing waited in vain. A year passed, and no sign of him, not so much as a letter.

A strange change had taken place within her; she could no longer summon up resentment at such unloving treatment. Resentment had turned to defiance. Why waste her feelings on this loveless husband of hers? There were other men. Her feelings clamoured for life and experience.

'In all these novels you seldom find a heroine who hasn't carried on with several men; to judge by them there's nothing unusual about a married woman taking a lover to make up for her husband's shortcomings. Who knows? Perhaps I committed some crime in an earlier life to be punished in this one with so heartless a husband. We had been married only a few months when he left me, thrust me aside. Since then more than a year has elapsed. Am I to suppose that in all this time a skirt chaser like him has controlled himself and kept away from the bypaths? It doesn't seem likely. Very well, what's sauce for the gander is sauce for the goose! Who will deny me the right to open a secret backdoor and let a someone, a lover, in? It's just too bad that the old man runs the house so strictly. Shut off like this from the outside world, I never even get to see a strange man . . .'

Arrived at this point in her thoughs, she was seized with new resentment, directed this time not against her faithless husband but against the domestic tyrant, her own father. She could not help toying with the wicked hope – ah, where was her filial piety now! – that he might soon depart for the Land of the Yellow Springs. Then she would be free to take a lover into the house.

And now this strange tenant farmer had suddenly turned up. From the very first she looked upon him exactly as a hungry hawk looks upon a chicken that has entered its field of vision: a welcome prey. His appearance was all one to her; let it be refined or vulgar, attractive or ungainly! Only one thing mattered: he was a man. And he wasn't so bad looking at that; in any case, he was powerfully built and that seemed promising. She planned to seize this man as a hawk seizes its prey.

At the thought of his mighty armament, the delicate young beauty felt just a wee bit frightened and ill at ease. Perhaps he would hurt her. Before he crawled under the covers, she pleaded with him:

'Don't be too violent. You'll be gentle with me, won't you? I know what a gigantic utensil you have. You won't hurt me, will you?'

'Why, the idea! How could I dare to injure the gracious young lady's precious body? I shall be ever so gentle and you may be sure that I won't hurt you.' These were his words, but he did not take her appeal very seriously, mistaking it for a coquettish challenge to show what he could do. Forgetting his promise, he started in with a brusque frontal assault.

But he was poorly received. She pushed him away angrily.

'Don't be so rough!' she fumed at him. 'You are hurting me! Is that how you keep your word?'

Contritely he broke off his attack. Apparently she had meant what she said. He would have to proceed more circumspectly.

'Forgive my enthusiasm, gracious lady. It has never before been my good fortune to embrace so beautiful a lady. Your bewitching presence robbed me of my reason; when I felt your silken skin, your tender flesh, I was as though drunk; I could not control my overwhelming desire – forgive me please and let me repair my wrong. I shall be doubly careful.' So he pleaded with her and renewed his promise. This time he kept it.

He gave up the idea of entering her pleasure house by force; instead, he let his ambassador reconnoiter the entrance and saunter about, first through the bushes on the fortress wall to east and west of the gate, then further down, in her valley of secret pleasures. Here his ambassador sauntered gaily up and down.

This was a trick he had learned from Aroma. At the beginning of their marriage, Aroma's pleasure portal had been approximately the same size as that of Noble Scent now; it had been no easy matter for his ambassador to gain admittance to her audience chamber and privy cabinet. Aroma herself had thought up an ingenious way of remedying the difficulty: by strolling about in her valley of secret joys, by rubbing gently against the 'back and shoulders' of her pleasure portal, his ambassador would call forth pleasant inner vibrations, which in turn would foster the dew of desire. Moistened by this dew, the intruder would be enabled to slip easily through the gate. Other expedients are often resorted to by youthful, inexperienced lovers, too excited to wait, but they are far from producing the same beneficial effect.

The dew of desire is very much like the spring floods in the upper Yangtse valley: a heavily laden junk has run aground on a sandbank; without the least exertion on the part of the boatmen, the flood waters lift it clear. The technical term for this stratagem which he had learned from Aroma is 'to coax the source into flowing by removing the pebbles'.

Noble Scent could not repress a giggle when she felt his ambassador wandering about, far from the object of his desires.

'Why are you fumbling around like that?' she asked. 'You must be lost.'

'Is it possible that you are unacquainted with this little variant?'

'Never heard of it. Seems to me you are all muddled.'

'Oh no, it's you who are very much mistaken. Just wait. In a minute you'll feel a pleasant sensation. Then you'll see who is muddled and who isn't.'

And indeed, after he had reconnoitered her valley of secret joys for a while, the dew of desire began to make the pathway smooth and slippery. 'The spring floods are coming,' he said to himself happily.

The junk was floating free – almost too free, he feared. Fearing that his ambassador might skid on the slippery path and miss the entrance, he requested his companion to guide him to the right spot with her tender little hand. She complied with some difficulty – it took all ten of her lotus shoots to hold the doughty ambassador. But soon, with her willing assistance, he had the difficult passage behind him and was presenting his credentials in her audience chamber.

Noble Scent's heart overflowed with gratitude. Thanks to her companion's delicacy and circumspection, she had not felt the least twinge of pain. The man was obviously an expert. She thanked him with a tender embrace.

'It seems very strange,' she said, 'I am told that you have never attached much importance to women, and I shouldn't be surprised to hear that this is your first try at gallantry. And what delicacy, what virtuosity! Especially when I think of my own young husband who regarded himself as a hero of the bedchamber and couldn't think of anything else! I'd like to know when he ever treated me with so much consideration and understanding. Really, I like you. I love you madly.'

Her praises increased his self-reliance and spurred him on to acquit himself of his task with redoubled zeal. And he held up his end so well that from then on she invited him into her bed night after night. She simply could not forego the unprecedented pleasures he offered her. He had become indispensable to her.

At first they carried on secretly, behind Ju-yi's back. But then they decided that since Ju-yi was bound to find out sooner or later, it would be better to tell her honestly and frankly how matters stood. To mollify her and keep her in a good humour, Noble Scent decided to stop treating her as an inferior and slave and to accord her the respectable status of a subsidiary wife; she herself, of course, would be the principal spouse.

Placated by this tactful treatment, Ju-yi put a good face on a business that was not altogether to her liking. From then on they formed a *ménage à trois*. Either the women, by turns, would share his couch all night, or else they would change places at midnight, or else all three would sleep together.

In the last case it sometimes happened that Honest Ch'üan, while only half awake, would mistake one for the other and address the lady's maid as *hsiao-chieh*, 'gracious young mistress,' and Noble Scent as Ju-yi. After making this blunder two or three times, he decided to use the neutral term *hsin-kan*, 'dearest,' for both of them.

The warning signal! Aunt Chen was on her way. It was time to take cover. With all their chatting and laughter they had failed to hear the first signal. Nimble as the waves, all four flung themselves on the pile of clothes, all reaching and grabbing at once.

Precious time was lost in the resulting confusion; the ladies had to content themselves with a meagre outer covering. But the Before Midnight Scholar's clothes were on the bottom of the pile and he couldn't get to them at all. Stark naked as he was, Scent Cloud pushed him into the trunk and closed it over him.

Immediately thereafter the visitor arrived, flanked by Pearl and Jade who, as good manners demand, had taken a few steps toward the rear of the house to welcome her.

The moment she set eyes on her two nieces, Aunt Chen had smelled a rat. Fear and embarrassment were written all over their faces as they stepped up to her in the middle reception hall as though to bar her way. Suspecting that something was amiss, she refused to waste time with the usual formalities of greeting, in which her nieces wished to involve her in the hope of delaying her. Instead, she made straight for the boudoir.

'Aha! All three of my beauties together! What a charming sight! How are you? Long time since we've seen each other!'

During these brief words of greeting, she looked searchingly about the room. She ignored the polite invitation to be seated, but pursued her customary inspection of the boudoir, approached the bed, looked into it and behind it, behind the cupboards and clothes racks, and squinted into every nook and corner.

But, to her vast disappointment, she couldn't find a thing. Had all those snakes and dragons been sheer imagination? Rather taken aback, she sat down on the proffered chair and began to talk about the weather.

The three nieces heaved an inward sigh of relief. Once again, thank goodness, the danger seemed to have blown over. For a moment they thought they were safe. But then – alack, alas! – they noticed something which they had quite forgotten in the excitement, something likely to create a peck of trouble: the Before Midnight Scholar's notebook with his select list of beauties. They had left it open on the desk. How stupid of them! Now they sat there on tenterhooks, waiting for the first opportunity to make it disappear.

But Aunt Chen's eye was quicker than their hands. Before they could do a thing, she caught sight of the notebook and a moment later she had it in her grasp. As gently and inconspicuously as possible, Pearl and Jade tried to wrest it away from her. Without the slightest success. Their aunt clung to her prey for dear life. Scent Cloud quickly thought up a different and – she thought – better means of warding off the impending calamity: a little deception.

'Let Aunt Chen have it if she wants it,' she said to her cousins in a tone of affected indifference. 'Let her keep it if it amuses her. We picked it up on the street. It doesn't mean a thing to us.'

'So kind of you,' said Aunt Chen. 'I'm sure it is quite without value. I simply cannot understand why you two were so dead set on taking it away from me. I think I'll have a look at it. You've made me curious.' With this she stood up and took a few steps toward the window. She opened the notebook and her eyes lit at once on the promising title: 'Vernal apparitions from far and wide.' 'Aha!' she thought, 'something about love.' And she decided the book must be full of pornographic pictures. With nervous eagerness she leafed through it, looking for illustrations which she thought would be more interesting than the text.

But though she leafed through the notebook from start to finish, there was not a sign of any 'vernal palace' pictures; nothing but text, written in a tiny 'fly-head' script.

She leafed back and began to read from the beginning. After skimming over the first few sections, she came to the conclusion that this strange list with its descriptions and critical notes must have been composed by some young academician full of wit and fine feeling. And how elegant, how poetic a style! It was a pleasure just to read it; this is much better, she thought, than some pretentious novel full of vernal episodes.

She was so entranced that she could not lay the thing down. She read and read. At last she came across a passage dealing with a certain 'dark beauty'. To her amazement she found that the description applied to her, stroke for stroke and line for line. Her heart began to pound. And three red circles were marked at the end of the commentary, showing that the unknown observer had put her in the highest class, that he regarded her as extra-special and outstanding.

Who, she wondered, could have composed this flattering portrait of her?

She pondered. Since her visit to the temple with her nieces, she hadn't left the house; no strange man could have laid eyes on her. Visit to the temple? Why yes, that was when that handsome and charming young man had so impetuously fallen on his knees and beat his forehead on the ground in their honour – he and no other must be the author! These were the thoughts that passed through her mind.

If she had the slightest doubts, they were dispelled when, leafing back through the notebook and skipping over two sections that had been crossed out, she came across the general heading:

'On such and such an hour of such and such a day of such and such a month, meeting with three great beauties . . .'

Hadn't the three of them gone to the temple together? Next came the two crossed-out passages. Obviously they had been crossed out only recently, because the heavy brush strokes still looked suspiciously fresh. The text was all smeared over, but there were still a few signs that she could decipher without difficulty. As, for example, the words:

'Gown of red and silver . . .'
'Her dress is the delicate light green of the lotus shoot . . .'

Didn't Jade have on a gown of red and silver that day, and hadn't Pearl been dressed in light green? And now, to cap it all, the freshly written quatrain, still glistening with fresh ink:

Are we, like a flock of wild geese,
To flutter about, looking for triumphal wreaths?
No – let us give age its due
And modestly retire.

Why, that was Pearl's handwriting! She knew it well. Aunt Chen could not help laughing to herself, and in her laughter bitterness was mingled with gleeful anticipation. Just wait. She would show them a thing or two.

Nonchalantly she dropped the telltale notebook into the depths of her sleeve pocket. She suddenly put on a solemn, stern countenance as though she had a very painful announcement to make.

'Ah yes,' she sighed. 'Our good ol Ts'ang Chieh (third millennium BC), the inventor of our script, was indeed a great sage.'

The three young ladies exchanged looks of puzzlement. A far-fetched remark if ever there was one. What could she be getting at?

'How so?' Scent Cloud asked.

'I am thinking of the characters he invented – everyone writes them differently, in his own personal way. With their help it is possible to convict criminals – of either sex! Let me ask you a question: the three of you live here under one roof. Am I right? – Is it not remarkable that the sign which wise old Ts'ang Chieh devised for the word adultery, should just happen to consist of "woman" written three times, as though he had foreseen thousands of years ago what is going on today here in your quarters. Am I right? Do you admit that there is something miraculous about wise old Ts'ang Chieh's script?'

Pearl tried to save the the situation:

'It is true that the three of us live here together. But what grounds have you for your outrageous suspicions? We have done no wrong.'

'No? And how did this compromising notebook come into your possession?'

'We found it in front of the house,' Scent Cloud insisted.

'You expect me to believe that? Why, a three-year-old child wouldn't fall for such fairy tales. And now let us be serious. Where have you hidden the author of the notebook? Confess. If you confess of your own free will, I shall be merciful and spare you the scandal. Otherwise I shall write your husbands in the capital and send them this notebook as evidence. What is more, I shall advise them to come home at once and call you to account.'

With courage born of despair, the three culprits persisted in their denail: 'We really found it quite by accident. We know nothing about the author, whether his name is Chang or Li, or where he lives. What more can we say?' But their words sounded very feeble and made no impression at all on the prosecuting attorney. Once again she looked round the boudoir, darting her glances to eastward and to westward, until they finally came to rest on a certain object. The bamboo trunk! She had overlooked it in her previous tour of inspection – And why was the lid closed? It had always been open before. There must be some explanation. She turned to Pearl and Jade:

'Since you refuse to confess, I shall adjourn our hearings for the moment. I really came for a very different purpose. I have always wanted to take a look at your picture scrolls but somehow I never got around to it. Won't you be so kind as to show me a few?'

Pearl and Jade exchanged looks of consternation.

'Oh,' they cried both at once, 'it's just too absurd! The trunk has been locked for a long while and we have mislaid the key somewhere; we have no idea where to look for it. But we shall look for it tomorrow, it must be somewhere about, and then we'll send the scrolls over to your house.'

'But I happen to be just in the mood to look at them now,' said Aunt Chen with an amiable smile. 'It doesn't matter about the key. I have heaps of keys at home, keys to fit every conceivable lock. I'll just send one of my maids for the key basket.' And that is exactly what she did. It was not long before the maid returned, struggling under the weight of a large basket. It must have contained several hundred keys.

Aunt Chen set to work at once, fitting keys in the lock.

The three young ladies stood there like statues, looking on in utter helplessness. They couldn't very well intervene, for that would only have confirmed her suspicions. Their last feeble hope was that none of the keys would fit. But it was quickly disappointed. Luck was on the side of their adversary. Their aunt had no need to try two keys or three keys, the very first one fit, the lock sprang open and she raised the lid.

And what a surprise! What did she see? No dead picture scrolls, no, an extremely living and well-shaped scroll of flesh and blood in the shape of a stark-naked, handsome youth. His skin was smooth and luminous. His truncheon – luckily for her, for otherwise the sight might have given her too great a shock – was lying in a quiet resting position across one thigh.

Even so she was so frightened that she quickly dropped the lid and closed the lock again. With a show of indignation, she turned to the three convicted culprits:

'A fine kettle of fish! So that's what you've been doing behind your husbands' backs. Since when have you had this individual in the house? And how many nights have you been carrying on with him? Confess. Where have you left your tongues?'

The three poor sinners were struck speechless. Their faces were the colour of parched earth.

'Very well,' said Aunt Chen sternly. 'Since you are so obstinate and refuse to confess, I have no other course but to report the matter to a magistrate. There will be a public scandal. You have brought it on yourselves.' She beckoned her two maids to come closer.

'I want you', she ordered, 'to run and tell the whole neighbourhood that triple adultery has been going on here in broad daylight. Tell them the offender has been caught in the act and that we have him safe under lock and key. Tell the people to come and look at him so they can testify when the case comes to court.'

The three sinners begged for a brief adjournment of the proceedings and retired to deliberate. They quickly concluded that the threat of a public scandal was not meant seriously, that their aunt merely wished to intimidate them in order to secure a share in their treasure. Very well, that could be discussed. The most sensible policy, they decided, was to propitiate her, to make concessions to negotiate a compromise, a *modus vivendi*.

They returned to the hall of judgment.

'We recognise the wrong we have done. We should never have done such a thing behind your back. A fault is a fault, we have no wish to deny it or embellish it. We throw ourselves on your mercy and ask your magnanimous indulgence; we further request that you open the trunk; its occupant would also like to make humble amends.'

'Very well. I agree to that. But there is one thing to be settled first. What form are his amends to take?'

Scent Cloud took the floor: 'We wish to inform our revered aunt that we cousins have so far enjoyed equal shares in this treasure of ours. From now on we shall be glad to offer you a one-quarter share, with the understanding that you as the oldest will take precedence over your nieces.'

Aunt Chen burst out laughing.

'That is an odd, not to say ridiculous, offer. Ha, ha! As I see it, you have hidden this certain someone here for heavens knows how long and taken your pleasure with him for heaven knows how many days and nights. And now you condescend to offer me a quarter share of the future pleasures. It is as though a judge should remit a thief's punishment – no torture, no imprisonment, no restitution of the stolen goods – and merely specify that he pay the authorities a small share of the proceeds of his future larcenies. You expect me to fall for that? Don't make me laugh.'

'What did you have in mind?' asked Pearl rather hesitantly.

'I am willing to let mercy prevail, to pass the matter over in silence on one condition: I will take this someone home with me and keep him for my bed companion until I have caught up on the pleasures you have swindled me out of. Once I am caught up, I shall return him to you, and you can sport with him again as you please. That is my offer. Should you decline it, I shall turn him over to the judge, and at the very best he will be thrashed until he looks like a lump of sausage with whom you will hardly wish to satisfy your appetites. Well, what have you to say?'

'In that case,' Jade suggested, 'we ought to specify the number of nights during which he will belong to you alone and at the end of which you must give him back. I trust that you don't mean to monopolise him for a whole month or a year.'

'Let us leave that question open for the present. When I get him home, I shall question him until I find out how many nights you have been carrying on together. I claim exactly as many nights for myself alone. Then and only then will I give him back. I have nothing more to add.'

The three told themselves inwardly that he would be sure to underestimate the number of nights he had spent with them in the hope of being sent back to them as quickly as possible. They said they had no objection.

'He has only been with us for two nights,' they added so loudly and distinctly that the someone in the trunk would be sure to hear. 'You can ask him when you get home. He will tell you the same thing.'

They now wished to let him out of the trunk so that he might escort their aunt home. To this she was opposed. She feared that once free he might give her the slip.

'It is still daylight. If we should arrive together, my staff would see him and wonder what is going on. I shouldn't like that. No, we must think up a way of transferring him unnoticed.'

'You go home now,' the nieces suggested. 'When it's dark, we shall send him over.'

Aunt Chen shook her head. That too struck her as unsafe. What assurance had she that these sly young snips would keep their word and not let him escape?

'I have it. A wonderful idea. There's no need to open the trunk. We shall let my servants carry it over just as it is, contents and all. I shall tell them it contains picture scrolls which are mine but which you had borrowed for a time. It's as simple as can be.'

Without even waiting for her nieces to answer, she sent one of her maids to summon her major-domo and four strong servants. They soon appeared, bringing ropes and carrying poles. At a terse command from their mistress the servants tied the ropes round the trunk and fastened them to the poles which they slung over their shoulders. A moment later the major-domo left the house followed by the servants and their burden. Aunt Chen brought up the rear with her two lady's maids.

Sad at heart, the three confederates looked after the receding procession. They felt like grieving widows looking after the coffin of a beloved husband and were very close to weeping and wailing. Away he went, their living vernal palace! And to make matters worse, they were worried. What would that man-crazy female do to him? It was perfectly possible that she would wear him out completely. Perhaps he would never return. That trunk was so like a coffin: an evil omen.

My esteemed readers will learn in the next chapter whether or not the Before Midnight Scholar was to find his way back to his beloved bamboo shoots.

In the meanwhile dinner was announced and all five sat down to the festive board. Of course the place of honour at one end of the table was reserved for Aunt Chen; at the other end sat the 'mutual friend'; the three cousins occupied the sides. Dish after dish of the choicest fare was served, accompanied by rich wines and sharp brandies. Soon the whole company was in the riotous mood which can so easily transform a merry dinner into a wild orgy.

The Before Midnight Scholar saw that a kind of chairman was needed who would take things in hand and enforce order. He suggested that they match fingers to choose a *ling-kuan*, an 'order giver'.

The winner, he proposed, should preside over the table and direct the subsequent entertainment. In this way confusion and quarrels would be avoided.

His suggestion was accepted unanimously – especially Aunt Chen was secretly delighted, for finger matching was her specialty. Five pairs of fists were raised at once, and each member of the company, from our scholar to Jade, the youngest of the cousins, had to show his skill at quick guessing. Quite as she had expected, Aunt Chen proved to be the quickest and shrewdest guesser. It was she who won the contest and was honoured with the post of chairman, or, if you will, chairwoman. She appointed the Before

Midnight Scholar *chien-ling-kuan*, her deputy. It was up to him to see that her commands were properly carried out.

From this point on all had to obey her commands. And when it came to giving orders, she was never at a loss. The first thing she did was to issue a detailed set of rules and regulations for the ensuing entertainment.

Her procedure was borrowed from the academic banquets held in the imperial Park of Rubies by candidates who have just passed the Palace examination. The *chuang-yüan*, or first victor, acts as chairman, seconded by the *pang-yen*, or second victor, and the *t'an-hua*, or third victor, who serve as his deputies.

Aunt Chen assumed the role of a *chuang-yüan*. And these were her orders: anyone whom the chairman, the *ling-kuan*, challenged to drink, must comply. And infringement on festive discipline would be punished by punitive cups. Whenever the aunt drank or imposed a drink on one of the cousins, the Before Midnight Scholar, as a gentleman, was obliged to 'keep company'. Little Jade was exempted from drinking. Having come out last in the finger matching, she was treated like a candidate who had flunked his examination, exempted not only from drinking, but also from active participation in the ensuing love contest, and constrained to serve as a kind of orderly, a maid of all work, performing such menial tasks as filling the cups and standing ready with hot towels. She was expected to stay sober. This ruling was quite acceptable to our little Jade, who was decidedly weak in both subjects, drinking and bed-battling.

The regulations provided that the love contest would be organised in the form of a lotto game with cards. The deck of cards was to be placed face down. Each of the three participants – as we have seen, Jade, the youngest, was exempted – was to pick the topmost card and then proceed, with the help of the Before Midnight Scholar, to act out the position represented on the face. As to the order of sequence, the chairwoman arranged it quite arbitrarily and entirely to her own advantage. Determined to follow recipe number three and improve her mood by listening to other people's sound effects, she laid down an order which was the exact opposite of what should have followed from the results of the finger matching: first Pearl, the loser, then Scent Cloud the second best, and finally the high and mighty chairwoman. Once a player had picked a card, she was forbidden to exchange it. Her regulations regarding the duration of the combact were equally autocratic. Pearl was granted one hundred ins-and-outs, and Scent Cloud two hundred, quite regardless of whether this allowance sufficed to make the cloud burst. Jade was instructed to count the ins-and-outs with the utmost precision. Any couple which exceeded or fell short of the prescribed number would be condemned to a number of punitive cups corresponding to the discrepancy. The chairwoman generously granted herself an unlimited number of ins-and-outs; the battle was to go on till the cloud burst. The participant who imitated the picture most authentically and elegantly was to be declared victor. Arbitrary deviations from the model were to be sanctioned by punitive cups and moreover entailed a reduction in the guilty party's allotted time and number.

At this point Pearl ventured a question:

'But what if the exalted *ling-kuan*, the chairman, should deviate from the model, what then?'

'Then I shall condemn myself to three punitive cups and begin again from the beginning,' said Aunt Chen graciously and without much reflection. 'If, in general, I should commit any breach of the regulations or injustice of any sort, you may set up a loud cry of protest. I have no wish to exert a dictatorship in the manner of the tyrant Chou-hsin of the Yin dynasty (1154–1122 BC).'

Here was a dangerous concession that could have grave consequences. The three cousins exchanged sly looks. Well would they mark their aunt's incautious words. But for the present they listened like obedient nieces, receiving their orders with humbly bowed heads. The Before Midnight Scholar took the liberty now and then of asking a question or raising a slight objection, and then a brief debate arose. But why were the three nieces so willing to accept regulations which obviously gave the chairman all the advantages and themselves all the drawbacks? There was a very special reason.

It was not for nothing that they had held a secret council of war. They had hatched out a plan so sly as to be positively diabolical. Just wait and see!

The rules having been established, the contest began. The chairman took a cup of wine and commanded Scent Cloud to take two; the deputy 'kept company'. Then Jade – this was one of her duties as an orderly – took a damp cloth and wiped the cards which had grown dusty from lying about unused for many years, shuffled them carefully in sight of all, and stacked them face down on the table.

Pearl was first to pick a card, which in accordance with the rules she showed the others. The picture represented the position designated as 'dragon-fly gliding over the waves': a nude beauty lies on the bed with legs parted wide but not raised; her companion, his arms resting on the coverlet, lies over her, his torso raised a good three feet, and plays about with her in the manner of a dragon-fly which skims over the surface of the water and does not dive in.

Pearl and the Before Midnight Scholar undressed, took the position of their model, and ran through the prescribed hundred ins-and-outs. As a favour to Aunt Chen, they affected a frenzy of passion long before they had got to the point, and emitted a wide variety of rutting sounds. Finally, Jade, who had been conscientously counting, ordered them to stop and handed them the damp towels which she held in readiness.

Next it was Scent Cloud's turn. The card she picked and showed around represented the position known as 'pushing the bark upstream'. A beauty is reclining in a light armchair, the lower part of her body raised high above the edge. Her companion, standing by the edge of the chair, has lifted her legs over his shoulders. His torso bent forward, his hands propped on the back of the chair, he is pushing with all his might, at every stroke moving the chair slightly forward.

Scent Cloud and her companion took the prescribed position and set conscientiously to work. The sound effects seemed more spontaneous and genuine than those emitted in the previous performance and put Aunt Chen into so high a mood, into such a lather of excitement, that she could hardly wait for the couple to finish their stint so that she herself could go on. Since on this occasion she was able to feast her eyes as well as her ears, it seems likely that she felt even more stirred up than in times past when she had coughed to let her husband know that his preparatory efforts had put her in a state of readiness.

No sooner was the second act concluded than she sprang from her chair and proclaimed in a tone of arrogant self-importance:

'And now make way! It is my turn to perform.'

Such was her haste that while one hand reached for the card, the other was already fiddling with her sash. She picked her card and looked at it. And what did she see? The hand holding it fell lifeless at her side.

'This card says . . . No, never,' she cried in a raucous voice, struggling to keep her composure. 'I'm going to exchange it.'

Hereupon her nieces set up a loud cry of protest. They tore the card from her fingers and quickly hid the rest of the stack away. Then they put their heads together and looked at the picture on the card. Goodness, what a surprise! In one camp bitter fury, in the other malicious joy!

The picture represented the objectionable 'I want to get married' position, in which the lover is forcing an entrance into his lady's upraised back yard. Was it only the malice of chance that had condemned the worthy aunt and chairwoman to perform in this position? No, it was something more.

To palm this card off on their aunt, that was the diabolical plan the cousins had hatched at their secret council of war. The execution had been entrusted to Jade, whose work it was to wipe and shuffle the cards. Once Aunt Chen had decided that the last turn would be hers,

Jade had deftly smuggled the topmost card into the third position. It was the cousins' shrewd calculation that their aunt would draw this card.

However, since the card was drawn in the normal way, it seemed possible that higher powers, spirits of vengeance, had a hand in the business and had allied themselves with human wit to punish Aunt Chen for her arrogance and domineering behaviour.

The nieces insisted that their aunt perform as scheduled. She put up a desperate struggle.

'Dear friends, please,' she begged tearfully. 'Won't you let me off? Be generous. You can't possibly expect such a thing of me.'

'Let you off?' cried the nieces. 'It's out of the question: Equal rights for all! What if one of us had picked this same card? Would you have let her off? I doubt it. You made up the rules. Once a card is picked, it cannot be exchanged under any circumstances. And didn't you boast that you knew all the positions by heart, that you wouldn't have to cling to Buddha's feet? Those were your very own words. If you thought that card was unsuitable, why didn't you remove it at the start? No, no. The rules are the rules. Off with your clothes. Or shall we undress you by force?'

The rebellious nieces turned to the Before Midnight Scholar: 'Hey, you. Why don't you say something? What are you deputy for? A fine deputy!'

'But my dear ladies. Far be it from me, as deputy, to take the part of our honoured chairwoman – but consider, if you please, how nature has endowed me. The thing is impossible, if only on technical grounds. Let us not be too cruel. I propose that we spare our worthy chairwoman this excessive punishment and condemn her to a certain number of punitive cups instead.'

But his attempted diplomacy served only to irritate rebellious youth.

'*Fang p'i!* Nonsense. If she is permitted to get away with punitive cups, why weren't we? Do you suppose we enjoyed the show we had to put on? You may be sure we would have been very glad to drain a few cups instead.'

The deputy could not deny the logic of their argument. There just wasn't anything plausible he could say. He fell silent for a time and pondered. The chairwoman was also at a loss. Finally the Before Midnight Scholar found his tongue:

'I have a proposal. Perhaps your ladyships, instead of insisting that the debt be paid in full, might remit just a few farthings. Let her, if you wish, strip to the skin in plain sight of us all. Let her take the prescribed pose and forgive her the rest.'

Scent Cloud and Jade raised a clamour, insisting mercilessly that the whole debt be paid. Pearl, however, declared without batting an eyelash that she accepted the proposed compromise.

'Very well, let her just undress and take the pose.'

The chairwoman and her deputy heaved a sigh of relief. Though with some resistance at first, she allowed him to remove her clothing. Then, reluctantly, but spurred on by encouraging remarks from all sides, she took the position on the edge of a divan: face and belly down, rear portal upraised.

The Before Midnight Scholar sent out his ambassador and, by way of stimulating the performance demanded by the rules, let him stroll about in the valley of secret joys and sniff at the hidden rear portal, but gave him strict orders not to force the gate. Even so, the exalted chairwoman yelled bloody murder. Then assuming that enough was enough and that she had honestly fulfilled her obligations, she prepared to rise.

But the saucy young ladies wouldn't hear of it. Pearl's acceptance of the compromise solution – that she should merely undress and take the pose – had not been meant seriously. It had only been a stratagem to delude the victim and disarm her resistance. Now that she had been fooled into taking the requisite position, the show must proceed. On this the young things insisted unanimously and in no uncertain terms.

Three pairs of hands sprang into action, pushing down the victim's head, her hands and shoulders pinned fast. As though clamped in a vice, she was unable to twist or even wriggle.

There was nothing she could do. Guided by an affectionate hand, the deputy's ambassador forced his way through the narrow portal. To make matters worse, one of the three young fiends stationed herself behind the Before Midnight Scholar and pushed with all her might to increase the ambassador's impetus.

By now he was halfway in. The victim screamed and whimpered, as though under torture: 'Have pity! I'm dying!' Frightened, the Before Midnight Scholar paused.

'We'd better stop. We wouldn't want to endanger her life.'

'Not until the cloud bursts,' cried the young fiends. 'That's what it says in her own rules.'

'Well, then, suppose we ask her how she's doing.'

'It's burst, it's burst,' moaned Aunt Chen. And then again: 'It's burst, it's burst.'

Finally the executioners relented and released their victim. With difficulty Aunt Chen struggled to her feet. Speechless and broken, she staggered out, supported by her maids.

For three days she lay sick in bed, racked with fever. A painful red swelling had formed on her rear portal.

Her three days of bed rest brought repentance. She recognised the wrong she had done her nieces with her arrogance. Though still a mite resentful, she felt that her punishment had been deserved.

As soon as she was able to go out, she returned next door and celebrated a solemn reconciliation with her former enemies. From then on the five of them – four women and one man – took their pleasure in perfect harmony and friendship on the same cushions and under the same blanket.

The Marquis de Sade (1740–1814)

Case Notes

Mad, bad and dangerous to know? Donatien Alphonse François de Sade makes Byron look like a model of tact and discretion. Not just because his surname was appropriated by Kraft-Ebbing in his *Psychopathia Sexualis* (1876) to describe the urge to rampant, pathological sexual domination (although the word *sadisme* had been in use in France since the 1830s) does he remain one of the few writers whose name genuinely shocks in the wrong company. Like Byron, he's a writer who is mythologised as much as a man as for his work. Lord Byron, however, made his own contribution to his myth, and played up the facets of his character that made him a proto rock-god, if you will, and – well – a Don Juan, of the early nineteenth century. He colluded in creating a vision of himself which took no heed of the undeniable beauty of some of his poetry, but which was great PR and undoubtedly helped him to enjoy the popularity in his own short lifetime denied to many of the writers who have posthumously entered one canon or another.

Sade, by contrast, though he undoubtedly bears some responsibility for this himself, had infamy thrust upon him from his earliest brush with the law. His card was marked. Contrary to playing up to it, that infamy was to plague him in very real ways all of his comparatively long life, and it was unjust even by the standards of a modern tabloid editorial. And yet, to my own disappointment, I find him impossible to write about without adopting the qualified tone of a social worker.

The sometimes tawdry events of Sade's own life have undergone unparalleled embellishment in the intervening centuries, both as the subject of censure, a literary Gilles de Rais, and praise, as one who turned a spotlight on the hypocrisy of the powerful of any stamp, imprisoned by three different regimes. To Simone de Beauvoir, he was the apotheosis of the misogynistic, pathologically objectifying male, to the surrealists he highlighted the absurdity of the established order. Baudelaire's original 'flower of evil', he is the ultimate non-joiner, his body of work a big 'fuck you' to belief in anything other than the irredeemably pathological, primeval nature of the beast within humankind. 'All universal moral principles are idle fantasies.'[1] Unbelievable as it may seem now, Customs and Excise only officially allowed the importation of his works into the UK in 1983. Today his life is undergoing another round of mythologising, as in the film *Quills* for example, for which he's fair game, and his writings seem relevant again.

At the turn of this century the world appears to be a brutalising dystopia. The last decade has seen a worldwide resurgence of ethnic hatreds from Rwanda to the Balkans and the Middle East, and the widespread acceptance that we can't, as a species, seem to put the world to rights so there's no point even trying. Or at least, that good intentions can bring about as much harm as ill intent. The gleeful bloodlust of such folly, so extreme that we can only make sense of it by thinking of its perpetrators as being transported in some way, makes Sade's world view seem more resonant than ever. Sade's notion that Nature compels the subjugation of the weak by the strong prefigures the baldest interpretation of evolutionary theory as espoused by would-be alpha males in pubs and bars

[1] *120 Days of Sodom.*

throughout the western world, 'We are no guiltier in following the primitive impulses that govern us than is the Nile for her floods or the sea for her waves.'[2]

In deciding whether or not he's actually any good, given how problematic he is, the question is whether he gives away more about himself or about the world, and how much he shares his protagonists' glee. 'It is not the object of debauchery that excites us, rather the idea of evil.'[3]

Much of Sade's work is pure pornographic fantasy, written to aid the private thrills of a bored and probably copiously masturbating prisoner. It becomes more and more Gothic and, according to Swinburne, ludicrous, the longer the period of his incarceration and the more he had to rely on his own fetid imagination rather than direct experience. And yet some of his earlier work is Swiftean satire which betrays a burning sense of social injustice. As any responsible pervert will know, there shouldn't be a contradiction here, any more than there is in dividing Graham Greene's work into his 'entertainments' and his religiose novels. Except that Sade did not make the distinction about his own work the way that Greene did. It runs the gamut confusingly between beyond-the-pale baroque torture and righteous indignation at the sufferings of the innocent. Sade confused his goals. Had he identified firmly whether he was in the mood to write pornography or polemic each time he sat at his desk, he might have made his life and his legacy a lot less confusing.

The story excerpted here, *Justine*, was written in 1787, during Sade's second period of imprisonment and a decade after his legal troubles had begun, and as such it falls into what we could deem the early period, before the disassociated excesses of pornographic imagination typified by *The One Hundred and Twenty Days of Sodom* (even though the latter was begun at around the same time). I've chosen it for inclusion here because of all his work it most exhibits the contradiction between social commentary and extreme

---

[2] *Aline and Valcour.*

[3] *120 Days of Sodom.*

SM detail unqualified by the fact that it's fantasy – in the sense that not all sexual fantasies are necessarily things we'd actually like to have happen – that is Sade at his most interesting.

We commonly think of Sade as a dealer in baroque visions, surrounded by the ghoulish tools of his pleasure like a literary Doctor Frankenstein. But he was a realist writer of sorts. Not in the sense that he had the literary ability to bring alive the social sufferings of eighteenth-century France, but it's easy to overlook the fact that he was every inch a man of his time, and an keen observer of it. The self-justifying ramblings of the aristocrats and priests in *The Misfortunes of Virtue*, and their bald assertions that might is right, are akin to Swift's famous solution to the Irish problem – that they eat their own babies. He takes a commonly espoused authoritarian view to its extreme to show its innate barbarity, and after all he lived in barbaric times. It was to his confusion more than anyone's, one feels, that this barbarism also turned him on.

The aristocratic indifference to the sufferings of the subjugated, which viewed them as fit only for one to take one's pleasure with, and the climate of institutionalised violence, led directly to the French Revolution. And it was Sade's independence of mind, the freedom from received ideas which allowed him to observe injustice, which led him also to the orgiastic lifestyle that got him into so much trouble and in which he was aided by his wife and later his mistress. For all his excesses – and his obesity – he had, it seems, a cad's charm.

Sade was both saved and cursed by the Revolution. Having been imprisoned largely at the whim of his mother in law, he had been transferred to the Bastille in 1784, and then to an insane asylum to the south-east of Paris, from which he was released under an amnesty issued in 1790 by the Revolutionary authorities, to include anyone incarcerated by the iniquitous system of *lettres de cachet*. As a moderate Revolutionary, Sade made his home in Paris and became president of his district. At this time he had the opportunity to send his mother in law, who as Presidente de Montrieul had been responsible for keeping him in prison for many years, to the guillotine. He didn't take it. In fact, his leniency made him a target of the Revolutionaries, suspicious that it betokened seditious opinions rather than compassion – he foreswore cruelty outside of a sexual context – and he was imprisoned once more in 1794. Sentenced to death, he was saved that same year when Robespierre fell, thereafter bitterly confirmed in his view of compassion as weakness.

Given his flawed intellectual honesty – he does nothing if not show us the worst of himself – we owe him the favour of seeing his work in the context of the things that both revolted and excited him. Eighteenth-century France was a brutal culture, where the powerful held unchecked lien over the abused poor, and where the ideas of the Enlightenment – such as the supremacy of law – were not known beyond the Paris salons. A routine judicial punishment was breaking on the wheel, and at such executions the gentlefolk would copulate behind the drawn blinds of their carriages as they watched the horror unfold. Until one realises that breaking on the wheel was not technically an execution as such, one cannot understand why Dr Guillotine was a humane man. But the executioner's art was to aim his blows at the victim's limbs, pelvic bone and ribs in such a way as to prolong the agony, often with the aid of various restorative draughts and preparations. A man may first have had his genitals wrenched off, and a woman her breasts. Once the wretch's broken limbs were contorted around the wheel and fastened in place such that they could be made to stare directly down at the upturned soles of their feet, they were hoisted aloft on a long pole and left to die as the birds pecked at their eyeballs, still aware as they began their inexorable transition into carrion. In this context, Sade starts to look like a bit of a pussycat.

Sodom contains relentless and at times unreadable detail of sexual terror, but in one way is a more straightforward – if harder – read than *Misfortunes*, since it qualifies itself as pornographic in intention. But it's also deeply flawed.

Written on the hoof during the topsy-turvy events of the Revolution, lost or destroyed once, and eventually finished in note form, it is a work without irony or levity, which asks few questions of itself, and which becomes pantomimic. Although admiring its atheism, Swinburne, with all the jaded insouciance of a sophisticated urbanite who'd been the subject of regular beatings at Eton, found it nothing more than 'an ingenious acrobatic performance'. One suspects he was affecting the unshockability *de rigeur* for a decadent like himself, however, for who cannot raise one's eyebrows at the one hundred and fifty murderous passions, narrated by Madame Desgranges, such as, 'His earlier passion was to squeeze the girl's neck, in later years he would tie the girl by the neck. Before her sits a sumptuous meal, but to reach it she must strangle; otherwise she dies of hunger.'[4] Or 'His first passion is for bestiality, his second is to sew the girl into untanned donkey's skin, her head protruding; he feeds and cares for her until the animal skin shrinks and crushes her to death.'[5] These things should not be written without qualification as fantasy of the kind one would be sickened by in reality, as evidence suggests Sade the man was. And yet to hold him culpable for thinking them is to subscribe to an Orwellian notion of thought-crime. My own counsel would be that Sade plead guilty to the lesser charge of taste-crime and throw himself on the mercy of the court!

In seeing the male sexual instinct as essentially murderous – and not just in the sense of conquest, of administering an orgasmic *coup de grace*, a *petit mort*, a consensual act, Sade seems convinced of the *rightness* of the lien the strong have over the weak. The truth is, the Sade who wrote *Sodom* had been perverted – in the wrong way – by bitterness. After years of imprisonment, he must've felt he owed no one any qualification of his barbarous thoughts. Much of his early work, such as *Misfortunes*, has a lightness of touch, a consistently satirical outlook, and

---

[4] Ibid..
[5] Ibid..

characterisation. He's flirting with his notion of the superiority of an indifferent Nature, of which we're part, as red in tooth and claw as anything else. In *Sodom*, he is, without apology, faithfully wedded to it, justifying Andrea Dworkin's thesis that all male sexuality springs from a murderous impulse. There's truth, perhaps, in the idea that *some* of it does.

But let's not take a madman, and one in denial, as the apotheosis of male sexuality. One can see a source of Sade's bitterness. If his first spell of incarceration had resulted from falling foul of his mother in law, and his second the Revolutionary authorities, his third – in which he was dispatched back to the asylum at Charenton – was on account of nothing other than falling foul of the new puritanism that was abroad at the end of the Terror. He had given of his intellectual honesty, as he saw it, and been censured for it. He didn't hold himself responsible for the excesses of his imagination. Sade's concern was to make sense of a barbaric world, and from it he concluded that Nature rewards the strong, and if there's no morality other than the natural order then that must make it right, or at least render right and wrong irrelevent. He was troubled and angered by the injustices of his time and place and this thesis was an attempt to come to terms with them, in order to achieve peace of mind and ease with the natural order, given that the events of his life had shown him his *own* powerlessness once he'd annoyed the wrong people. Perhaps his haughty country-squire ego could not take that. Perhaps he just felt sorry for himself. Whatever, his sin was to admit that the semiotics of crime and punishment also excited him.

To Sade's mind, Nature takes no account of the individual, the species is everything, and its survival is assured at the cost of individual suffering. He's not out so much to justify his own rampant urges as to come to terms with suffering – his own, perhaps, as much or more than others' – and achieve peace of mind. He's wrong, for all around us are examples of compassion and collaborative behaviour, from the rearing of children to the combined efforts at survival that a marooned party of sailors or explorers might make, which suggest that empathy and compassion aren't just the fruits of lilly-livered liberalism but are at least as essential to our evolutionary success as pathological brutality and murder.

Sade's work is deeply flawed, but give him the time. He tried to make sense of what excited him, and was honest enough to admit it. Politically he was hardly a Revolutionary, and accepted the *droit de signeur* that was his by birth, but he identified the illegitimacy and hypocrisy inherent in the exercise of power as much as any anarchist, because he believed that it came from the same fetid wellspring as his own sexual instincts. He both attracted and revolted himself, and tried to come to terms with the beast within, pretty hard when you're too embittered to make sense of the difference between reality and fantasy. His writing's not always that great, either. With regard to *The One Hundred and Twenty Days of Sodom*, for example, it's fair to say that one could almost originate a 'write like Sade' software program of which the first requirement would be to insert 'while being sodomised' as the last clause in every third sentence. (Considering their decadent slack-arsed gape, however, that particular vice is never too much of an arduous torment for our heroes.)

If you don't think I have already, then I'm not even going to attempt to justify the wilder excesses of his fiction, except to say that he must've been very bored. Nor especially de Beauvoir's charge, based on the fact that his work is pretty much all male dom/fem sub, except to say that, well, that's just the way he swung. Politically, he would have agreed with these words of Dostoyevsky: 'A harsh whipping with a cane is the worst kind of torture practised in our country. Though it may seem impossible, five hundred lashes, even just four hundred, is all it takes to kill a man. The right to corporal punishment exercised by one man over another is one of the evils that afflicts society, it is a sure means to smother any seed of civilisation and to cause it to decompose.' That was, thought Sade, a process which had long since been completed, had the seed of civilisation ever taken root at all.

Perhaps it's true to say, as the psychoanalyst Alfred Adler might have, that his *real* fantasy isn't about sex at all, but about power. It's hardly surprising that Mummy's little Alphonse should, after a lifetime of imprisonment that was little if ever justified by the extent of his real crimes and misdemeanours, create for himself a world in which the untrammeled absolute power of the socially privileged male such as himself held lien over the lives – and deaths – of those in subjection to him. It's unusual, in *The Misfortunes of Virtue*, that he goes to great lengths to explain realistically how the gleeful evildoings of the monks at Father Clement's monastery go undetected by the outside world for so long. By contrast, it's frequently part of the fantasy that the law itself, if not explicitly enshrining such a feudal code, simply doesn't apply to such an area. Such activities are often presented simply as being above the law, as if taking place in a mythical principality, let's call it Pornotopia. In the context of the property rights of *ancien regime* France, in which it was pretty much just an aristocratic decency that you didn't kill the poor, it's not hard to see where this derives from.

His prose style often reinforces the idea that it's solely the power that really counts for him. Perhaps it's partly the fault of situations in which he rushed his writing, but we don't get much sense of sweat-sheened, taughtened skin, of squeals and slaps, the kind of gratifying sexual onomatopoeia you'd expect of a modern SM novel. Likewise we get little of the psychology of submission and domination as it happens in reality – there's no indignation on part of sub, ciphers or sex-dolls to a woman, none of the Stockholm Effect come to that. In short, none of the emotional power such extreme situations could have in the hands of someone like Nexus's own Penny Birch. Perhaps he'd simply been incarcerated for so long, the victim in a power-play of a different sort, that he'd forgotten what it was like. What you *do* get is bucketloads of imagination and ideas.

In his will he wrote, 'I flatter myself that my memory will disappear from the minds of men.' The divine Marquis to many, a *bête noir* to even more, Sade was not granted his wish. He lives in infamy, perfect shorthand for all that's beyond the pale. So leave your preconceptions here, and make up your own mind. That's what he'd have really wanted, after all.

Justine

On the way he said, 'I feel much better now, thanks to you.'

Justine then took the liberty of asking him how a rich man such as he travelled without attendants and exposed himself to the danger of being attacked, as had just happened to him.

'I'm young and pretty strong and have always travelled this way alone, on business. I've never been molested before. If I take no one with me it's not because of the expense; I'm rich, as you'll soon see for yourself, and money doesn't bother me; but I enjoy travelling alone better. Those two men who just knocked me down are two shabby gents of this distrct from whom I won some money last week in a gambling house at Vienne. They promised to pay me and I was satisfied with their word of honour and met them today and that was how they paid me off. But,' he said, 'it'll be soon getting dark; we'd better hurry. I know a place about two miles from here where we can stop overnight. Tomorrow we'll get fresh horses there and be able to reach home the same evening.'

Quickening their pace, they did finally reach the inn he mentioned.

They had supper pleasantly together. Later he recommended Justine to the care of the mistress of the house and they both retired separately. She had never felt so happy.

The next morning on two hired mules, escorted by the valet of the inn, they reached the borders of Dauphiny, still steering their course toward the mountains.

The journey being too long to make in one day, they pulled up at Virieu, where Justine received the same cares, the same consideration from her new master. They continued on their way the following day.

About four in the afternoon they got to the foot of the mountains. There the road became almost impassable and Roland, fearing some mishap, charged the muleteer not to leave Justine. They penetrated deep into the narrow passages. The road curved so continuously, rising and descending, that after travelling about four miles, with every beaten track and sign of life behind them, Justine fancied she was at the end of the world.

In spite of herself, a little uneasiness started to come over her which Roland could not help noticing; but he said nothing. His silence made her even more uneasy.

At last they beheld a castle, perched on top of a mountain at the brink of a deep precipice, into which it seemed ready to sink. No road leading to it appeared and they had to follow a goat-path, cluttered with stones on all sides.

'There's my house,' said Roland.

Justine expressed her surprise that he lived in such a wild, desolate place.

'It suits me!' he answered.

This reply redoubled her fears, so much indeed that she now hung upon his every word, gesture and shade of tone to find some reassurance for her growing anxiety. She could do nothing else, and kept silent.

About a quarter of a mile from the castle Roland alighted from his mule and got Justine to do the same. He handed both mules to the muleteer, paid him and ordered him to return.

His procedure gave Justine a great deal of fresh worriment. Roland was aware of it and said, 'What ails you, Therese? You're not out of France. We're on the border of Dauphiny and very near Grenoble.'

'I know,' she answered, 'but what makes you settle down in a place like this?'

'Because those who live in it are very honest folk, that's why. Maybe you'll learn something!'

'Ah, sir!' she said to him, 'how you frighten me! Where are you taking me?'

'Nowhere – just a gang of counterfeiters.'

He grabbed her arm and forced her to cross a little bridge which was lowered at their arrival and raised again immediately after.

As soon as they had entered he showed her a deep grotto at the bottom of the yard, where four chained women were making a wheel turn. 'Do you see this well,' he said, 'there are your companions, and that'll be your job. Provided you work ten hours daily, turning this wheel, and satisfy us like those women, you'll be allowed black bread and a plate of beans every day. As for your freedom, forget about it – you haven't a chance! When you're old and worn out you'll be thrown into that hole there alongside of the well, with about sixty others like you waiting for you inside of it – and then we'll get somebody to replace you.'

'Oh God, please!' she cried, throwing herself at his feet, 'remember how I saved you. . . . You promised to make me happy and protect me . . . how can you forget what I did for you?'

'What do you mean "What I did for you"!' he said. 'Why, you bitch, what were you doing when you came to help me – wasn't it to satisfy an impulse of your own heart! Didn't satisfying it give you pleasure! How in hell can you ask me to be grateful to you for the pleasures you give yourself! And what makes you think that a man like myself, floating in wealth, can owe you anything – a slut like you! If you saved me you did it to satisfy and enjoy your own sentiment – I owe you nothing. . . . To work, slave, to work!'

He gave her no time for further delay and ordered two attendants to strip and chain her with the rest. She had to get right to work, without being permitted to rest herself after the tiresome journey she had just made.

Many hours later Roland approached her and making her stop in her tracks, chained to the wheel, forced her to listen to him as he sat himself comfortably down.

'I want you to know, Therese,' he said, 'that civilisation in overthrowing the principles of nature still leaves the latter some rights, however. In the beginning, you know, nature created strong and weak beings. She intended that the weak be subordinated to the strong. But the dexterity, the intelligence of man diversified the position of individuals; it was no longer physical force that determined ranks, it was money. The richest man became the strongest; the poorest, the weakest. So you see, as long as the priority of power is established, nature is indifferent to whether it be the weak or the poor who are crushed by the man of riches, or the man of strength. Now as for the feeling of gratitude you claim I owe you – it was never nature's intention that one who received a favour should forego his rights over the other who yielded to the pleasure of obliging him. Do you find such sentiments among animals? The pride of an elevated soul should never allow itself to be bowed down by an obligation. Is not he who receives always humiliated? And does not this humiliation which he feels, sufficiently pay the benefactor, who by that alone finds himself raised above the other? Is it not an enjoyment for pride, to raise oneself above the other? Does he who obliges need any other? And if the obligation, in humbling him who receives, becomes a burden to him, why force him to keep it? Why must I allow myself to be humiliated every time one who has obliged me looks at me! Ingratitude, therefore, instead of being a vice, is really the virtue of proud souls, just as expecting gratitude is that of weak souls. Let people oblige me as much as they like, but let them ask nothing in return for having enjoyed the sentiment of obliging.'

He then armed himself with a bull's pizzle and saluted her with twenty stripes. He said, 'I don't do this, Therese, for any fault already committed by you, but merely to give you an idea how I act when you do. This is just how you'll be dealt with when you are lax in your duties.'

He greeted her tears with light mockery. 'Ah,' he said, 'I shall hear more of them; your troubles are first beginning.' And he left her.

Their time was up and Justine as well as her companions were untied. After having been given their daily portion of water, bread and beans, they were locked in for the night.

Under a grotto round this vast well there were six small dark cells, which were locked up like dungeons. There the girls spent the night.

Justine was lost in sombre reflection when the door of her cell was opened and in walked Roland, who seemed nervous and irritable. He gazed at Justine a moment with eyes that made her start.

'Follow me!' he said.

And he got hold of her by the arm and dragged her along. He led her with his right hand, and with his left held a small lantern which dimly lighted their way. After several turnings they got to the door of a cave. He opened it and forcing her in first, told her to descend while he locked the door behind. Much farther on they met a second one which was opened and shut the same way. But when they got into the second cave there were no steps, but a narrow road which, curving around, kept going down.

They walked along about twenty minutes, the sickly blur of light from his lantern occasionally lighting up in the damp stone walls niches containing huge chests of money.

He was silent all the way.

They had got far down into the bowels of the earth. At last they came to a bronze gate which opened into a large round vault about thirty feet in diameter. It was a dark dismal place, furnished with black hangings, and on the walls skeletons of every size, bones formed crosswise, leering death-heads, rods, whips, switches, daggers and pistols. A lamp was suspended from one of the corners of the vault, and in the centre a long rope fell to about ten feet above the ground. On the right stood a coffin, with a kneeling desk alongside, above which hung a crucifix placed between two large black candles. On the left fastened to a cross there was a wax effigy of a naked woman, so real and lifelike that for some time Justine was actually deceived by it. It was nailed to the cross breastwise, so that all its hind parts were clearly exposed. The flesh seemed horribly mortified, and the blood oozed, dripping down along the thighs. Covered with fine hair, its head was turned, appearing to implore forgiveness. All the contorted expressions of suffering on its face seemed so real, even the tears flowing from the protruding, blood-stained eyes. The end of the vault was taken up by a vast black sofa.

'If you ever get the idea into your head to get away, here's where you'll meet your finish!' Roland said. And merely making this threat inflamed him and made him twitch.

Molesting her furiously, he told her that since he now held her in this den it was just as well she didn't leave it, which would save him the trouble of bringing her all the way down again.

She rushed to his knees and tried to remind him again of the good turn she had done him. This irritated him still further and he ordered her to hold her tongue, knocking her down upon the floor with a blow of his knee.

'Come!' he said, hauling her up by the hair, 'come, get ready! I'm certainly going to sacrifice you now!'

'Master . . . master . . .'

'No, no! you must die! I'm sick of hearing myself reproached with your trifling favours; I like to owe nothing to anybody! You must die, I tell you . . . get into this coffin, see if it fits you!'

He flung her into it, locked her in, then went out of the vault, pretending he was leaving her there. But he soon came back and took her out.

'You look swell in there!' he said. 'It was just made for you. But to let you die quietly in there would be too fine a death. I have a better one for you, not half so comfortable. Come, wench, implore your God! Beg him to come and save you; if he really has the power of doing it!'

She threw herself upon the kneeling stool, and while in a loud voice she poured out her heart to the Eternal, Roland tortured her still more cruelly. He scourged her with a hammer studded with steel spikes, every blow of which forced the blood to spurt and spatter into his face. And he continued raving, 'Well! your prayers don't help you! Your unhappy virtue only makes you suffer! It gives way before the hands of wickedness . . . oh, what a delicious irony that is, Therese! Come, your prayer must be over!'

He set her on the sofa again. 'You must die, Therese, I told you so, didn't I!'

He gripped her arms and, tying them to her legs, passed round her neck a black silk cord, both ends of which he held in his hands. At will, he was able to tighten the cord around her neck and choke her to death.

'This torture, Therese,' he said, 'is sweeter than you think. You will feel death through exquisite sensations of pleasure. The squeezing that this cord effects upon the mass of your nerves, will set you on fire. If all persons condemned to this torture knew in what intoxication it brings death they would be less frightened by this punishment and commit their crimes oftener and with far more assurance. This delightful operation, Therese,' he continued, 'will just about redouble my own pleasure too!'

His fury knew no bounds. The more he succeeded, the tighter he pulled the cord round her neck. This amused him and he egged her on to yell louder and louder, modulating the pressure of the cord according to the degree of his pleasure. Then all at once he pulled so violently that the colour in Justine's face turned blue and her senses slowly slipped from under her and her voice gradually died out.

When she opened her eyes she found herself unbound, and he said to her, 'Well, Therese, tell me the truth, didn't you get any pleasure out of it! It doesn't matter; I'm worried more about my own pleasure. It was so good that I'm going to try it again in just a few moments.'

Raising her up on a stool, he threw round her neck the rope hanging from the ceiling, and firmly fastened it. He then tied a cord to the stool, and holding the end, sat down in an armchair opposite. He had given Justine a sharp knife with which she was to cut the rope hanging above her just at that moment when by means of the cord he pulled the stool from under her feet.

'Therese,' he said, 'it all depends on yourself. If you miss your aim I certainly shall not miss mine. Am I wrong in telling you your life depends on yourself?'

He sat down and intended to pull the stool away the moment he reached the high moment of his intoxication.

He was in his full glory and, teasing Justine's already overstrained nerves, often made a feint at pulling the stool. But soon the violence of his feelings betrayed him into making the fatal movement; the stool slipped away, she cut the rope and fell safely to the ground.

The knife in her hand, she might have taken him by surprise and rushed upon him; but she knew it would be useless. She hadn't the keys and, not knowing the way, she would have been dead before she got half-way out of this hidden catacomb. Moreover, he was always armed.

Pleased with her mildness and quite satisfied, he beckoned her to go out, and they both went upstairs again.

Next day Justine examined her companions more closely. The four girls with her were all from about twenty-five to thirty years old. Though stupefied by misery and deformed by their severe labour they still retained a few relics of their former beauty. They were all well built, and the youngest, Suzanne, was especially lovely, with fine eyes and very pretty hair. Roland had taken her at Lyons and carried out away to this castle about three years ago. She more than the others suffered Roland's ferocities. By dint of being lashed with the bull's pizzle her buttocks had become as callous and hard as a cow's hide dried in the sun.

It was she who informed Justine that Roland was soon to set out for Venice, if the large sums he lately had gotten passed in Spain returned him the bills of exchange he was awaiting in Italy. He did not like to carry his gold beyond the mountains, and never sent any there; and was wont to get his forged monies passed in a different country from the one in which he wished to settle down. By this means, rich with the bills of another country, he could never be found out. But any minute everything might go wrong, and the retreat he was contemplating depended on this last transaction in which the principal amount of his treasures was at stake. If his *piasters*, *zechins* and *louis* were accepted at Cadiz and he got, accordingly, bills of Venice, Roland would be happy for the rest of his life. But if his fraud were discovered, one day alone would suffice to ruin him.

'Great god!' cried Justine, 'I hope they get him!'

About twelve o'clock the girls were allowed two hours' rest, by which they generally profited going singly to their rooms to eat and breathe and relax. But at two they were tied up again and forced to work until night.

They were mostly naked not only because of the heat, but much rather to be in a better way of receiving the stripes of the bull's pizzle which their master came occasionally to lay on. In cold weather they were supplied with a pair of trousers and waistcoat so tight to the skin that their bodies were nevertheless just as well exposed to the blows of a man whose pleasure was to thrash them.

That same night, Roland came again for Justine in her dungeon, and, falling into a passion at the sight of his cruelties, started to molest and abuse her again. When he appeared assuaged, she took advantage of his moment's calmness and entreated him to ease her lot. But, alas, she was still not aware that if in such natures the moment of delirium renders their passion for cruelty more active, calmness does not on the other hand soften them; or that they are possessed by a fire, even though under ashes, which burns nevertheless at all times, because of an inextinguishable supply of fuel constantly keeping it up.

'And why should I?' he answered. 'By what right do you ask that I ease your lot? Is it because of the pleasure you have given me? But am I going at your feet begging for the favours you grant me? I ask nothing from you – I take. I do not see why, because I use a right over you, I must abstain from exacting a second one. There is no love in my case. Love is a chivalrous sentiment thoroughly despised by me, and my heart has never felt it. I make use of a woman from necessity as one makes use of a round hollow vase in a different need. But I never bestow either esteem or tenderness upon an individual whom my money or strength submits to my passions. I owe only to myself for what I rob. Never requiring submission, why should I show gratitude? Does a man who steals another's purse owe him any thanks? It is the same with a crime committed on a woman. There's always good cause to commit a second one, but never sufficient reason for making amends.' He was a very outspoken man.

'Oh, sir! to what height you carry wickedness!'

'To the highest point, Therese, to the highest point! There isn't anything I have not given way to, nothing that I have not done! My principles excuse and make legitimate every one of them. I have always found in evil an attraction. Crime kindles my lust, and the more frightful it is the more it excites me. I enjoy in committing it the same kind of pleasure ordinary people taste in a woman – even more, much more. On a thousand occasions when I've found myself thinking of crime – giving myself up to it, or having just committed it – it put me in the same state as one is when beside a lovely naked woman; it stirs my senses up in the same way. I perpetrate it in order to be inflamed. Without it I am impotent.'

'Oh, sir! what you say is awful, but I have seen examples of it before.'

'There are a thousand of them, Therese. You must not imagine that it is a woman's beauty which stirs up the spirit. It is really the crime involved that makes possession attractive to me. The more criminal, the more inflamed one is. The man who enjoys a woman he steals from her husband, a girl he seduces, is undoubtedly far more delighted than the husband who merely enjoys his wife. And the more worthy of respect the bonds severed, the more delightful is the act. When one has tasted all, he wants his obstacles increased in order to cause pains and have greater difficulty surmounting them. Now, if crime seasons an enjoyment, separate from this enjoyment, it can be a pleasure in itself. Yes, crime alone can be an enjoyment. Otherwise, how could it lend savour if it weren't itself savoury. These theories lead far, I know. I'll even prove it to you before long just how far. But it doesn't matter, as long as one enjoys. Was there, for instance, my child, anything simpler or more natural than to see me enjoy you? You didn't think so. You thought I was under an obligation to you. But I yield to nothing; I break all the ties which ensnare fools. I subject you to my desires, and out of the simplest, the most monotonous enjoyment I make a truly delightful one. Yield therefore, Therese, yield and learn. When you return to the world as one of the strong, misuse likewise your rights and you shall see how lively and acute every pleasure will be!'

Roland walked out and left her absorbed in bitter reflections.

Justine had already been in this den about six months, serving all Roland's whims, when one evening he walked into her cell with Suzanne.

'Come, Therese,' he said, 'it seems to me a long time since I've taken you down to that vault which had frightened you so much. Follow me, both of you; but don't you both expect to come back; I must leave one behind – we'll see to whose lot it'll fall.'

Justine stood up and cast bewildered looks at Suzanne, whose eyes were clouded with tears. They went down.

Hardly were they shut up in the underground vault when Roland gloated over them with wild eyes. He took special pleasure in repeating their doom, and in convincing them that one of the two would certainly remain behind.

'Come,' he said, seating himself and making them stand straight up before him, 'she who pleases me best will get the prize.'

'It's not right,' said Suzanne, 'she who pleases you best ought to be the one to be forgiven.'

'Not at all! The moment I find out who is best, I will be certain then that *her* death will give me most pleasure. Besides, if I were to pardon the one who pleased me the more, you'd both set to work with such ardour that you would perhaps cast my senses into the ecstasy before the complete consummation of the sacrifice, and this is just what I don't want.'

'The completion of your ecstasy is all you should want, and if you attain it without crime, why must you commit one!' said Justine.

'Ah! because I shall reach it more deliciously, and I came down here to commit one, and commit one I'm going to!

That lovely skin, Therese,' he said to Justine, 'is still very far from being as hard and callous as Suzanne's. One could set fire to that dear girl's rumps and she would not feel it. But yours, Therese, but yours . . .'

This threat really tranquillised her. Since he intended to subject her to fresh cruelties it was obvious to her that he had not as yet a mind to immolate her.

'I don't think,' he said to Suzanne, 'that the most frightful lashes could draw another drop of blood from that back of yours!'

He frisked about, as animated as a young cold in spring.

'Suzanne,' he said at last, 'you win. I don't know what I should like to do to you!'

'Oh, sir, have pity on her, she is in enough pain!' Justine pleaded.

Oh, yes! Ah, if I only had that famous Emperor Kie here we should indeed do something different. I am too mild, Therese, quite a stranger to it all, a mere school boy!'[1]

'Come, Therese,' he said, 'come, dear girl, let's have a little game of rope cutting.'[2]

---

[1] The Chinese Emperor Kie was one of the greatest scoundrels ever seen on the throne. His wife was as cruel and debauched. Between them they shed for their pleasure floods of blood daily.

We are told that, immolating their victims, they used to prolong their lives in the cruellest agonies of death, and in such a state of suffering that they were ever on the point of giving up the ghost; but by the inhuman cares of those monsters they were sustained; and fluctuated from relief to torture, restored one moment to life only to die the next. Inside their palace they had a secret closet where the victims were sacrificed under their eyes, while they were enjoying.

Theo, one of the Emperor's successors, had a very cruel wife, also. They had a column which they used to redden, upon which people were bound under her eyes. 'The Princess,' says the historian from whom these extracts are borrowed, 'used to be amused immensely at the writhings and screeches of these unfortunate victims; she was not pleased unless her husband frequently afforded her this spectacle.' *Hist. des Conj.*, page 43, tome VII.

[2] This game, which was described further back, was greatly in vogue among the Celts, from whom we descend. (See *Histoire des Celts.*) Nearly all these debaucheries and strange, brutal passions of libertinism, rigorously repressed today, were formerly either pastimes or legal

She got upon the stool with the rope round her neck. He set himself before her and Suzanne attended him. Armed with the knife, Justine cut it at just the right moment and fell to the ground without any harm.

'All right,' said Roland, 'it is your turn, Suzanne. Good luck to you if you get out of it with as much skill!'

And so she was next raised up on the tripod. But her he hung.

'Let's go out, Therese, you'll not come back here again until your turn comes.'

The next day her companions asked Justine what had become of Suzanne. She told them and they were not at all surprised. It seemed they were all awaiting the same doom, and even eagerly desired it.

At last tidings were spread through the castle that Roland not only received the immense quantity of bills he had requested for Venice, but that he was also asked for another six million of forged money.

Such were the new state of things when Roland went to Justine to take her down for the third time to the underground vault. Recalling the threats he made her the last time they were there, she was tense with anxiety.

'Cheer up, Therese,' he said, 'you have nothing to fear – it's about something concerning myself, a strange sensation I wish to enjoy; but it will make you run no risk.'

She followed him down, and as soon as the door was shut he said, 'Therese, you're the only one in the house whom I could rely on. I prefer you even to my sister.'

She was filled with surprise and asked him to explain himself.

'Listen,' he said, 'my fortune is made, but at any time I may be ruined. I may be watched and they may grab me during

---

customs or religious ceremonies. In many pious ceremonies of the Pagans flogging was used. Several nations were wont to use these same tortures or passions for the initiation of their young warriors. This was called *Huscanaver*. (See the *Ceremonies religieuses de tous les peuples de la terre*.)

the conveyance I'm going to make of my riches. If that happens, the rope'll be my end. As punishment they'll give me the same pleasure I delight in making women taste. Now, I'm convinced that this death is much more mild than cruel. But as the women whom I made feel its first pangs were never really truthful with me, I want to find out for myself its sensation. I want to have it tried on my own person, and know from my own experience if the squeezing does not really bring on pleasure. Once persuaded that this death is but a pastime, I shall more easily face it when my time comes. It is not that I am afraid of death – I no more fear hell than I expect paradise; but I should not like to suffer while dying. So let's try it, Therese. You will do everything to me that I did to you. I am going to strip and get up on this stool; you will fasten the rope and I'll excite myself. As soon as you see that I'm about getting ready you'll pull away the stool, and let me hang for a while. You'll let me hang until you see my pleasure complete, or notice symptoms of suffering. In the second case you will set me loose at once, but in the first case you will let nature take its full course and loose me only afterwards. You see, Therese, I put my life in your hands. Your freedom, fortune, will be the price of your good conduct.'

'Ah, sir,' said Justine, 'it's an extravagant proposal!'

'No, Therese, you must!' he answered, undressing. 'But behave well. See what proof I give you of my confidence and esteem.'

What would have been the good of her wavering – was he not master of her?

He got upon the stool, the rope round his neck, and wanted Justine to rail at him, curse him with all the horrors of his life, all which she did. He got ready and beckoned her to pull away the stool.

Hanging by his neck for a while, his tongue was lolling half way out, his eyes bulging; but soon, beginning to swoon away, he motioned feebly to Justine to set him loose.

On being revived he said, 'Oh, Therese! one has no idea of such sensations, what a feeling! It surpasses anything I know! Now they can hang me if they want! But, Therese, again you're going to find me very grateless. But what can I do, my dear – people do not correct themselves at my age. You dear creature, you have just given me my life, and never was I so bent on taking yours. You complained of Suzanne's fate, well, I'm going to have you join her. I am going to throw you alive into that hole she's buried in.'

He dragged her, screaming, to a huge cylindrical hole concealed in a far corner of the vault. He opened the lid and lowered a lamp into it so that she could better distinguish the host of dead bodies with which it was filled. He then slipped a long rope under her arms, which were tied behind her back, and let her down about thirty feet into the hole, half-way to the bottom. In this position she suffered frightfully, and it seemed to her that her arms were being pulled from their sockets. The loathsome smell almost stifling her, she thought she was about to end her days in midst of the heap of dead bodies. And way above her she heard him raving with delirium and threatening to cut the rope. However, he merely took pleasure in threatening, but didn't really do it, and after some time drew her up again.

'Were you afraid, Therese?'

'Oh, sir! oh . . . oh!'

'That's how you'll die, Therese, be sure of it!' he said. 'I just want you to get used to it!'

At last Roland was ready to take his leave. On the eve of his departure he went in to see Justine to pay her his last respects.

She threw herself at his feet and begged him to set her free, and to give her a little money to get to Grenoble.

'To Grenoble? Certainly not, you would squeal on us there.'

'Well, kind sir,' she implored with tears, 'I promise you never to go there. To convince you of it take me as far as Venice. I swear never to give you any trouble!'

'I won't give you a franc!' he replied. 'Pity and gratitude, as I told you a thousand times already, is not in me, and were I three times as rich as I am, I wouldn't give any poor man a sou. The sight of misfortune only excites me, amuses me. These are principles I never turn from, Therese – I told you. Poverty is a natural thing, and it was nature's intention that civilisation should not change this primary law. To relieve the needy man is to destroy the order of nature and overthrow that balance which is the basis of her most sublime arrangements; it is to teach indolence and slothfulness, it is to teach the poor an equality dangerous to society!'

'Oh, sir, would you speak like that if you were not rich?'

'That may be, Therese. Everyone has his own way of seeing things; such is mine and I shall not change it. People complain of the beggars in France. If they wanted to, they could hang seven or eight thousand of them and they'd all be gone. Would a man devoured by vermin allow them to live upon him through pity? Why act differently in this case?'

'But virtue!' Justine cried, 'benevolence! Humanity!'

'They are stumbling blocks to happiness. If I have made myself happy it's mostly because I have rid myself of all the stupid prejudices of men. I have mocked divine and human laws and always sacrificed the weak man when I found him in my way. In cheating the public, gullible as they are, in ruining the poor man and robbing the rich, I have arrived where I am. Why didn't you do as I did; you had the same opportunity. But you preferred imaginary and fantastic virtues instead – was it worthwhile? But it's too late, Therese, too late – weep for your faults, it's all you can do.'

And finishing this conversation, again he forced her to stoop to his aberrant desires and whims, almost strangling her. When he felt thoroughly allayed, he took out the bull's pizzle and branded her body with lash upon lash; and he told her she had good cause to be happy, as he had not enough time to give her more of them.

The next day before actually setting out he had a farewell scene of fresh atrocities. Roland was an avid reader of the Roman historians, and some of his methods of torture and ferocity he slavishly borrowed from the annals of Nero, Adronicus and Tiberius.

It was thought that Roland's sister would leave with him, as he had taken her out of the castle fully dressed. But before mounting his horse he ordered her to take her post alongside of the other women and said, 'My comrades think I was smitten with this slut; but I'll leave her behind as a pledge. Since I'm going to take such a dangerous trip I might as well try out my pistols on one of these bitches – there are more here than are wanted, anyway.'

And he loaded one of his pistols and stuck it into the breast of every one of the girls lined up before him, but only when he reached his sister, who was last in line, did he discharge it.

She did not instantly expire but struggled for a long while under her chains.

On the day after Roland's departure everything changed. His successor was a mild and reasonable man and had the girls instantly released from their chains and labour.

'That is no work for women,' he kindly said to them. 'The trade we carry on is bad enough without making it worse by such terrible things.'

Instead they were all given work in the castle, cutting the coins and stamping them, work which wasn't really very hard, and for their labour were given good rooms and excellent food.

At the end of about two months Dalville, Roland's successor, informed the girls of the safe arrival of his colleague.

It was now quiet and nice at the castle, and under the kind, new master the work, though criminal, went on smoothly and merrily.

But one day the doors were suddenly broken in, the fences scaled and the house filled, before the men had time to think of their defence, with a batallion of soldiers. There was nothing to do but surrender. They were all chained like beasts, tied upon horses and conveyed to Grenoble.

The case of the counterfeiters was soon tried. When the brand on Justine's shoulder was seen, they almost spared themselves the trouble of questioning her, and she was about to be condemned to the fate of the others, to be hung, when she obtained some pity from one of the magistrates, who was the most influential man of this tribunal, an upright judge and a man celebrated for his good sense and kindliness. He listened attentively to her and was convinced by her manner of her good faith and the truth of her misfortunes. He himself pleaded for her, and because of his power and influence she was found innocent, though misled; and was given her full liberty. Her protector even took up a small collection for her. She thought her troubles were now at last over and wept for sheer joy.

Justine had gone to live near the suburbs in an inn facing the water. Following the advice of the man who got her her freedom, it was her intention to stay there for some time and try to get work in town; but if she did not succeed, to return to Lyon with letters of recommendation from her influential protector.

The second day at the inn, while having her lunch in the dining room, she noticed that she was being closely watched by a stout, well dressed woman sitting at a nearby table, who had herself styled, *Baroness*.

Justine looked more closely at the woman and wondered where she had seen her before; and then they caught each other's eye and both started to stare, trying to place one another. The Baroness finally rose, came over to Justine's table and, very gracious, asked was she mistaken – was it not Therese she was speaking to, the same Therese she rescued ten years ago from jail – did she not recall La Dubois?

Justine was little flattered by this discovery, but answered her politely, being aware that she had to do with a clever, crafty woman.

Madame Dubois loaded her with courtesy and attentions. She said that she had been worried about Justine's recent scrape with the authorities, but that she had learned of it too late; she would otherwise have gotten in touch with the magistrates, among whom were some of her bosom friends.

Feeble as usual, Justine allowed herself to be led on in this way, and Madame Dubois easily ingratiated herself. Justine was soon telling her all the misfortunes she experienced since their last meeting.

'My dear friend,' Madame Dubois said, embracing her, 'I'm so sorry to hear it. I've wanted to see you so long, Therese! But everything will be all right now. I have lots for both of us. Look,' showing her hands covered with glittering diamonds. 'That's the result of my profession. You see, Therese, if I had been virtuous like you, today I'd be locked in jail or hung!'

'Oh, madame!' Justine answered, 'if you got all that through crime, it won't always last. Providence always punishes evil in the end!'

'You're mistaken, Therese. Don't think that providence always befriends virtue. Don't let the good luck you're running in now for a little while lead you astray. It is all one to providence whether Paul does evil or Peter good. Nature requires both, and crime even more than virtue is the most indifferent thing in the world to her. Listen, Therese!' as she bent over closer to her, 'you're intelligent, my child, and I'd like to convince you, really! It is not a question of *choosing* between virtue and vice; that doesn't make a man happy – both are simply ways of conducting oneself. But what makes a man happy is to do as everybody else – that's what counts. He who doesn't follow the mob is always wrong. In a wholly virtuous world I would recommend virtue to you, because then only virtue would be rewarded, and happiness would depend completely upon just that. But in a wholly corrupted world like ours, vice is the only thing. He who does not fall in with the rest hasn't a chance; everybody steps all over him – he is weak and hopelessly crushed. The laws vainly try to talk virtue to the mass, but it's just talk. The people who make the laws are really too biased towards evil and never carry out their fine talk – they merely make a stab at it for the sake of appearances, that's all. These same men who are always in power realise the advantage of vice and unscrupulousness and wish everybody else to be virtuous so that they alone might have the greater benefit of this advantage, and get the upper hand. Can't you see that corruption is the general interest of men – that he who will not be corrupted with them struggles against the general interest? Now what happiness can a man expect who thwarts the interest of others? I suppose you'll tell me that it is vice which is opposed to men's interest. That's true, I admit, in a world composed of an equal share of good and bad people, because then the interest of the one would evidently clash with the interest of the other. But that doesn't hold in a wholly corrupted society such as ours, where one's vices could only wrong the wicked; but who in turn are given the opportunity of other vices which indemnify them; and so they all find themselves happy. It is a mutual exchange of injuries, one compensating for the other. Vice only hurts virtue, which really shouldn't exist; and when it no longer exists, vice can hurt only the wicked, but no longer virtue itself. Then it will be just vice pitted against vice; and instead of hurting each other they will merely stimulate one another. Do you see, dear child, what I'm driving at? It's no wonder that you have failed a thousand times in your life – taking every road but the one everybody was following. If you had followed the general current you would have been as well off and happy as I am now. Is it as easy going up a river as down it? Another thing, you're always talking to me about providence, that it loves order, and virtue. Isn't it constantly giving you examples of its injustices and irregularities – sending men war, famine, plagues, floods and earthquakes? Isn't it a universe vicious in all its parts and ways? Is that your idea of a providence loving virtue! Why do you insist that vicious individuals displease it, since it acts itself only through vices, since all is evil and corruption in its works, since all is crime and disorder in its will! Moreover, Therese, from whom do our passions for evil come if not from its own hand? Isn't that the work of providence, too! A little more philosophy in the world would soon set everything right, and judges and legislators would soon see that the crimes they blame and punish in others but not in themselves, is far more useful sometimes than those virtues they preach; but which they never reward; or practise themselves.'

'But supposing that I adopted your theories,' said Justine, 'how about my conscience – wouldn't I suffer from remorse almost every minute of the day!'

'Remorse – why, Therese, remorse is just an illusion, merely the whining of a cowardly soul – too cowardly to stifle and kill it!'

'Can remorse be stifled?' asked Justine.

'Of course, nothing is easier, Therese. People repent only what they're not in the habit of doing. If you have remorse for anything you do, do it again and again, and you'll see how easily you forget about your conscience. And anyway who said that remorse proves a crime – it simply shows a weak soul, easily subdued. People have remorse for the most trivial sins. Crime is the most meaningless thing in the world, though sometimes necessary. All you have to do is convince yourself of this, Therese. Let us analyse what men generally call crime and you'll see for yourself. Isn't crime just violating the national laws and customs? But what is called a crime in France isn't one a couple of hundred miles from here. Is there any action considered criminal universally, by every nation on the globe? It is merely a matter of opinion, climate, location, taboos, Therese. What might be thought vicious and criminal here in France might be considered praiseworthy and virtuous elsewhere. And so isn't it absurd to try and force ourselves to practise virtues which are vice in some other place, and be afraid of committing crimes considered excellent actions in another country! Now, I ask you, Therese, why worry about having for your own interest committed a crime in France which is really a virtue in China? And why put yourself out doing good deeds they would hang you for in Siam? Can't you see that remorse doesn't spring from the act itself, but only because it is prohibited? Study the customs and morals of all nations, and you'll agree that remorse is the sole fruit of ignorance and prejudice. You'll learn that there is no real evil in anything and that it's stupid to repent and not do what is useful and agreeable to you. I am forty-five;

I committed my first crime at fourteen and have never at any time been bothered with my conscience. When a thing didn't work out right I might have blamed myself for my awkwardness; but remorse – pff!'

'All right – I grant that, madame,' Justine answered, 'but let me reason according to your own logic. Why do you expect my conscience to be as firm as yours, since it has not been accustomed from infancy like yours to overcome the same prejudices? Why do you ask that my mind, so different from yours, be able to grasp the same theories? You yourself say that there is good and bad in nature – well there must be a certain number of people on the side of the good. That is the side I take it, which is also according to nature. Then why do you want me to wander from the rules that that same nature which you worship so much lays down for me. Moreover, you mustn't think everybody is as lucky as you and always goes unpunished. You saw what happened to that gang of counterfeiters. Out of fifteen, fourteen died at the gallows in disgrace.'

'Do you call that a disgrace, Therese? When one has outgrown these petty principles and childish prejudices he is indifferent to such meaningless things as honour, disgrace or reputation; and it makes little difference to him whether he dies on the scaffold or in bed. You see, there are two sorts of scoundrels in this world, Therese: one, who is rich and has power and influence; the law seldom reaches him. The other is *nobody* and, to make up for the immunity of the first scamp, the laws and authorities are doubly down on him. But, being born without wealth, if he has any sense he should have one aim: to get money anyway he can. If he succeeds he is a great success; if not, he is stretched on the rack. But what matter – he has nothing to regret as there was nothing to lose.'

'I cannot bear to listen to your sophisms and blasphemies any longer!' Justine said, rising from the table indignantly.

'Just a minute, Therese!' said Madame Dubois, holding her back. 'Sit down a minute, please – I want to talk to you – I want to help you! Listen, if you don't refuse to help me a little, here are a thousand francs – yours soon as the deed's done.'

'What is it?'

'Did you notice that young merchant from Lyons who has been eating here the last four or five days?'

'Who, Dubreuil?' Justine asked.

'Yes, that's right!'

'Well?'

'He is in love with you,' Madame Dubois said with a drop in her voice. 'He has confided it to me. He thinks you're awfully nice. He thinks you are really beautiful, so modest and gentle and reserved. And I don't blame him, I think so myself. Well, this romantic young man is worth close to a million and his house is full of treasures. I want you to just let me make this man believe you like him too, and will listen to him. What do you say, Therese? I'll talk him into taking a walk with you and all you've got to do is amuse him and keep him out as long as possible while I rob him. I won't leave town immediately, and he'll never suspect us. Eventually, I'll leave quietly. You'll follow me and get your money once we're out of France. How about it, Therese?'

'All right,' Justine fell in with her. Her real intention was to appraise Dubreuil of Madame Dubois' plans. And wishing to further mislead her she said, 'But wait a minute! If Dubreuil is in love with me I can, on either warning him or yielding to him, get more from him than you're offering me to betray him.'

'Good!' Madame Dubois answered. 'You're learning – that's what I call a good pupil. I'm beginning to think you were more cut out for a career of crime than myself. Well, I'll make it five thousand then, is that better – you satisfied now?'

For Justine the situation was very perplexing. Of course she had no intention of carrying out her agreement with Madame Dubois, for any amount of money. But to be compelled to expose Madame Dubois also grieved her. She hated to bring any creature into danger. What is more, she felt indebted to Madame Dubois for having ten years before freed her from prison. She very much preferred preventing the crime without anybody suffering for it; and with anybody but a consummate rogue like madame she might have succeeded.

It was a finally arranged, and that same evening Justine began putting Dubreuil more at his ease. She was convinced he really had a sincere liking for her. In short time a warm intimacy sprung up between them and they set a day to take a long stroll or ride together out into the open country.

On the day appointed Madame Dubois invited them both to have lunch with her in her room. After lunch, which was a long drawn out affair, they sat around a while and chatted pleasantly together. But Justine grew restless and said it was time for them to say goodbye and start out on their little jaunt.

They left Madame Dubois and went downstairs to get their horses ready; but before actually setting out Justine was alone a minute with Dubreuil.

'Dubreuil . . .' she said to him very quickly. 'Listen to me closely . . . say nothing . . . do what I tell you! Have you got a reliable friend close by?'

'Yes, my partner – Valbois . . .'

'Good! Let us go at once and tell him not to leave your room a minute all the time we're out!'

'But I've got the key . . . why worry . . . why all this fuss . . .?'

'Do as I tell you, please – it's important – otherwise I don't go out with you. Dubois arranged this walk so as to rob you – she is watching us . . . she's dangerous – hurry – give him your key and tell him not to leave until we're back – I'll explain everything later!'

Dubreuil did as he was cautioned, and after installing his friend Valbois in his room he set out with Justine. On the way out, at some distance from the inn, she gave him a lengthy explanation of everything and told him how she had become acquainted with a woman like Madame Dubois. And she also told him of all her unhappy experiences and misfortunes. He was very grateful and sympathetic. In a transport of emotion he offered to marry her. He told her that all her troubles were now over, and sketched for her in a faltering voice the fine life for many years to come that they would both have together. It was a flattering offer and she could not refuse it; but it seemed she could not accept it either without trying to make him see that all might give him cause to repent later his hasty offer. He was pleased with her delicacy and only pressed her the more eagerly.

The quick and embarrassed flow of their conversation had already carried them about three or four miles outside of the town. They were just going to alight and enjoy the cool shade of a wood along the river bank where they intended leisurely to stroll together, when Dubreuil suddenly said he was feeling very sick; and he leaned against the saddle and started to retch violently. They speedily drove back to town.

Dubreuil was so sick by the time they returned that he had to be carried to his room. A doctor then came and said he was poisoned. On hearing this Justine immediately ran to Madame Dubois' apartment, but finding that she was gone, hastened directly to her own room and discovered it had been rifled, her money and clothes stolen. There was no doubt now in her mind who was behind it all.

She went back to Dubreuil's room but was not allowed to come in. He was dying and very near his end. He was certain Justine was innocent and had expressly forbidden her being prosecuted.

Valbois, Dubreuil's friend, later came out and told her that it was all over. She wept bitterly and he tried to quiet her. He himself felt the loss of Dubreuil very deeply and sincerely. And though he pitied Justine when she told him of all her troubles and misfortunes, yet he blamed her for the over-tenderness which had hindered her from lodging a complaint as soon as she had been apprised of Madame Dubois' plans.

They both figured it would now be too late having Madame Dubois pursued, which would, moreover, involve considerable expense. And then again, her prosecution might embroil Justine. Valbois did not conceal from her the fact that if the whole of this last misadventure were made public the depositions he would be forced to make would compromise her, however guarded he might be, because of both her sudden intimacy with Dubreuil, and her last suspicious jaunt with him. He tried to impress upon her how easily she could be put under a cloud of suspicion. He thought it would be best to drop the entire matter and that Justine leave town immediately without seeing anybody at all. For his part he assured her that he would never act against her, and that in all that had occurred he believed her innocent and could only accuse her of feebleness. She then and there made up her mind and decided to do as he advised; it was certain even to herself that all appearances of guilt were against her.

'I'm sorry,' Valbois said, handing her some money, 'that I can't help you much. I haven't an awful lot of money myself and can only spare a little. But I know a woman who is leaving here some time tonight or tomorrow for Chalon, which is my home town. I'll ask her to help you. Let me see – yes . . . right – come on, I'll take you to her right now, that's an idea, come on!' They both hurried out.

Introducing Justine to his friend and townswoman, Valbois said, 'Madame Bertrand, this is Therese, a very good friend of mine. When are you leaving – tomorrow? Well, I want you to take Therese with you and look after her as if she were my own sister. She's going your way and is looking for work. See what you can do for her, will you? Don't charge her anything – I'll settle with you later. That's fine, thanks!'

He kissed Justine on the cheek. 'Goodbye, Therese,' he said, 'Madame Bertrand is leaving early tomorrow morning. I hope you have better luck. I'll see you again soon. Goodbye!'

Justine floundered in bewilderment before the sudden rush of events, and her heart was like a stone in her body. She wandered about the streets aimlessly, so shrunk with confused despair that she drew the attention of passers-by; and to avoid the embarrassing and prying notice of others she made for the river bank, for some isolated spot where she could be alone with her thoughts and memories and free the clogging feeling in her breast.

There she sat for hours musing and thinking upon many sad reflections. As on many occasions before she also thought of her sister, Juliet; and wondered what had become of her, and if she, too, was so terribly unhappy. Justine had a terrible longing to see her; for she felt she now had to have someone to comfort her, but it made her miserable to think Juliet was gone forever out of her life.

So completely was she carried away by the current of her thoughts that the sun sunk beneath the water and the night's darkness soon spread over the town without her being aware of it. When three men got hold of her, one putting his hand on her mouth, only then was she roused from her deep reverie. They threw her headlong into a carriage which just then pulled up; and they sped through the town, going at the same pace for about twenty minutes.

The coach finally arrived at a house where they rolled through wide gates opened to let them in.

They crossed many long, dark rooms, in one of which, where a feeble light crept through the chinks of the door, they locked her in. A stout woman shortly came in with a candle in her hand. It was Madame Dubois. 'Come,' she said to Justine, 'come, little innocence and receive the reward of your virtue.' She pushed Justine impatiently into a room where an elderly man who had a face like a faun out of a Greek fable, but with a more stolid and not half so clever or lively an expression, was seated.

'Monseigneur,' said Madame Dubois, pulling Justine in front of him, 'here's the little girl you've wanted so badly – yes, the celebrated Therese, herself. There's nothing like her! She's a much better prize than the other little girl I'm bringing from the convent, who'll be here any minute, too. The other has physical virtues, but this one – ah! what sentiments! Sentiments are her whole existence, and you couldn't find a more frank or upright creature – how about it. Therese! Both girls are yours and you can do whatever you want with them. But I've got to beat it – there's a man dead in this town and it's no longer safe here.'

'No, no, darling!' said Monseigneur, 'stay here. There's nothing to be afraid of – you're under my protection. How can I do without you . . . but this Therese is really pretty . . .' And to Justine, 'How old are you, my child?'

'Twenty-six, Monseigneur, and many sorrows.'

'Sorrows . . . misfortunes – yes, I know all about it. Huh, it's amusing – really funnier than I thought it was. I'll put an end to all your troubles, my child – just twenty-four hours and it'll be all over. Isn't that right, Dubois?' he laughed.

'Of course!' Madame Dubois answered. 'If Therese was not a good friend of mine I would never have brought her to you.'

He made Justine lean her head upon his chest, and lifting her hair he closely examined the nape of her neck. He had hard bony hands with powerful fingers that gripped like a vice. 'Oh, it's delightful!' he cried, vigorously pressing down on her collar-bone, 'I have never seen one fastened so well – it'll be great fun slicing that head off!'

A knock was just then heard at the door, and Dubois went out and forthwith brought in the young girl from the convent about whom they had just spoken. Her name was Eulalie, a lovely girl to look at. 'Good heavens, madame, where have you taken me!' she said. But Monseigneur was already pulling her roughly towards him, and with his long fingers proceeding to stroke her neck passionately. Wrinkling his forehead as if making some mental calculation, he sharply twisted her head from one side to the other.

'Come!' he said. 'These two girls will give me great pleasure. You'll be well paid for this, Dubois. Let us go into my boudoir – come with us, Dubois, I want you to help me.'

They were all compelled to go with him.

On a table to the right were many kinds of wines and strong liquors and a great supply of food.

He took Eulalie first, and abetted by Dubois, his wild revel lasted for more than an hour. As Eulalie's severed head finally rolled heavily to the floor only then was he completely appeased. But he was completely exhausted, and staggered to the table and sat down.

It was his wish to prolong the agony of Justine's suspense. He was in none too great a hurry; and he and Dubois drank heavily to revive their strength. But they sat at the table so long and gorged themselves with so much food and wine, making merry between them, that they eventually rolled to the floor blind-drunk. Justine, seeing this, grabbed whatever clothes were within reach, which happened to be Madame Dubois', and rushed madly out toward the stairs. Through the long empty apartments she stumbled and fell in the darkness; and on the other side of the corridor she heard a door slam and the dull tread of steps on the heavy carpets. She drew up rigid and clung close to the wall in the dark empty room, until the sound died away in the distance. She finally reached the gate without encountering any resistance, and got safely back to Grenoble.

It was very late when she reached town. But she immediately went to Valbois' room and knocked on his door. He woke up startled, and opening the door, his eyes swollen with sleep, he stared at Justine several seconds before recognising her, such was the state she was in – what with the ghastly expression on her face and Madame Dubois' clothes all awry, hanging loosely about her. He asked what had happened, and gasping, she told him. 'Can't you have her arrested?' she aspirated, 'she's not far from here and I think I remember the way. The wretch! she took the money you gave me today, too!'

'God, Therese! you certainly are the most unfortunate girl in the world; something's always happening to you! No, we'll leave Dubois alone, for the same reasons I told you today. The less we mess with people of that sort, so much the better. The thing for you is to get out of this town. Here is some more money; there's enough for you to get some other clothes, too. Now, go and get some sleep and don't forget to meet Madame Bertrand early tomorrow. Good night, Therese, good luck.'

'O virtuous young man. . . .'

'Yes . . . good night, Therese, good night . . . good luck to you. . . .'

Early the next day Justine left Grenoble. Though in that town she did not find the happiness she had always fancied she would, yet there at least she had received more pity than in any other, and that greatly consoled her.

Madame Bertrand and she were travelling in a small closed carriage driven by one horse. Madame Bertrand, a pretty nasty, suspicious, prattling, gossiping, troublesome, shallow-brained woman, was still suckling a little girl about fifteen months old. Everything went well right up to Lyons, where madame had to stop over for three days to carry out some of her business transactions.

In this town Justine had an encounter she was far from expecting. With one of the girls from the inn, whom she had begged to accompany her, she happened to be walking along the waterfront. A bright, clear day, they were enjoying the afternoon sunshine and watching the leisurely crowd of people go by. Suddenly, just a short distance ahead of her she espied the hermit Dom Antonin of the temple of Mota. Erect and beatific, he was walking gingerly towards her and she could not possibly avoid him. He bowed very grandly as he accosted her graciously in a low, smooth, unctuous voice.

'Therese, my child, how are you? Was that kind, running away like that? That wasn't nice, my child, leaving us the way you did! And who is this dear creature . . .' he addressed himself to the girl accompanying Justine, holding her chin paternally in his hand.

He told Justine that he was now first brother of the house of the Shaamanite Order situated in this town. He also said, in a low voice, that she ran great risk of being retaken by the temple in Burgundy if he merely sent word there. But he promised not to if she and her friend would come to see him in his new abode. He insisted that they come right along with him, that later they might have difficulty finding the place alone, as it was hard to get it. 'We'll pay both of you well, Therese. We are ten in our house and I promise you at least a couple of francs from each one of us.'

Justine blushed at these proposals and tried to make the idolater believe he was mistaken; but he was not to be put off. At length, upon her repeated refusals to follow him, he confined himself to merely asking for their address. To get rid of him Justine gave him a wrong number, which he jotted down in his pocket book. He left, assuring them that he would soon see them again.

Returning to the inn Justine explained to her companion, as well as she could, her acquaintance with the brother. But whether what she told did not satisfy the girl, who said, 'I think he's awfully cute!' or, which is more likely, because the girl was vexed, having been deprived by Justine's virtuousness of an adventure bringing profit and pleasure – be that as it may, she tattled and told Madame Bertrand about it. Madame was greatly displeased, with Justine's virtue or lack of it is hard to say, and thereafter she seemed to nourish a ranking grudge against her.

They left Lyons very late and arrived at Villefranche about six in the evening. A long trip was ahead of them the next day and they were anxious to have supper immediately and go right to bed.

Many hours after retiring, the whole inn was roused by great smoke which was rapidly filling all the rooms. The fire spread quickly, and Justine and Madame Bertrand, half naked, threw open their door. All about them they heard the deafening crash of falling walls, the cracking of timber breaking under the flames, and the shrill screams of people scurrying to safety. They were panic-stricken as the fire roared on all sides and they rushed haphazard through it and found themselves tied up with a knot of people, partly dressed and hysterical, trying to get out. Justine just then recalled that Madame Bertrand had forgotten her child behind in their room, and ran back and picked it up, holding it close in her arms. The flames were now raging more furiously; and she was burnt in several places, dodging falling plaster and timber, as she scampered back with the child in her arms to where Madame Bertrand was still huddled together with the same group of pushing men and women. Trying to step upon a half-burnt plank, her foot missed, and by a natural impulse Justine threw up her hands in front of her face, letting go of the child. It slipped from her grasp, and right under its mothers eyes fell and was buried under a heavy, falling, simmering debris. There was a terrifying scream as Justine felt herself dragged and pulled outside. In the general confusion she thought she was being dragged to safety; but when outside she found herself thrown into a coach where a woman dug a pistol into her ribs, she gathered her wits and recognised Madame Dubois staring menacingly at her. 'You bitch! a word out of your mouth and I'll blow you out of your seat! I've got you now, and you won't get away again!'

'You here, madame?' Justine said, bewildered.

'You bet I'm here! That fire is my doing. It was through a fire I rescued you from jail and saved your life, and through a fire you're going to lose it! I would have chased you even to hell! I almost had you at Lyons – I just missed you! But I soon got on your trail again all right! I arrived here in Villefranche just an hour after you did. I knew you were in this inn and had my men set fire to it. I was going to get you dead or alive! You're going back to Monseigneur. He was furious when he learned of your getaway. He gives me a couple of thousand for every girl I get him. He was so mad he wouldn't pay me for Eulalie. We won't get out of this coach until we get to his house. And I'll teach you for robbing my clothes! And you just try and get away, you bitch!' Madame Dubois said furiously as the horses galloped rapidly on.

Leopold von Sacher-Masoch (1836–1895)

Travails with my Aunt

If Sade can be unreadably robust at times, Sacher-Masoch is, by contrast, the pervert you can read between scenes without ruining your appetite. Born in Galicia in 1836 to the family of Prague's chief of police, he was a man of a different era to Sade. He is a less quixotic figure, with none of the philosophical pretensions that Sade brings to his pornography. He is also a finer prose stylist. Although Sade's earlier works occasionally impress with their concise satire, before he abandoned characterisation pretty much completely, Sacher-Masoch often has the nimbler turn of phrase. All the more surprising considering the clause-heavy sentence structure of many German novels of the period.

He can be criticised for being Vaudevillian perhaps. If they don't excite you, then his haughty dominatrices can seem a little like the Wicked Witch of the West. But that is to miss the element of pastiche he brings to his own work, and the pornographic context they're intended to occupy. Sacher-Masoch himself was an insatiable flagellant, and it seems that the demands he made of the women in his life were no less taxing because they required the dishing out, rather than the taking, of pain. The writings of his wife Wanda will, I hope, be covered in a future volume.

He'll be most known to today's reader, I'd suggest, thanks to the Velvet Underground's 'Venus in Furs', a paean to the haughty, imperious heroine of Sacher-Masoch's most well-known novel of that name, Wanda von Dunajew. The song, like the book, is narrated by Severin, her indentured sex-slave and Sacher-Masoch's thinly-veiled alter ego. The novel is Sacher-Masoch's most autobiographical, based firmly on a liaison he enjoyed with Fanny Pistor, scene-name the Baroness Bogdanov. With John Cale's delicate viola cadence repeated inexorably to the ritualised beating of Mo Tucker's tambourine, the song is a powerful evocation of a CP scene, if a little self-conscious by today's standards. (For that, perhaps, visit Death in Vegas's 'Dirge'.)

But *Venus in Furs* differs from Sacher-Masoch's other stories in that it is not a fable, but autobiographical in a similar way to the contemporary vogue for confessional literature. Most of his tales, like Sade's, feature fabulistic storytelling and the same broad sweeps of fortune and misfortune, in which vice is rewarded – his heroines lie and cheat their way to wealth and social standing – and virtue never. But there are few similarities beyond that. Had Kraft-Ebbing not appropriated the term *masochism* along with *sadism* in his *Psychopathia Sexualis* (1876), the two would seldom be mentioned in the same breath, other than as fellow members of the canon of pervy literature.

In many ways, Sacher-Masoch is the classic pervert of Freudian case-study: his one-track minded sexual concerns, which dominated the course of his life, at his own admission stemmed from a single incident in which he could be said to have been 'arrested'. Of a childhood sojourn with an aunt on his father's side, Havelock Ellis writes:

> He was playing with his sisters at hide-and-seek and had carefully hidden himself behind the dresses on a clothes-rail in the Countess's bedroom. At this moment the Countess suddenly entered the house and ascended the stairs, followed by a lover, and the child, who dared not betray his presence, saw the Countess sink down on a

sofa and begin to caress her lover. But a few moments later the husband, accompanied by two friends, dashed into the room. Before, however, he could decide which of the lovers to turn against the Countess had risen and struck him so powerful a blow in the face with her fist that he fell back streaming with blood. She then seized a whip, drove all three men out of the room, and in the confusion the lover slipped away. At this moment the clothes-rail fell and the child, the involuntary witness of the scene, was revealed to the Countess, who now fell on him in anger, threw him to the ground, pressed her knee on his shoulder, and struck him unmercifully. The pain was great, and yet he was conscious of a strange pleasure. While this castigation was proceeding the Count returned, no longer in a rage, but meek and humble as a slave, and kneeled down before her to beg forgiveness. As the boy escaped he saw her kick her husband. The child could not resist the temptation to return to the spot; the door was closed and he could see nothing, but he heard the sound of the whip and the groans of the Count beneath his wife's blows.[1]

In *Venus in Furs* Savarin chronicles how a fur-clad aunt he hated had bound and whipped him until he bled, with an evil smile on her face, then forced him to his knees to thank her for his treatment. 'Under the lash of a beautiful woman my senses first realised the meaning of womanhood. In her fur jacket she seemed to me like a wrathful queen, and from then on my aunt became the most desirable woman on God's earth.'

Sacher-Masoch spent his literary career continually sculpting his mistress like a prose Pygmalion, fetishising the rustle of her clothes, her haughty demeanour. He's a broken record if you don't have a taste for this, but not nearly as relentless as Sade, if you don't have a taste for him either! The evil vixen bitch figure has become a staple of fetish fiction. There are many formulaic dungeon novels

[1] *Studies in the Psychology of Sex*.

featuring a Machiavellian chatelaine or countess who directs events to increase her number of recalcitrant but strangely attracted slaves. But we can also see his influence, at a pinch, in the vengeful vixens of Eric Stanton's zestful strip cartoons, who, given due cause by some cad, bind, beat and enforcedly feminise their way to revenge. Or even in the brutal Varla, Tura Satana's character in Russ Meyer's *Faster, Pussycat! Kill! Kill!* whose murderous disdain for men is pure Sacher-Masoch heroine turned American gang-girl.

Sacher-Masoch's men, by contrast, are well-intentioned, civilised individuals in helpless thrall to their fiendish mistresses, and often unmoved by their faithful and decorous wives at home. Like the upright teacher destroyed by Dietrich's Lola in von Sternberg's *The Blue Angel*, they are brought low and, in their debasement, whatever social standing they had hitherto enjoyed seems to exist at that moment only to counterpoint their fall, their dignity defiled.

Sacher-Masoch's writing brought him a degree of literary success that's perhaps surprising to those of us used to thinking of erotic writing as a genre pursuit on the margins of today's mass-market fiction. He fitted perfectly with the Victorian taste for semi-explicit but salacious novels in which the moral balance is ultimately redressed and the reader allowed a degree of distance from the subject that's not dissimilar to one of today's red-top Sunday papers, at whose gossip we can tut-tut comfortably regardless of our own moral rectitude.

But, despite his success, his single-interest concerns did not allow him to be a happy man, it seems. After Fanny Pistor, he spent his time seeking another woman to take on the mantle – and responsibility – of being the incarnation of his vision of female desirability, and perhaps never found her. In her *Confessions*, his wife Wanda complains that throughout their ten-year marriage he forced her to wield the whip non-consensually. How does one compel another into a dominant act? Simple economics, according to Wanda – she had known the horrors and compromises of poverty, and Leopold was paying the rent. So given his one-track mindedness, it's worth looking at how his heroines function as pornographic objects of attraction. We all want, at times, the things we can't have, and untouchability, like the glass in a shop window, increases desire. So Sacher-Masoch's heroines become more beautiful for rendering themselves untouchable to all but their lady's maids. And for their salivating, kneeling slaves it's the ultimate extension of Courtly Love.

It goes without saying that Sacher-Masoch's thrill was also a matter of humiliation as much as pain. He wasn't simply an endorphin junkie, going for the burn of CP, happy to direct if required, with no more emotional baggage than that with which one might go to a gym for a work-out. He wanted his face rubbed in the shame of his position, he craved the debasement of the true masochist. With desperation, he wanted a woman who could do it *right.* He wanted to be (un)pleasantly surprised. Part of the humiliation, and one which could only increase the sense of his mistress's untouchability, was being made to view his mistress and not touch. Like Savarin, he craved being helpless. 'Nothing can intensify my passion more than tyranny, cruelty, and especially the faithlessness of a beautiful woman.'[2] By extension, he loved the thought of being helplessly made to watch his wife make love with another man, even though penetration was never at the core of his sexual fantasies, so it seems, as they applied to himself.

For Sacher-Masoch, whether the sexual act is followed through to completion or not is irrelevant next to the receiving of pain. And he took a prodigious amount of pain. After all, bites and bruises are trophies of how sexually transported one has been. It betokens the height of sexual ecstasy to interpret pain as pleasure. Anyone who's ever woken up with marks they hadn't noticed the night before – and not through the numbing effects of drink – will know it doesn't take a spell in a baroque dungeon to realise that. So if that accounts for the

---

[2] *Venus in Furs.*

significance of pain to sex, as betokening you've hit the spot, what about pain without sex, pain as the sole object of contact, and inflicted not in the context of a state of arousal, but to bring one about? Pain as foreplay for an act that'll never happen? There'll always be something *outré* about that. And a perv like Sacher-Masoch wouldn't have it any other way – for then it can only add to the shame.

In so far as Sacher-Masoch claims any philosophical position for himself at all, it is to explain his tastes, no more. Like Sade, Sacher-Masoch saw that nature rewards the strong. In so far as he felt the need to examine it at all, he ascribed his fixation to this. As with Sade, it would be anachronistic to talk about evolutionary theory (remember – I only said the former's thoughts *prefigured* its more populist interpretations), but Sacher-Masoch thinks of it as survival behaviour for the weak to cleave to the strong. In *The Female Hyena of the Hungarian Plain*, Anna Klauer leads a band of robbers and even becomes known, in local legend, as a she-wolf. In *Venus in Furs*, Savarin says the following:

> In woman and her beauty I saw something divine, because the most important function of existence – the continuation of the species – is her vocation. To me, woman represented a personification of nature, Isis, and man was her priest, her slave. In contrast to him she was cruel like nature herself, who tosses aside whatever has served her purposes as soon as she no longer has need for it. To him her cruelties, even death itself, still were sensual raptures.

Sacher-Masoch's hyperbolic ragbag of goddess-worship doesn't explain his attraction to this particular chosen image of strength, nor why he conceived of himself as weak. But that's to miss the point that this is the voice of Savarin, part of a narrative, it's not meant as overarching theory. Truth is, he functioned perfectly well in his daily life and wasn't an especially weak man in his dealings with the world. He was even a decorated soldier. In his masochism he was a classic case, in that he sought to have a bit of a breather from the responsibilities of life and perhaps the guilt of being a child of authority – his father was chief of police during a rebellion, and Sacher-Masoch himself had witnessed the 1846 revolt of the Polish peasantry against the landowners two years before. Hangings, burnings and even crucifixion were sights that had greeted the impressionable child. Maybe the Freudian interpretation is characteristically simplistic after all.

The cruel indifference of his heroines is akin to the indifference of Sade's whole world towards the individual, except Sacher-Masoch doesn't consider himself a philosopher – instead he's a prose writer of some grace, who would have liked to bear comparison with Goethe more than Sade. He writes to gratify, and – to the extent that his stories have the motivation and narrative drive a nineteenth-century reading audience required – to gratify people other than himself. In that paradoxical sense he's more of a pornographer than Sade who, one feels, only wished to extend his poor, incarcerated imagination so far as to please his dystopic self. Except that Sacher-Masoch's work was evidently perfectly well within the envelope of popular Victorian reading!

At times vaudevillian too, his writing has no revolutionary agenda, even though he witnessed violent revolution as a boy. It's unlikely that Sacher-Masoch felt bitter or let down like Sade, for whom decades of imprisonment must have impacted unimaginably on so willful a psyche. A god, of some form or another, was in his heaven, even if poor winsome Leopold wasn't always sexually fulfilled. Contrast the attitude robber Mikulev expresses towards religion (in explaining why he'd robbed a church) in the short story *Bajka* – limited to criticising the venality of organised religion, but not theism itself – with Sade's firm denial of the existence of God, in which even so he was saying no more than many Paris radicals of the time: 'Before God? Do you think he looks upon the vessels in which the Eucharist is offered? What does he care for gold and silver? He sees men's deeds, he looks into their hearts and judges them accordingly. He is not deceived by prayer and incense.' In criticising the venality of the organised Church, he's doing no more than picking up a common thread in salacious writing from Boccaccio to Dom B's *The Lascivious Monk.* 'What are these priests, these monks and nuns, except a bunch of liars and hypocrites? To us they promise the Kingdom of Heaven, but they are clever enough to keep the earth for themselves, and while we go hungry and homeless and cold, they wax fat at our expense and commit all those sins for which they keep Hell hot for us.' Fine rhetoric but nonetheless a million miles from the crystal-clear atheism of Sade or Mirbeau.

Despite what he'd claim for them, Sacher-Masoch's women are not representative of universal human nature, or anything more than the lust objects he makes them. They're she-devils made flesh, haughty, statuesque, with a well-turned ankle and a demeanour of the most smouldering contempt. Unlike Sade's parade of broken Copelias, Sacher-Masoch's women are attractive because of how they think, for the poetry in the cruelty of their sadism. Trapping her quarry in a pit, like a wild animal, Bajka glories in her own hypocrisy in giving up the robber to the authorities for her own thirty pieces of silver. It's not that she doesn't have the independence of mind to see that the robber has a point, she's simply that amoral. At the close of *Bajka*, having brought about Mikulev's fall, see how the heroine rubs her triumph in! 'As Mikulev was led up to the gallows, Bajka stood erect in her little ox-drawn cart and nodded to him. She was wearing the new sheepskin that the Abbess had given her, the coral-bead necklace and earrings that the robber had presented her with. At her feet stood two bags of gold, the price that the government had placed on the robber's head.'

Bajka is a fable but it's not a morality tale. Its power lies in its ambivalence, its indifference to anything but its heroine's Machiavellian cruelty, in its pornographic value. I mention it here, before *Venus in Furs*, since in his stories told in the third person there's perhaps more of a distillation of the kind of female mind that turned Sacher-Masoch on.

Now I Wanna be your Dog

It's worth contrasting another of Sacher-Masoch's melodramatic third-person stories with the intimacy of *Venus in Furs*, which follows. *The Female Hyena of the Hungarian Plain* charts Anna Klauer's metamorphosis from penniless moppet to murderous evil bitch writ large. She's taken under the wing of the cravenly submissive Baron von Steinfeld, who sets her up as his Mistress – with a capital 'M' – and the two enjoy a strong bond and an intimately kinky tryst in which the Baron, in Iggy Pop's words, can lie right down in his favourite place. When he feels compelled, however, to marry according to position, Anna, hitherto unrepressedly free of such social considerations, takes it badly to say the least. Having shot the Baron apparently fatally, she runs off to a circus in Munich, where she becomes an invaluable addition to its cast and an iconic image of female domination. She decides to compete on the Baron's terms and advance her position within society. She pays her dues. Submitting at first to the rigorous regime of circus discipline, controlled and taught with a whip by a riding master who trains people like animals, she flowers into Sarolta, a bareback rider and lion tamer, exercising imperious, precise, gymnastic control over the feral instincts of the beasts at her command. Like Eliza Doolittle in *My Fair Lady*, she is schooled, too, in polite manners, elocution and deportment, and her newfound social skills are not unlike Dumbo's magic feather, serving to give her confidence in the abilities she already had.

> ... whenever Signora Arabella ventured to come to the riding-school and to prompt her with a stroke of the whip, Sarolta invariably kissed her hand after the lesson, saying with platitudinous assurance that she considered herself fortunate to be struck by her, for 'The hand that loves well does well to chastise!'
>
> Thus she managed, little by little, to win over everyone, to make herself indispensable to everyone, and, without being aware of it herself, to make the most of everyone.

From the circus director and his wife she learned good Italian, from Monsieur Jacques the most elegant French; Mr Brown, who in reality was a Hungarian named Matschlausie, taught her Magyar, his own language, which she soon succeeded in speaking like a real Hungarian woman. As for Miss Stanette, whose name was actually Wilhelmine Sporner, a native of Hanover, she helped her to exchange the soft Viennese dialect for the harsh but correct High German.

When at last, at Frankfurt-am-Main, she appeared for the first time in public and carried off a dazzlingly successful performance, she – hitherto so mistreated and made fun of – became the spoilt child of the director and of the whole troupe; it was now her turn to play the tyrant of those who had tyrannised over her.

No matter where the troupe gave shows, Sarolta was pursued by the assiduities of the most handsome and wealthiest men in all the places she went to; but she affected such an incredible frigidity towards their advances that she soon acquired the universal nickname of 'The Virtuous Equestrienne'.

Needless to say, before long she attracts the attentions of another recklessly masochistic aristo, the Prince Parkany:

'My dear lady,' said the Prince, 'do not take it amiss if I come straight to the point. I know of your virtue, as I am aware also of your despotic character; I realise that you tolerate only slaves.

'I will not say anthing to you of Love, but I will permit myself to tell you that, ever since I saw you in your riding act yesterday evening for the first time, I have worshipped you, as I never have worshipped any woman before; that everything I possess is at your disposal, and that I desire nothing but the right to be your slave.'

'Oh, come now! You must want something more than that!' Sarolta replied with a playful smile. 'I should be lying if I were to say to you: "I love you". It may well be that I am quite incapable of loving any man. Be that as it may, you do awaken an extraordinary interest in me. Perhaps I may today put to you the same question that you yourself yesterday, from your own box, put to me, and to which never, in the course of my entire career, have I permitted myself to answer in a positive way to anybody, whoever it might be.'

'You make me inexplicably happy!' exclaimed the Prince. 'Then you will have the graciousness to permit me to serve you as if you were my mistress and I your humble servant?'

'I am not accustomed to pretend and I am sometimes inconsiderate in my frankness', was Sarolta's reply, 'because I am too proud to conceal my sentiments or to hide my thoughts. For that reason I must ask you to listen to what I expect from you:

'If the thrill that the professional equestrienne inspires in you evaporates, then you must leave me and forget me. Not only will I not bear you any malice for so doing, but I will be grateful to you for it. If, on the other hand, your feelings concerning that woman are such as you say they are and you are furthermore convinced that that woman retains the hold that attracts you to her only through the dread that your enthusiasm may prove to be a blazing straw and that, if she were to give herself to you, she would lose all the dazzling advantages that she derives from her profession, then I will be yours.'

'Can you be serious in what you are saying, Sarolta?' exclaimed the Prince exultantly.

'I have never been more serious.'

'Then, you belong to me.'

As Mistress of the Prince's ancestral pile, she makes the most of the possibilities of the almost feudal hegemony she enjoys in her new home:

If any servant or peasant had done anything remiss as far as this female tyrant was concerned, he was ordered to report immediately to Sarolta in her bedchamber, where he generally found her reclining on a luxurious divan; she would remind him of his faults and announce the punishment that he had incurred.

No sooner did he hear the sentence than he was seized from behind by the two wenches, who, until then, had remained concealed behind a heavy curtain. The two women, before he had even had time to realise what was about to happen, had bound him securely hand and foot.

While all the time taunting the unfortunate victim with the cruellest jokes, Sarolta's two assistant executioners would open the trap door that led to the ground floor and drag the poor wretch down a winding staircase to a kind of dungeon situated at the bottom of the stairs, followed by the cruel tyrant herself.

There the condemned fellow would be tied to a stake, while Sarolta, assisted by Iela and Ersabeth, lashed him with a pair of long whips until the blood ran, deriving from this work a kind of diabolical pleasure.

Then they would leave him there all day long, his body faint with hunger and tugging at his aching limbs. To see men suffer had become for the former equestrienne a source of sensual delight.

Not long after their union, she poisons Prince Parkany with the aid of the local witch! Clad in widow's weeds for a requisite time, she's soon up to her intrigues once again, bestowing her haughty favours on the slimy churchman, Father Pistian, the complicit confessor of her infamy. And pursuing the hapless, priggish Emerich Bethlemy, a Hungarian Angel Clare whose 'get thee behind me' attitude only serves to increase her obsession.

Meanwhile, she sets herself up as the tyrant-leader of a local band of robbers, spurring them into ever greater offences and becoming infamous in local legend. Her deal with Eula Bartamy, their thuggish, henchman-like leader, keeps everyone involved happy – his gang keeps the profits of their crimes and delivers the human booty to her, to toy with at her pleasure – in a Ms Hyde incarnation of the seemingly grieving widow and social doyenne. This secret life is kept opaque from her friends among the chattering class, on whom, nonetheless, she has managed to inflict lesser though ingenious humiliations nonetheless: '... friends and neighbours who visited the Parkany castle and took part in the dazzling banquets, the hunts and sleigh-parties organised by Sarolta, constituted a kind of court for this imperious and petulant woman, although they had had, too, on more than one occasion, to endure her sovereign whims and capricious cruelties.

'One day, she caused a veritable torrent to pour from the ceiling on the assembled company; on another occasion, she made all her guests at dinner sit upon stinging-nettles.'

Then, in a plot development that's a piece of sadomasochistic sitcom, who should move on to the neighbouring lands but baron von Steinfeld, the servile wretch who first broke her heart. The Baron, of course, doesn't recognise the woman who lives in fine style as the Princess Parkany as the young waif Anna Klauer. Unsatisfied with his compliant wife at home, he begins a murderous liaison in which the now older woman has still not forgiven him for her original embitterment. Not for the passionate Princess the easy cynicism of an older and more worldly woman towards her youthful expectations. At its culmination, she reveals herself to him alone as the infamous leader of her band of brigands, and her terrible revenge takes a leaf straight out of the methods of the Spanish Inquisition, but von Steinfeld, a cipher for the author's own fascination with his heroine, is only more enthralled and, in his maimed state, even helps her to undress!

> 'Finish him off, Sarolta, my sweet little dove. He is very low. He can't last much longer!'
>
> 'But I don't want to!' exclaimed the beautiful Hyena, stamping her foot with rage.
>
> 'Then he will be dead too soon,' replied the witch.
>
> 'Oh, all right, then, stop!' Sarolta ordered her two female executioners, who removed one by one the instruments of torture and released Steinfeld.

'Use all the resources of your art, old woman, to revive him. He must recover consciousness and remain conscious until the end.'

The sorceress came back with all kinds of phials and flasks and soon set to work at the task. After a number of attentions, Steinfeld's eyelids fluttered and he looked at her.

'That didn't cost you your life, did it?' exclaimed Sarolta. 'But you have atoned enough and now the most beautiful reward awaits you. Come to me, I want to be merciful and give you your life and give myself to you. Come, we shall celebrate our wedding.'

'Can this be true, Anna? No more cruelties?' asked Steinfeld, as if recovering from a bad dream.

'Don't ask me anthing more. I am yours,' exclaimed the beautiful woman, holding out her arms to him.

He tried to approach, but fell down before he could reach her. The girls picked him up and placed him at Sarolta's feet.

'So you are mine?' stammered the Baron, as she put her superb arms around him and kissed him.

With a glance she dismissed the two servants. The old hag laid a costly sable fur coat by the Princess's head on the cushion of the couch and retired also.

'I want to make myself more beautiful,' said Sarolta with a gay laugh, 'as beautiful as Venus Anadyomene.'

Steinfeld helped her to undress and then handed her the sable fur in which she wrapped herself with inimitable grace and which reached to the soles of her feet; then she pressed her diabolical lips against his until, crazy with joy, he fell at her feet.

'Finish me off,' he implored her in sudden ecstasy.

'Indeed I will,' said Sarolta with a sinister look.

She made a slight sound and, in the twinkling of an eye, Steinfeld was once again seized by the servants, who then chained him to an iron ring fixed in the wall above the marble font.

'What does this mean?' he shouted. 'What has come over you?'

'You will soon find out,' said Sarolta, rising.

Then the servants tore off all his clothes.

'You robbed me of my youth, you swine,' continued Sarolta, 'and now you shall pay it back with your own blood!'

'What? Am I mad?'

'Have you never heard of that Hungarian Countess who took baths in human blood and so remained eternally young? Today I want to experiment with that strange beauty secret.'

'My God! Can this be possible?' groaned Steinfeld. 'Surely I must be dreaming!'

'Then wake up!' exclaimed the beautiful Hyena.

She threw off her fur coat and climbed into the marble font.

Father Pistian, his usefulness at an end, is not spared this fate either. Next she turns her gaze on poor Bethlemy once more. Incensed that he should be keeping company with a common tavern wench, ' a naughty and wanton little devil . . . but as beautiful and tricky as a grass snake,' while spurning her own imperious sexuality, she bribes his lover Ursa to give him up one night to her gang of robbers, who at her direction stuff his head into the nest of a rather unpleasant species of ant, who will eat it alive, through to the bone. I'd leave the question of plausibility to an entomologist. Dismayed by the murderous scene she happens upon, and guilty, Ursa frees Bethlemy once the robbers have left, and participates in an ambush by the authorities in which they're killed. On the run, the Princess flees, only to meet, in the end, a worse fate at the hands of a mob than that which would have befallen her at the hands of the authorities. Justice is served:

'Pity! Have pity . . .' she begged.

'Did you have pity on your victims, you wretch?' replied the old peasant. 'Kill her, all of you, without the slightest mercy!'

The peasants went on with their frightful execution. Sarolta had received more than a hundred blows and was bleeding from an almost equal number of wounds· at last she fell unconscious.

'That's enough!' ordered the old man.

'But she's still alive,' pleaded a peasant woman.

'That's the point,' exclaimed the old man. 'She can't stand any more blows, but we are going to hang her while she's still living.'

'That's it, hang her!' shouted all the crowd.

In vain did Sarolta give vent to the most hideous curses, in vain did she implore mercy, in vain did her mortal anguish and suffering draw tears from her eyes.

A peasant girl struck her a blow on the back of the neck, two other blows fell at once, and after a while her body was swinging from the branch of an alder-tree.

Her death throes lasted only a few minutes, and then this vile female monster gave up the ghost.

The peasants cut down her corpse, threw it on to a dung-cart, and thus she was taken to the Commissariat.

In *The Female Hyena*, the author keeps his sympathies, and ours, distant from his heroine enough for us to conclude that we're being asked to hate-fuck her, with all the prurient opprobrium of right-thinking hypocrites throughout the ages. At least, Sacher-Masoch is making that appeal to our imagination. Sarolta's no Tess of the D'Urbevilles, more sinned against than sinning. When wretched payback for all her misdeeds befalls her, Sacher-Masoch allows himself a good dollop of penny-dreadful salaciousness – in keeping with the Victorian melodrama of the story as a whole – in his description of her ignominy and shame. If one can argue the toss, on a fable-like reading, about the end that Sarolta metes out to Baron von Steinfeld, one can't pretend her intended torture of Emerich Bethlemy, though he has spurned her, is motivated by anything other than sheer – well – sadism. There's no moral ambiguity here, and the moral redress she suffers strikes a conservative note in keeping the story within the confines of narrative fiction, and in keeping her character, as a woman corrupted but also corrupt, distant from our sympathy and more resonant as wank material for one of Sacher-Masoch's turn of mind. And – not to overlook the importance of the practical over the critical – more conventionally publishable.

Sacher-Masoch serves Sarolta up as a lust-hate figure, and betrays, for all his slavish love of an imperious woman, a big dollop of *schadenfreude* towards his heroine. There may be no more tender way to make love than to make your partner tender, but Sacher-Masoch's women take no prisoners with their captives – they're vituperative, venomous, remorseless forces of a cruel Nature, who taunt their slaves even until the point of death, a death which serves to confirm their insignificance for them in an irrevocably final and therefore climactic, orgasmic way.

Sacher-Masoch is ultimately a conservative writer; he doesn't play mind-games and he inhabits the moral status quo. For Sade, the illegitimacy of power, as exercised by the powerful and ruthless of the world and observed as acutely as by any bleeding-hearted anarchist, provides the individual dom's excuse for his – and in Sade's case it is 'his' – own libertinage and liberties taken. Sacher-Masoch acknowledges the legitimacy of the social order (even in the lynch law of the common folk as can be seen in *Hyena*). He may as well, for *Hyena* is unapologetically entertainment – a nineteenth-century Gothic B-movie, if that's not too clunky a comparison. It would be missing the point that this story is pornographic pastiche to observe that Sacher-Masoch's heroine is a pretty two-dimensional character. Unlike in the works of Sade, we are let in on the submissive's head-trip, but that's only because Sacher-Masoch *was* the sub. He is as self-centred in his way as Sade is, in that his dominants are as much ciphers as Sade's submissive broken dolls. How much more challenging had Sarolta got away. Sade would probably have let her. But then, when it came to his villains at least, Sade was often an old softie.

And so to *Venus in Furs* – far more personal, intimate and representative a tale. It's worth noting something about Sacher-Masoch's view of fur itself, since it provides such an important motif, and was so personally important to Sacher-Masoch the man, as well as the author. We may think of them as betokening decadence and amorality today, but in chilly Mittel Europe in the nineteenth century, furs were as everyday a sight as a polar fleece today, as of course were horsewhips. Just as Sade was fascinated by the macabre instruments of restraint which must have been present in his daily life from time to time, if not used directly on an aristocratic prisoner such as himself, Sacher-Masoch's particular fetish wasn't the stuff of fevered flights of fancy, but an everyday accoutrement for most, one in which he could delight secretly, deliciously, whether its wearer was ignorant of the pleasures her clothes afforded him or not, with the added thrill of stealing pleasure where it's not conventionally found. Just as, in our own time, *haute couture* can accommodate overt fetish fashion as much as it likes, but true fetishism remains a private thrill, based firmly on, and continually reinforced by, the everyday.

Venus in Furs

> MY BELOVED – I do not care to see you today, or tomorrow, and not until evening the day after tomorrow, and then *as my slave*.
>
> Your mistress
> WANDA

'As my slave' was underlined. I read the note which I received early in the morning a second time. Then I had a donkey saddled, an animal symbolic of learned professors, and rode into the mountains. I wanted to numb my desire, my yearning, with the magnificent scenery of the Carpathians.

I am back, tired, hungry, thirsty, and more in love than ever. I quickly change my clothes, and a few moments later knock at her door.

'Come in!'

I enter. She is standing in the centre of the room, dressed in a gown of white satin which floods down her body like light. Over it she wears a scarlet *kazabaika*, richly edged with ermine. Upon her powdered, snowy hair is a little diadem of diamonds. She stands with her arms folded across her breast, and with her brows contracted.

'Wanda!' I run towards her, and am about to throw my arms about her to kiss her. She retreats a step, measuring me from top to bottom.

'Slave!'

'Mistress!' I kneel down, and kiss the hem of her garment.

'That is as it should be.'

'Oh, how beautiful you are.'

'Do I please you?' She stepped before the mirror, and looked at herself with proud satisfaction.

'I shall become mad!'

Her lower lip twitched derisively, and she looked at me mockingly from behind half-closed lids.

'Give me the whip.'

I looked about the room.

'No,' she exclaimed, 'stay as you are, kneeling.' She went over to the fireplace, took the whip from the mantelpiece, and, watching me with a smile, let it hiss through the air; then she slowly rolled up the sleeve of her fur jacket.

'Marvellous woman!' I exclaimed.

'Silence, slave!' She suddenly scowled, looked savage, and struck me with the whip. A moment later she threw her arm tenderly about me, and pityingly bent down to me. 'Did I hurt you?' she asked, half-shyly, half-timidly.

'No,' I replied, 'and even if you had, pains that come through you are a joy. Strike again, if it gives you pleasure.'

'But it doesn't give me pleasure.'

Again I was seized with that strange intoxication.

'Whip me,' I begged, 'whip me without mercy.'

Wanda swung the whip, and hit me twice. 'Are you satisfied now?'

'No.'

'Seriously, no?'

'Whip me, I beg you, it is a joy to me.'

'Yes, because you know very well that it isn't serious,' she replied, 'because I haven't the heart to hurt you. This brutal game goes against my grain. Were I really the woman who beats her slaves you would be horrified.'

'No, Wanda,' I replied, 'I love you more than myself; I am devoted to you for death and life. In all seriousness, you can do with me whatever you will, whatever your caprice suggests.'

'Severin!'

'Tread me underfoot!' I exclaimed, and flung myself face to the floor before her.

'I hate all this play-acting,' said Wanda impatiently.

'Well, then maltreat me seriously.'

An uncanny pause.

'Severin, I warn you for the last time,' began Wanda.

'If you love me, be cruel towards me,' I pleaded with upraised eyes.

'If I love you,' repeated Wanda. 'Very well!' She stepped back and looked at me with a sombre smile. '*Be then my slave, and know what it means to be delivered into the hands of a woman.*' And at the same moment she gave me a kick.

'How do you like that, slave?'

Then she flourished the whip.

'Get up!'

I was about to rise.

'Not that way,' she commanded, 'on your knees.'

I obeyed, and she began to apply the lash.

The blows fell rapidly and powerfully on my back and arms. Each one cut into my flesh and burned there, but the pains enraptured me. They came from her whom I adored, and for whom I was ready at any hour to lay down my life.

She stopped. 'I am beginning to enjoy it,' she said, 'but enough for today. I am beginning to feel a demonic curiosity to see how far your strength goes. I take a cruel joy in seeing you tremble and writhe beneath my whip, and in hearing your groans and wails; I want to go on whipping without pity until you beg for mercy, until you lose your senses. You have awakened dangerous elements in my being. But now get up.'

I seized her hand to press it to my lips.

'What impudence.'

She shoved me away with her foot.

'Out of my sight, slave!'

After having spent a feverish night filled with confused dreams, I awoke. Dawn was just beginning to break.

How much of what was hovering in my memory was true; what had I actually experienced and what had I dreamed? That I had been whipped was certain. I can still feel each blow, and count the burning red stripes in my body. And *she* whipped me. Now I know everything.

My dream had become truth. How does it make me feel? Am I disappointed in the realisation of my dream?

No, I am merely somewhat tired, but her cruelty has enraptured me. Oh, how I love her, adore her! All this cannot express in the remotest way my feeling for her, my complete devotion to her. What happiness to be her slave!

She calls me from her balcony. I hurry upstairs. She is standing on the threshold, holding out her hand in friendly fashion. 'I am ashamed of myself,' she says, while I embrace her, and she hides her head against my breast.

'Why?'

'Please try to forget the ugly scene of yesterday,' she said with quivering voice. 'I have fulfilled your mad wish, now let us be reasonable and happy and love each other, and in a year I will be your wife.'

'My mistress,' I exclaimed, 'and I your slave!'

'Not another word of slavery, cruelty, or the whip,' interrupted Wanda. 'I shall not grant you any of those favours, none except wearing my fur jacket; come and help me into it.'

The little bronze clock on which stood a cupid who had just shot his bolt struck midnight.

I rose, and wanted to leave.

Wanda said nothing, but embraced me and drew me back on the ottoman. She began to kiss me anew, and this silent language was so comprehensible, so convincing –

And it told me more than I dared to understand.

A languid abandonment pervaded Wanda's entire being. What a voluptuous softness there was in the gloaming of her half-closed eyes, in the red flood of her hair which shimmered faintly under the white powder, in the red and white satin which crackled about her with every movement, in the swelling ermine of the *kazabaika* in which she carelessly nestled.

'Please,' I stammered, 'but you will be angry with me.'

'Do with me what you will,' she whispered.

'Well, then whip me, or I shall go mad.'

'Haven't I forbidden you,' said Wanda sternly, 'but you are incorrigible.'

'Oh, I am so terribly in love.' I had sunk to my knees and was burying my glowing face in her lap.

'I really believe,' said Wanda thoughtfully, 'that your madness is nothing but a demonic, unsatisfied sensuality. *Our unnatural way of life must generate such illness*. Were you less virtuous, you would be completely sane.'

'Well then, make me sane,' I murmured. My hands were running through her hair and playing tremblingly with the gleaming fur, which rose and fell like a moonlit wave upon her heaving bosom, and drove all my senses into confusion.

And I kissed her. No, she kissed me – savagely, pitilessly, as if she wanted to slay me with her kisses. I was in a delirium, and had long since lost my reason, but now I, too, was breathless. I sought to free myself.

'What is the matter?' asked Wanda.

'I am suffering agonies.'

'You are suffering –' she broke out into a loud amused laughter.

'You laugh!' I moaned, 'have you no idea –'

She was serious all of a sudden. She raised my head in her hands, and with a violent gesture drew me to her breast.

'Wanda,' I stammered.

'Of course, you enjoy suffering,' she said, and laughed again, 'but wait, I'll bring you to your senses.'

'No, I will no longer ask,' I exclaimed, 'whether you want to belong to me for always or for only a brief moment of intoxication. I want to drain my happiness to the full. You are mine now, and I would rather lose you than never have had you.'

'Now you are sensible,' she said. She kissed me again with her murderous lips. I tore the ermine apart and the covering of lace and her naked breast surged against mine.

Then my senses left me –

The first thing I remember is the moment when I saw blood dripping from my hand, and she asked apathetically, 'Did you scratch me?'

'No, I believe, I have bitten you.'

It is strange how every relation in life assumes a different face as soon as a new person enters.

We spent marvellous days together we visited the mountains and the lakes, we read together, and I completed Wanda's portrait. And how we loved one another, how beautiful her smiling face was!

Then a friend of hers arrived, a divorced woman somewhat older, more experienced, and less scrupulous than Wanda. Her influence is already making itself felt in every direction.

Wanda wrinkles her brows, and displays a certain impatience with me.

Has she ceased loving me?

For almost a fortnight this unbearable restraint has lain upon us. Her friend lives with her, and we are never alone. A circle of men surrounds the young women. With my seriousness and melancholy I am playing an absurd role as lover. Wanda treats me like a stranger.

Today, while we were out walking, she fell behind with me. I saw that this was done intentionally, and I rejoiced. But what did she tell me?

'My friend doesn't understand how I can love you. She doesn't think you either handsome or particularly attractive otherwise. She is telling me from morning till night about the glamour of the frivolous life in the capital, hinting at the advantages to which I could lay claim, the large parties which I would find there, and the distinguished and handsome admirers I would attract. But of what use is all this, since it happens that I love you.'

For a moment I lost my breath, then I said: 'I have no wish to stand in the way of your happiness, Wanda. Do not consider me.' Then I raised my hat, and let her go ahead. She looked at me surprised, but did not answer a syllable.

When by change I happened to be close to her on the way back, she secretly pressed my hand. Her glance was so radiant, so full of promised happiness, that in a moment all the torments of these days were forgotten and all their wounds healed.

I now am aware again of how much I love her.

'My friend has complained about you,' said Wanda today.

'Perhaps she feels that I despise her.'

'But why do you despise her, you foolish young man?' exclaimed Wanda, pulling my ears with both hands.

'Because she is a hypocrite,' I said. 'I respect only a woman who is actually virtuous, or who openly lives for pleasure's sake.'

'Like me, for instance,' replied Wanda jestingly; 'but you see, child, a woman can only do that in the rarest cases. She can neither be as gaily sensual, nor as spiritually free as a man; her state is always a mixture of the sensual and spiritual. Her heart desires to enchain man permanently, while she herself is ever subject to the desire for change. The result is a conflict, and thus usually against her wishes lies and deception enter into her actions and personality and corrupt her character.'

'Certainly that is true,' I said. 'The transcendental character with which woman wants to stamp love leads to her deception.'

'But the world likewise demands it,' Wanda interrupted. 'Look at this woman. She has a husband and a lover in Lemberg and has found a new admirer here. She deceives all three and yet is honoured by all and respected by the world.'

'I don't care,' I exclaimed, 'but she is to leave you alone; she treats you like an article of commerce.'

'Why not?' the beautiful woman interrupted vivaciously. 'Every woman has the instinct or desire to draw advantage out of her attractions, and much is to be said for giving oneself without love or pleasure because if you do it in cold blood, you can reap profit to best advantage.'

'Wanda, what are you saying?'

'Why not?' she said, 'and take note of what I am about to say to you. *Never feel secure with the woman you love*, for there are more dangers in woman's nature than you imagine. Women are neither as *good* as their admirers and defenders maintain, nor as *bad* as their enemies make them out to be. *Woman's character is characterlessness.* The best woman will momentarily go down into the mire, and the worst unexpectedly rises to deeds of greatness and goodness and puts to shame those that despise her. No woman is so good or so bad but that at any moment she is capable of the most diabolical as well as of the most divine, of the filthiest as well as of the purest, thoughts, emotions and actions. In spite of all the advances of civilisation, woman has remained as she came out of the hand of nature. She has the nature of a savage, who is faithful or faithless, magnanimous or cruel, according to the impulse that dominates at the moment. Throughout history it has always been a serious deep culture which has produced moral character. Man even when he is selfish or evil always follows *principles*, woman never follows anything but *impulses*. Don't ever forget that, and never feel secure with the woman you love.'

Her friend has left. At last an evening alone with her again. It seems as if Wanda had saved up all the love, which had been kept from her, for this superlative evening; never had she been so kind, so dear, so full of tenderness.

What happiness to cling to her lips, and to die away in her arms! In a state of relaxation and wholly mine, she rests her head against my breast, and with drunken rapture our eyes seek each other.

I cannot yet believe, comprehend, that this woman is mine, wholly mine.

'She is right on one point,' Wanda began, without moving, without opening her eyes, as if she were asleep.

'Who?'

She remained silent.

'Your friend?'

She nodded. 'Yes, she is right, you are not a man, you are a dreamer, a charming cavalier, and you certainly would be a priceless slave, but I cannot imagine you as my husband.'

I was frightened.

'What is the matter? You are trembling?'

'I tremble at the thought of how easily I might lose you,' I replied.

'Are you made less happy now because of this?' she replied. 'Does it rob you of any of your joys, that I have belonged to another before I did to you, that others after you will possess me, and would you enjoy me less if another were made happy simultaneously with you?'

'Wanda!'

'You see,' she continued, 'that would be a way out. You won't ever lose me then. I care deeply for you and intellectually we are harmonious, and I should like to live with you always, if in addition to you I might have –'

'What an idea,' I cried. 'You fill me with a sort of horror.'

'Do you love me any the less?'

'On the contrary.'

Wanda had raised herself on her left arm. 'I believe,' she said, 'that to hold a man permanently, it is vitally important not to be faithful to him. What honest woman has ever been as devotedly loved as a hetaira?'

'There is a painful stimulus in the unfaithfulness of a beloved woman. It is the highest kind of ecstasy.'

'For you, too?' Wanda asked quickly.

'For me, too.'

'And if I should give you that pleasure,' Wanda exclaimed mockingly.

'I shall suffer terrible agonies, but I shall adore you the more,' I replied. 'But you would never deceive me, you would have the demonic greatness of saying to me: I shall love no one but you, but I shall make happy whoever pleases me.'

Wanda shook her head. 'I don't like deception, I am honest, but what man exists who can support the burden of truth. Were I to say to you that this serene, sensual life, this paganism is my ideal, would you be strong enough to bear it?'

'Certainly. I could endure anything so as not to lose you. I feel how little I really mean to you.'

'But Severin –'

'But it is so,' said I, 'and just for that reason –'

'For that reason you would –' she smiled roguishly – 'have I guessed it?'

'Be your slave!' I exclaimed. 'Be your unrestricted property, without a will of my own, of which you could dispose as you wished, and which would therefore never be a burden to you. While you drink life at its fullest, while, surrounded by luxury, you enjoy the serene happiness and Olympian love, I want to be your servant, to put on and take off your shoes.'

'You really aren't so far from wrong,' replied Wanda, 'for only as my slave could you endure my loving others. Furthermore the freedom of enjoyment of the ancient world is unthinkable without slavery. It must give one a feeling of being like unto a god to see a man kneel before one and tremble. I want a slave, do you hear, Severin.'

'Am I not your slave?'

'Then listen to me,' said Wanda excitedly, seizing my hand. 'I want to be yours, as long as I love you.'

'A month?'

'Perhaps, even two.'

'And then?'

'Then you become my slave.'

'And you?'

'I? Why do you ask? I am a goddess and sometimes I descend from my Olympian heights to you, softly, very softly, and secretly –

'But what does all this mean,' said Wanda, resting her head in both hands with her gaze lost in the distance, 'a golden fancy which never can become true.' An uncanny brooding melancholy seemed shed over her entire being; I have never seen her like that.

'Why inachievable?' I began.

'Because slavery doesn't exist any longer.'

'Then we will go to a country where it still exists, to the Orient, to Turkey,' I said eagerly.

'You would – Severin – in all seriousness?' Wanda replied. Her eyes burned.

'Yes, in all seriousness, I want to be your slave,' I continued. 'I want your power over me to be sanctified by law; I want my life to be in your hands, I want nothing that could protect or save me from you. Oh, what a voluptuous joy when once I feel myself entirely dependent upon your absolute will, your whim, at your beck and call. And then what happiness, when on occasion you deign to be gracious, and the slave may kiss the lips which mean life and death to him.' I knelt down, and leaned my burning forehead against her knee.

'You are talking as in a fever,' said Wanda agitatedly; 'and you really love me so endlessly?' She held me to her breast, and covered me with kisses. 'You really want it?'

'I swear to you now by God and my honour, that I shall be your slave, wherever and whenever you wish it, as soon as you command,' I exclaimed, hardly master of myself.

'And if I take you at your word?' said Wanda.

'Please do!'

'All this appeals to me,' she said then. 'It is different from anything else – to know that a man who worships me, and whom I love with all my heart, is so wholly mine, dependent on my will and caprice, my possession and slave, while I –'

She looked strangely at me.

'If I should become frightfully frivolous you are to blame,' she continued. 'It almost seems as if you were afraid of me already, but you have sworn.'

'And I shall keep my oath.'

'I shall see to that,' she replied. 'I am beginning to enjoy it, and, heaven help me, we won't stick to fancies now. You shall become my slave, and I – I shall try to be *Venus in Furs*.'

I thought that at last I knew this woman, understood her, and now I see I have to begin at the very beginning again. Only a little while ago her reaction to my dreams was violently hostile, and now she tries to carry them into execution with the soberest seriousness.

She has drawn up a contract according to which I give my word of honour and agree under oath to be her slave, as long as she wishes.

With her arm around my neck she read this, unprecedented, incredible document to me. The end of each sentence she punctuates with a kiss.

'But all the obligations in the contract are on my side,' I said, teasing her.

'Of course,' she replied with great seriousness, 'you cease to be my lover, and consequently I am released from all duties and obligations towards you. You will have to look upon my favours as pure benevolence. You no longer have any rights, and no longer can lay claim to any. There can be no limit to my power over you. Remember, that you won't be much better than a dog, or some inanimate object. You will be mine, my plaything, which I can break to pieces whenever I want an hour's amusement. You are nothing, I am everything. Do you understand?' She laughed and kissed me again, and yet a sort of cold shiver ran through me.

'Won't you allow me a few conditions –' I began.

'Conditions?' She contracted her forehead. 'Ah! You are afraid already, or perhaps you regret, but it is too late now. You have sworn, I have your word of honour. But let me hear them.'

'First of all I should like to have it included in our contract that you will never completely leave me, and then that you will never give me over to the mercies of any of your admirers –'

'But Severin,' exclaimed Wanda with her voice full of emotion and with tears in her eyes, 'how can you imagine that I – and you, a man who loves me so absolutely, who puts himself so entirely in my power –' she halted.

'No, no!' I said, covering her hands with kisses. 'I don't fear anything from you that might dishonour me. Forgive me the ugly thought.'

Wanda smiled happily, leaned her cheek against mine, and seemed to reflect.

'You have forgotten something,' she whispered coquettishly, 'the most important thing!'

'A condition?'

'Yes – that I must always wear my furs,' exclaimed Wanda. 'But I promise you I'll do that anyhow because they give me a despotic feeling. And I shall be very cruel to you, do you understand?'

'Shall I sign the contract?' I asked.

'Not yet,' said Wanda. 'I shall first add your conditions, and the actual signing won't occur until the proper time and place.'

'In Constantinople?'

'No. I have thought things over. What special value would there be in owning a slave where everyone owns slaves. What I want is to *have a slave*, *I alone*, here in our civilised sober, Philistine world, and a slave who submits helplessly to my power solely on account of my beauty and personality, not because of law, of property rights or compulsions. This attracts me. But at any rate we will go to a country where we are not known and where you can appear before the world as my servant without embarrassment. Perhaps to Italy, to Rome or Naples.'

We were sitting on Wanda's ottoman. She wore her ermine jacket, her hair was loose and fell like a lion's mane down her back. She clung to my lips, drawing my soul from my body. My head whirled, my blood began to seethe, my heart beat violently against hers.

'I want to be absolutely in your power, Wanda,' I exclaimed suddenly, seized by that frenzy of passion when

I can scarcely think clearly or decide freely. 'I want to put myself absolutely at your mercy for good or evil without any condition, without any limit to your power.'

While saying this I had slipped from the ottoman, and lay at her feet looking up at her with drunken eyes.

'How beautiful you now are,' she exclaimed, 'your eyes half-broken in ecstasy fill me with joy, carry me away. How wonderful your look would be if you were being beaten to death, in the extreme agony. You have the eyes of a martyr.'

Sometimes, nevertheless, I have an uneasy feeling about placing myself so absolutely, so unconditionally into a woman's hands. Suppose she did abuse my passion, her power?

Well, then I would experience what has occupied my imagination since my childhood, what has always given me the feeling of seductive terror. A foolish apprehension! It will be a wanton game she will play with me, nothing more. She loves me, and she is good, a noble personality, incapable of a breach of faith. But it lies in her hands – *if she wants to she can*. What a temptation in this doubt, this fear!

Now I understand Manon Lescaut and the poor chevalier, who, even in the pillory, while she was another man's mistress, still adored her.

Love knows no virtue, no profit; it loves and forgives and suffers everything, because it must. It is not our judgement that leads us; it is neither the advantages nor the faults which we discover that make us abandon ourselves or that repel us.

It is a sweet, soft, enigmatic power that drives us on. We cease to think, to feel, to will; we let ourselves be carried away by it, and ask not whither.

A Russian prince made his first appearance today on the promenade. He aroused general interest on account of his athletic figure, magnificent face and splendid bearing. The women particularly gaped at him as though he were a wild animal, but he went his way gloomily without paying attention to anyone. He was accompanied by two servants, one a negro, completely dressed in red satin, and the other a Circassian in his full gleaming uniform. Suddenly he saw Wanda, and fixed his cold piercing look upon her; he even turned his head after her, and when she had passed, he stood still and followed her with his eyes.

And she – she veritably devoured him with her radiant green eyes – and did everything possible to meet him again.

The cunning coquetry with which she walked, moved and looked at him, almost stifled me. On the way home I remarked about it. She knit her brows.

'What do you want,' she said, 'the prince is a man whom I might like, who even dazzles me, and I am free. I can do what I please –'

'Don't you love me any longer –' I stammered, frightened.

'I love only you,' she replied, 'but I shall have the prince pay court to me.'

'Wanda!'

'Aren't you my slave?' she said calmly. 'Am I not Venus, the cruel northern Venus in furs?'

I was silent. I felt literally crushed by her words; her cold look entered my heart like a dagger.

'You will find out immediately the prince's name, residence and circumstances,' she continued. 'Do you understand?'

'But –'

'No argument, obey!' exclaimed Wanda, more sternly than I would have thought possible for her, 'and don't dare to enter my sight until you can answer my questions.'

It was not till afternoon that I could obtain the desired information for Wanda. She let me stand before her like a servant, while she leaned back in her armchair and listened to me, smiling. Then she nodded, she seemed to be satisfied.

'Bring me my footstool,' she commanded shortly.

I obeyed, and after having put it before her and having put her feet on it, I remained kneeling.

'How will this end?' I asked sadly after a short pause.

She broke into playful laughter. 'Why things haven't even begun yet.'

'You are more heartless than I imagined,' I replied, hurt.

'Severin,' Wanda began earnestly. 'I haven't done anything yet, not the slightest thing, and you are already calling me heartless. What will happen when I begin to carry your dreams to their realisation, when I begin to lead a gay, free life and have a circle of admirers about me, when I begin actually to fulfil your ideal, tread you underfoot and apply the lash?'

'You take my dreams too seriously.'

'Too seriously? I can't stop at make-believe when once I begin,' she replied. 'You know I hate all play-acting and comedy. You have wished it. Was it my idea or yours? Did I persuade you or did you inflame my imagination? I am taking things seriously now.'

'Wanda,' I replied, caressingly, 'listen quietly to me. We love each other infinitely, we are very happy, will you sacrifice our entire future to a whim?'

'It is no longer a whim,' she exclaimed.

'What is it?' I asked frightened.

'Something that was probably latent in me,' she said quietly and thoughtfully. 'Perhaps it would never have come to light, if you had not called it to life, and made it grow. Now that it has become a powerful impulse, now that it fills my whole being, now that I enjoy it, now that I cannot and do not want to do otherwise, now you want to back out – you – are you a man?'

'Dear, sweet Wanda!' I began to caress her, kiss her.

'Don't – you are not a man –'

'And you,' I flared up.

'I am stubborn,' she said, 'you know that. I haven't a strong imagination, and like you I am weak in execution. But when I make up my mind to do something, I carry it through, and the more certainly, the more opposition I meet. Leave me alone!'

She pushed me away, and got up.

'Wanda!' I likewise rose, and stood facing her.

'Now you know what I am,' she continued. 'Once more I warn you. You still have the choice. I am not compelling you to be my slave.'

'Wanda,' I replied with emotion and tears filling my eyes, 'don't you know how I love you?' Her lips quivered contemptuously. 'You are mistaken, you make yourself out worse than you are; you are good and noble by nature –'

'What do you know about my nature?' She interrupted vehemently, 'You will get to know me as I am.'

'Wanda!'

'Decide, will you submit, unconditionally?'

'And if I say no.'

'Then –'

She stepped close up to me, cold and contemptuous. As she stood before me now, the arms folded across her breast, with an evil smile about her lips, she was in fact the despotic woman of my dreams. Her expression seemed hard, and nothing lay in her eyes that promised kindness or mercy.

'Well –' she said at last.

'You are angry,' I cried, 'you will punish me.'

'Oh no!' she replied, 'I shall let you go. You are free. I am not holding you.'

'Wanda – I, who love you so –'

'Yes, you, my dear sir, you who adore me,' she exclaimed contemptuously, 'but who are a coward, a liar, and a breaker of promises. Leave me instantly –'

'Wanda! –'

'Wretch!'

My blood rose in my heart. I threw myself down at her feet and began to cry.

'Tears, too!' She started to laugh. Oh, this laughter was frightful. 'Leave me – I don't want to see you again.'

'Oh my God!' I cried, beside myself. 'I will do whatever you command, be your slave, a mere object with which you can do what you will – only don't send me away – I can't bear it – I cannot live without you.' I embraced her knees, and covered her hand with kisses.

'Yes, you must be a slave, and feel the lash, for you are not a man,' she said calmly. She said this to me with perfect composure, not angrily, not even excitedly, and that was what hurt most. 'Now I know you, your dog-like nature that adores where it is kicked, that rejoices the more it is maltreated. Now I know you and now you shall come to know me.'

She walked up and down with long strides, while I remained cowering on my knees; my head was hanging limply, tears flowed from my eyes.

'Come here,' Wanda commanded harshly, sitting down on the ottoman. I obeyed her command, and sat down beside her. She looked at me sombrely, and then a light suddenly seemed to illuminate the interior of her eye. Smiling, she drew me towards her breast, and began to kiss the tears out of my eyes.

The odd part of my situation is that I am like the bear in Lily's park, I can escape and don't want to; I am ready to endure everything as soon as she threatens to set me free.

If only she would use the whip again. There is something uncanny in the kindness with which she treats me. I seem like a little captive mouse with which a beautiful cat prettily plays. She is ready at any moment to tear me to pieces, and my heart of a mouse threatens to burst.

What are her intentions? What does she purpose to do with me?

It seems she has completely forgotten the contract, my slavehood. Or was it actually only stubbornness? And she gave up her whole plan as soon as I no longer opposed her and submitted to her imperial whim!

How kind she is to me, how tender, how loving! We are spending marvellously happy days.

Today she had me read to her the scene between Faust and Mephistopheles, in which the latter appears as a wandering scholar. Her glance hung on me with strange pleasure.

'I don't understand,' she said when I had finished, 'how a man who can read such great and beautiful thoughts with such expression, and interpret them so clearly, concisely and intelligently, can at the same time be such a visionary and supersensual ninny as you are.'

'Were you pleased?' said I, and kissed her forehead.

She gently stroked my brow. 'I love you, Severin,' she whispered. 'I don't believe I could ever love anyone more than you. Let us be sensible, what do you say?'

Instead of replying I folded her in my arms; a deep inward, yet vaguely sad happiness filled my breast, my eyes grew moist, and a tear fell upon her hand.

'How can you cry!' she exclaimed, 'you are a child!'

On a pleasure drive we met the Russian prince in his carriage. He seemed to be unpleasantly surprised to see me by Wanda's side, and looked as if he wanted to pierce her through and through with his electric grey eyes. She, however, did not seem to notice him. I felt at that moment like kneeling down before her and kissing her feet. She let her glance glide over him indifferently, as though he were an inanimate object, a tree, for instance, and turned to me with her gracious smile.

When I said goodnight to her today she seemed suddenly unaccountably distracted and moody. What was occupying her?

'I am sorry you are going,' she said when I was already standing on the threshold.

'It is entirely in your hands to shorten the hard period of my trial, to cease tormenting me –' I pleaded.

'Do you imagine that this compulsion isn't a torment for me, too,' Wanda interjected.

'Then end it,' I exclaimed, embracing her, 'be my wife.'

'*Never, Severin,*' she said gently, but with great firmness.

'What do you mean?'

I was frightened in my innermost soul.

'*You are not the man for me.*'

I looked at her, and slowly withdrew my arm which was still about her waist; then I left the room, and she – she did not call me back.

* * *

A sleepless night; I made countless decisions, only to toss them aside again. In the morning I wrote her a letter in which I declared our relationship dissolved. My hand trembled when I put on the seal, and I burned my fingers.

As I went upstairs to hand it to the maid, my knees threatened to give way.

The door opened, and Wanda thrust forth her head full of curling-papers.

'I haven't had my hair dressed yet,' she said, smiling. 'What have you there?'

'A letter –'

'For me?'

I nodded.

'Ah, you want to break with me,' she exclaimed, mockingly.

'Didn't you tell me yesterday that I wasn't the man for you?'

'*I repeat it now!*'

'Very well, then.' My whole body was trembling, my voice failed me, and I handed her the letter.

'Keep it,' she said, measuring me coldly. 'You forget that it is no longer a question as to whether you satisfy me as a man; as a *slave* you will doubtless do well enough.'

'Madame!' I exclaimed, aghast.

'That is what you will call me in the future,' replied Wanda, throwing back her head with a movement of unutterable contempt. 'Put your affairs in order within the next twenty-four hours. The day after tomorrow I shall start for Italy, and you will accompany me as my servant.'

'Wanda –'

'I forbid any sort of familiarity,' she said, cutting my words short; 'likewise you are not to come in unless I call or ring for you, and you are not to speak to me until you are spoken to. From now on your name is no longer Severin, but Gregor.'

I trembled with rage, and yet, unfortunately, I cannot deny it, I also felt a strange pleasure and stimulation.

'But, madame, you know my circumstances,' I began in confusion. 'I am dependent on my father, and I doubt whether he will give me the large sum of money needed for this journey –'

'That means you have no money, Gregor,' said Wanda, delightedly, 'so much the better, you are then entirely dependent on me, and in fact my slave.'

'You don't consider,' I tried to object, 'that as a man of honour it is impossible for me –'

'I have indeed considered it,' she replied almost with a tone of command. 'As a man of honour you must keep your oath and redeem your promise to follow me as slave whithersoever I demand and to obey whatever I command. Now leave me, Gregor!'

I turned towards the door.

'Not yet – you must first kiss my hand.' She held it out to me with a certain proud indifference, and I, the dilettante, the donkey, the miserable slave pressed it with intense tenderness against my lips which were dry and hot with excitement.

There was another gracious nod of the head.

Then I was dismissed.

Though it was late in the evening my light was still lit, and a fire was burning in the large green stove. There were still many things among my letters and documents to be put in order. Autumn, as is usually the case with us, had fallen with all its power.

Suddenly she knocked at my window with the handle of her whip.

I opened and saw her standing outside in her ermine-lined jacket and in a high round Cossack cap of ermine of the kind which the great Catherine favoured.

'Are you ready, Gregor?' she asked darkly.

'Not yet, mistress,' I replied.

'I like that word,' she said then, 'you are always to call me mistress, do you understand? We leave here tomorrow morning at nine o'clock. As far as the district capital you will be my companion and friend, but from the moment we enter the railway-coach you are my slave, my servant. Now close the window, and open the door.'

After I had done as she had demanded, and after she had entered, she asked, contracting her brows ironically, 'well, how do you like me.'

'Wanda, you –'

'Who gave you permission?' she gave me a blow with the whip.

'You are very beautiful, mistress.'

Wanda smiled and sat down in the armchair. 'Kneel down – here beside my chair.'

I obeyed.

'Kiss my hand.'

I seized her small cold hand and kissed it.

'And the mouth –'

In a surge of passion I threw my arms around the beautiful cruel woman, and covered her face, arms and breasts with glowing kisses. She returned them with equal fervour – the eyelids closed as in a dream. It was after midnight when she left.

At nine o'clock in the morning everything was ready for departure, as she had ordered. We left the little Carpathian health-resort in a comfortable light carriage. The most interesting drama of my life had reached a point of development whose denouement it was then impossible to foretell.

So far everything went well. I sat beside Wanda, and she chatted very graciously and intelligently with me, as with a good friend, concerning Italy, Pisemski's new novel, and Wagner's music. She wore a sort of Amazonesque travelling-dress of black cloth with a short jacket of the same material, set with dark fur. It fitted closely and showed her figure to best advantage. Over it she wore dark furs. Her hair wound into an antique knot, lay beneath a small dark fur hat from which a black veil hung. Wanda was in very good humour, she fed me sweetmeats, played with my hair, loosened my neckcloth and made a pretty cockade of it; she covered my knees with her furs and stealthily pressed the fingers of my hand. When our Jewish driver persistently went on nodding to himself, she even gave me a kiss, and her cold lips had the fresh frosty fragrance of a young autumnal rose, which blossoms alone amid bare stalks and yellow leaves and upon whose calyx the first frost has hung tiny diamonds of ice.

We are at the district capital. We get out at the railway station. Wanda throws off her furs and places them over my arm, and goes to secure the tickets.

When she returns she has completely changed.

'Here is your ticket, Gregor,' she says in a tone which supercilious ladies use to their servants.

'A third-class ticket,' I reply with comic horror.

'Of course,' she continues, 'but now be careful. You won't get on until I am settled in my compartment and don't need you any longer. At each station you will hurry to my car and ask for my orders. Don't forget. And now give me my furs.'

After I had helped her into them, humbly like a slave, she went to find an empty first-class coupé. I followed. Supporting herself on my shoulder, she got on and I wrapped her feet in bearskins and placed them on the warming bottle.

Then she nodded to me, and dismissed me. I slowly ascended a third-class carriage, which was filled with abominable tobacco-smoke that seemed like the fogs of Acheron at the entrance of Hades. I now had the leisure to muse about the riddle of human existence, and about its greatest riddle of all – *woman*.

Whenever the train stops, I jump off, run to her carriage, and with doffed cap await her orders. She wants coffee and then a glass of water, at another time a bowl of warm water to wash her hands, and thus it goes on. She lets several men who have entered her compartment pay court to her. I am dying of jealousy and have to leap about like an antelope so as to secure what she wants quickly and not miss the train.

In this way the night passes. I haven't had time to eat a mouthful and I can't sleep, I have to breathe the same oniony air as Polish peasants, peddlers and common soldiers.

When I mount the steps of her coupé, she is lying stretched out on cushions in her comfortable furs, covered up with the skins of animals. She is like an oriental despot, and the men sit like Indian deities, straight upright against the walls and scarcely dare to breathe.

She stops over in Vienna for a day to go shopping, and particularly to buy a series of luxurious gowns. She continues to treat me as her servant. I follow her at the respectful distance of ten paces. She hands me her packages without so much as deigning to bestow a kind look, and laden down like a donkey I pant along behind.

Before leaving she takes all my clothes and gives them to the hotel waiters. I am ordered to put on her livery. It is a Cracovian costume in her colours, light-blue with red facings, and red quadrangular cap, ornamented with peacock-feathers. The costume is rather becoming to me.

The silver buttons bear her coat of arms. I have the feeling of having been sold or of having bonded myself to the devil.

My fair demon leads me from Vienna to Florence. Instead of linen-garbed Mazovians and greasy-haired Jews, my companions now are curly-haired *contadini*, a magnificent sergeant of the first Italian Grenadiers and a poor German painter. The tobacco smoke no longer smells of onions, but of salami and cheese.

Night has fallen again. I lie on my wooden bed as on a rack; my arms and legs seem broken. But there nevertheless is an element of poetry in the affair. The stars sparkle round about, the Italian sergeant has a face like Apollo Belvedere, and the German painter sings a lovely German song.

'Now that all the shadows gather
And endless stars grow light,
Deep yearning on me falls
And softly fills the night.

Through the sea of dreams
Sailing without cease,
Sailing goes my soul
In thine to find release.'

And I am thinking of the beautiful woman who is sleeping in regal comfort among her soft furs.

Florence! Crowds, cries, importunate porters and cab-drivers. Wanda chooses a carriage and dismisses the porters.

'What have I a servant for?' she says. 'Gregor – here is the ticket – get the luggage.'

She wraps herself in her furs and sits quietly in the carriage while I drag the heavy trunks hither, one after another. I break down for a moment under the last one; a good-natured *carabiniere* with an intelligent face comes to my assistance.

She laughs. 'It must be heavy,' said she, 'all my furs are in it.'

I get up on the driver's seat, wiping drops of perspiration from my brow. She gives the name of the hotel, and the driver urges on his horse. In a few minutes we halt at the brilliantly illuminated entrance.

'Have you any rooms?' she asks the portier.

'Yes, madame.'

'Two for me, one for my servant, all with stoves.'

'Two first-class rooms for you, madame, both with stoves,' replied the waiter who had hastily come up, 'and one without heat for your servant.'

She looked at them, and then abruptly said: 'They are satisfactory, have fires built at once; my servant can sleep in the unheated room.'

I merely looked at her.

'Bring up the trunks, Gregor,' she commands, paying no attention to my looks. 'In the meantime I'll be dressing, and then I'll go down to the dining-room, and you can eat something for supper yourself.'

As she goes into the adjoining room, I drag the trunks upstairs and help the waiter build a fire in her bedroom.

He tries to question me in bad French about my employer. With a brief glance I see the blazing fire, the fragrant white poster-bed, and the rugs which cover the floor. Tired and hungry I then descend the stairs, and ask for something to eat. A good-natured waiter, who used to be in the Austrian army and takes all sorts of pains to entertain me in German, shows me the dining-room and waits on me. I have just had the first fresh drink in thirty-six hours and have the first bite of warm food on my fork, when she enters.

I rise.

'What do you mean by taking me into a dining-room in which my servant is eating,' she snaps at the waiter, flaring with anger. She turns around and leaves.

Meanwhile I thank heaven that I am permitted to go on eating. Later I climb the four flights upstairs to my room. My small trunk is already there, and a miserable little oil-lamp is burning. It is a narrow room without fireplace, without a window, but with a small air hole. If it weren't so beastly cold, it would remind me of one of the Venetian *piombi*, those notorious prisons under the leaden roof of the Palace of the Doges. Involuntarily I have to laugh out aloud, so that it re-echoes, and I am startled by my own laughter.

Suddenly the door is pulled open and the waiter, with a theatrical Italian gesture, calls, 'You are to come down to madame, at once.' I pick up my cap, stumble down the first few steps, finally arrive in front of her door on the first floor and knock.

'Come in!'

I enter, shut the door and stand to attention.

Wanda has made herself comfortable. She is sitting in a négligé of white muslin and lace on a small red divan with her feet on a footstool that matches. She has thrown her fur cloak about her. It is the identical cloak in which she appeared to me for the first time as the goddess of love.

The yellow lights of the candelabra which stand on projections, their reflections in the large mirrors, and the red flames from the open fireplace play beautifully on the green velvet, the dark-brown sable of the cloak, the smooth white skin, and the red, flaming hair of the beautiful woman. Her clear, but cold face is turned towards me, and her cold green eyes rest upon me. 'I am satisfied with you, Gregor,' she began.

I bowed.

'Come closer.'

I obeyed.

'Still closer,' she looked down, and stroked the sable with her hand. 'Venus in Furs receives her slave. I can see that you are more than an ordinary dreamer, you don't remain far in arrears of your dreams, you are the sort of man who is ready to carry his dreams into effect, no matter how mad they are. I confess, I like this; it impresses me. There is strength in this, and strength is the only thing one respects. I actually believe that under unusual circumstances, in a period of great deeds, what seems to be your weakness would reveal itself as extraordinary power.

'Under the early emperors you would have been a martyr, at the time of the Reformation an anabaptist, during the French Revolution one of those inspired Girondists who mounted the guillotine with Ma Marseillaise on their lips. But you are my slave, my –'

She suddenly leaped up; the furs slipped down, and she threw her arms with soft pressure about my neck.

'My beloved slave, Severin, oh, how I love you, how I adore you, how handsome you are in your Crocavian costume! You will be cold tonight up in your wretched room without a fire. Shall I give you one of my furs, dear heart, the large one there –'

She quickly picked it up, throwing it over my shoulders, and before I knew what had happened I was completely wrapped up in it.

'How wonderfully becoming furs are to your face, they bring out your noble lines. As soon as you cease being my slave, you must wear a velvet coat with sable, do you understand? Otherwise I shall never put on my fur jacket again.'

And again she began to caress me and kiss me; finally she drew me down on the little divan.

'You seem to be pleased with yourself in furs,' she said. 'Quick, quick, give them to me, or I will lose all sense of dignity.'

I placed the furs about her, and Wanda slipped her right arm into the sleeve.

'This is the pose in Titian's picture. But now enough of joking. Don't always look so solemn, it makes me feel sad. As far as the world is concerned you are still merely my servant; you are not yet my slave, for you have not yet signed the contract. You are still free, and can leave me any moment. You have played your part magnificently. I have been delighted, but aren't you tired of it already, and don't you think I am abominable? Well, say something I command it.'

'Must I confess to you, Wanda?' I began.

'Yes, you must.'

'Even if you take advantage of it,' I continued, 'I shall love you the more deeply, adore you the more frantically, the worse you treat me. What you have just done inflames my blood and intoxicates all my senses.' I held her close to me and clung for several moments to her moist lips.

'Oh, you beautiful woman,' I then exclaimed, looking at her. In my enthusiasm I tore the sable from her shoulders and pressed my mouth against her neck.

'You love me even when I am cruel,' said Wanda, 'now go! – you bore me – don't you hear?'

She boxed my ears so that I saw stars and bells rang in my ears.

'Help me into my furs, slave.'

I helped her, as well as I could.

'How awkward,' she exclaimed, and struck me in the face again. I felt myself growing pale.

'Did I hurt you?' she asked, softly touching me with her hand.

'No, no,' I exclaimed.

'At any rate you have no reason to complain, you want it thus; now kiss me again.'

I threw my arms about her, and her lips clung closely to mine. As she lay against my breast in her large heavy furs, I had a curiously oppressive sensation. It was as if a wild beast, a she-bear, were embracing me. It seemed as if I were about to feel her claws in my flesh. But this time the she-bear let me off easily.

With my heart filled with smiling hopes, I went up to my miserable servant's room, and threw myself down on my hard couch.

'Life is really amazingly droll,' I thought. 'A short time ago the most beautiful woman, Venus herself, rested against your breast, and now you have an opportunity for studying the Chinese hell. Unlike us, they don't hurl the damned into flames, but they have devils chasing them out into fields of ice.

'Very likely the founders of their religion also slept in unheated rooms.'

During the night I startled out of my sleep with a scream. I had been dreaming of an ice-field in which I had lost my way; I had been looking in vain for a way out. Suddenly an Eskimo drove up in a sleigh harnessed with reindeer; he had the face of the waiter who had shown me to the unheated room.

'What are you looking for here, my dear sir?' he exclaimed. 'This is the North Pole.'

A moment later he had disappeared, and Wanda flew over the smooth ice on tiny skates. Her white satin skirt fluttered and crackled; the ermine of her jacket and cap, but especially her face, gleamed whiter than the snow. She shot towards me, enclosed me in her arms, and began to kiss me. Suddenly I felt my blood running warm down my side.

'What are you doing?' I asked horror-stricken.

She laughed, and as I looked at her now, it was no longer Wanda, but a huge, white she-bear, who was digging her claws into my body.

I cried out in despair, and still heard her diabolical laughter when I awoke, and looked about the room in surprise.

* * *

Early in the morning I stood at Wanda's door, and the waiter brought the coffee. I took it from him, and served it to my beautiful mistress. She had already dressed, and looked magnificent, all fresh and roseate. She smiled graciously at me and called me back when I was about to withdraw respectfully.

'Come, Gregor, have your breakfast quickly too,' she said, 'then we will go house-hunting. I don't want to stay in the hotel any longer than I have to. It is very embarrassing here. If I chat with you for more than a minute, people will immediately say: "The fair Russian is having an affair with her servant – you see, the race of Catherines isn't extinct yet." '

Half an hour later we went out; Wanda was in her cloth-gown with the Russian cap, and I in my Cracovian costume. We created quite a stir. I walked about ten paces behind, looking very solemn, but expected momentarily to have to break out into loud laughter. There was scarcely a street in which one or the other of the attractive houses did not bear the sign *Camere ammobiliate*. Wanda always sent me upstairs, and only when the apartment seemed to answer her requirements did she herself ascend. By noon, I was as tired as a stag-hound after the hunt.

We entered a new house and left it again without having found a suitable habitation. Wanda was already somewhat out of humour. Suddenly she said to me: 'Severin, the seriousness with which you play your part is charming, and the restrictions which we have placed upon each other are really annoying me. I can't stand it any longer; I do love you; I must kiss you. Let's go into one of the houses.'

'But, my lady –' I interposed.

'Gregor?' She entered the next open corridor and ascended a few steps of the dark stairway; then she threw her arms about me with passionate tenderness and kissed me.

'Oh, Severin, you were very wise. You are much more dangerous as slave than I would have imagined, you are positively irresistible, and I am afraid I shall have to fall in love with you again.'

Don't you love me any longer then?' I asked, seized by a sudden fright.

She solemnly shook her head, but kissed me again with her swelling, adorable lips.

We returned to the hotel. Wanda had luncheon, and ordered me also quickly to get something to eat.

Of course, I wasn't served as quickly as she, and so it happened that just as I was carrying the second bite of my steak to my mouth, the waiter entered and called out with his theatrical delivery: 'Madame wants you at once.'

I took a rapid and painful leave of my food, and tired and hungry, hurried towards Wanda, who was already in the street.

'I wouldn't have imagined you could be so cruel,' I said reproachfully. 'With all these fatiguing duties you don't even leave me time to eat in peace.'

Wanda laughed gaily. 'I thought you had finished,' she said, 'but never mind. Man was born to suffer, and you in particular. The martyrs didn't have any beefsteaks either.'

I followed her resentfully, gnawing at my hunger.

'I have given up the idea of finding a place in the city,' Wanda continued. 'It will be difficult to find an entire floor which is shut off and where you can do as you please. In such a strange, mad relationship as ours there must be no jarring note. I shall rent an entire villa – and you will be surprised. You have my permission now to satisfy your hunger, and look about a bit in Florence. I won't be home till this evening. If I need you then, I will have you called.'

I looked at the Duomo, the Palazzo Vecchio, the Loggia di Lanzi, and then I stood for a long time on the banks of the Arno. Again and again I let my eyes rest on the magnificent ancient Florence, whose round cupolas and towers were drawn in soft lines against the blue, cloudless sky. I gazed on its splendid bridges, beneath whose wide arches the lively waves of the beautiful yellow river ran, and the green hills which surrounded the city, bearing slender cypresses and extensive buildings, palaces and monasteries.

It is a different world, this one in which we are – a gay, sensuous, smiling world. The landscape too has nothing of the seriousness and sombreness of ours. It is some distance to the last white villas scattered among the pale green of the mountains, and yet there isn't a spot that isn't bright with sunlight. The people are less serious than we; perhaps they think less, but they all look as though they are happy.

It is also maintained that death is easier in the south.

I have a vague feeling now that such a thing as beauty without thorn and love of the senses without torment does exist.

Wanda has discovered a delightful little villa and rented it for the winter. It is situated on a charming hill on the left bank of the Arno, opposite the Cascine. It is surrounded by an attractive garden with lovely paths, grass plots and a magnificent meadow of camellias. It is only two storeys high, quadrangular in the Italian fashion. An open gallery runs along one side, a sort of loggia with plaster-casts of antique statues; stone steps lead from it down into the garden. From the gallery you enter a bath with a magnificent marble basin, from which winding stairs lead to my mistress's bedchamber.

Wanda occupies the second storey by herself.

A room on the ground floor has been assigned to me; it is very attractive, and even has a fireplace.

I have roamed through the garden. On a round hillock I discovered a little temple, but I found its door locked. However, there is a chink in the door and when I glue my eye to it, I see the goddess of love on a white pedestal.

A slight shudder passes over me. It seems to me as if she were smiling at me saying: 'Are you there? I have been expecting you.'

It is evening. An attractive maid brings me orders to appear before my mistress. I ascend the wide marble stairs, pass through the ante-room, a large salon furnished with extravagant magnificence, and knock at the door of the bedroom. I knock very softly for the luxury displayed everywhere intimidates me. Consequently no one hears me, and I stand for some time in front of the door. I have a feeling as if I were standing before the bedroom of the

Great Catherine, and it seems as if at any moment she might come out in her green sleeping furs, with the red ribbon and decoration on her bare breast, and with her little white powdered curls.

I knock again. Wanda impatiently pulls the door open.

'Why so late?' she asks.

'I was standing in front of the door, but you didn't hear me knock,' I reply timidly. She closes the door, and clinging to me she leads me to the red damask ottoman on which she had been resting. The entire arrangement of the room is in red damask – wallpaper, curtains, *portières*, hangings of the bed. A magnificent painting of Samson and Delilah decorated the ceiling.

Wanda receives me in an intoxicating deshabille. Her white satin dress flows gracefully and picturesquely down her slender body, leaving her arms and breast bare, and carelessly they nestle amid green velvet. Her red hair falls down her back as far as the hips, only half held by strings of black pearls.

'Venus in furs,' I whisper, while she draws me to her breast and threatens to stifle me with her kisses. Then I no longer speak and neither do I think; everything is drowned out in an ocean of unimagined bliss.

'Do you still love me?' she asks, her eye softening in passionate tenderness.

'You ask!' I exclaimed.

'You still remember your oath,' she continued with an alluring smile, 'now that everything is prepared, everything in readiness, I ask you once more, is it still your serious wish to become my slave?'

'Am I not ready?' I asked in surprise.

'You have not yet signed the papers.'

'Papers – what papers?'

'Oh, I see, you want to give it up,' she said, 'well then, we will let it go.'

'But Wanda,' I said, 'you know that nothing gives me greater happiness than to serve you, to be your slave. I would give everything for the sake of feeling myself wholly in your power, even unto death –'

'How beautiful you are', she whispered, 'when you speak so enthusiastically, so passionately. I am more in love with you than ever and you want me to be dominant, stern and cruel. I am afraid it will be impossible for me to be so.'

'I am not afraid,' I replied smiling, 'where are the papers?'

'So that you may know what it means to be absolutely in my power, I have drafted a second agreement in which you declare that you have decided to kill yourself. In that way I can even kill you, if I so desire.'

'Give them to me.'

While I was unfolding the documents and reading them, Wanda got pen and ink. She then sat down beside me with her arm about my neck, and looked over my shoulder at the paper.

The first one read:

Agreement between Mme von Dunajew
and Severin von Kusiemski

Severin von Kusiemski ceases with the present day being the affianced of Mme Wanda von Dunajew, and renounces all the rights appertaining thereunto; he on the contrary binds himself, on his word of honour as a man and nobleman, that hereafter he will be her *slave* until such time that she herself sets him at liberty again.

As the slave of Mme von Dunajew he is to bear the name Gregor, and he is unconditionally to comply with every one of her wishes, and to obey every one of her commands; he is always to be submissive to his mistress, and is to consider her every sign of favour as an extraordinary mercy.

Mme von Dunajew is entitled not only to punish her slave as she deems best, even for the slightest inadvertence or fault, but also is herewith given the right to torture him as the mood may seize her or merely for the sake of whiling away the time. Should she so desire, she may kill him whenever she wishes; in short, he is her unrestricted property.

Should Mme von Dunajew ever set her slave at liberty, Severin von Kusiemski agrees to forget everything that he has experienced or suffered as her slave, and promises *never under any circumstances and in no wise to think of vengeance or retaliation.*

Mme von Dunajew on her behalf agrees as his mistress to appear as often as possible in her furs, especially when she purposes some cruelty towards her slave.

Appended at the bottom of the agreement was the date of the present day.

The second document contained only a few words.

Having become increasingly weary of existence and its illusions, I have of my own free will put an end to my worthless life.

I was seized with a deep horror when I had finished. There was till time, I could still withdraw, but the madness of passion and the sight of the beautiful woman who lay all relaxed against my shoulder carried me away.

'This one you will have to copy, Severin,' said Wanda, indicating the second document. 'It has to be entirely in your own handwriting; this, of course, isn't necessary in the case of the agreement.'

I quickly copied the few lines in which I designated myself a suicide, and handed them to Wanda. She read them, and put them on the table with a smile.

'Now have you the courage to sign it?' she asked with a crafty smile, inclining her head.

I took the pen.

'Let me sign first,' said Wanda, 'your hand is trembling; are you afraid of the happiness that is to be yours?'

She took the agreement and pen. While engaging in my internal struggle, I looked upward for a moment. It occurred to me that the painting on the ceiling, like many of those of the Italian and Dutch schools, was utterly unhistorical, but this very fact gave it a strange mood which had an almost uncanny effect on me. Delilah, an opulent woman with flaming red hair, lay extended, half-disrobed, in a dark fur cloak, upon a red ottoman, and bent smiling over Samson who had been overthrown and bound by the Philistines. Her smile in its mocking coquetry was full of a diabolical cruelty; her eyes, half-closed, met Samson's and his with a last look of insane passion clung to hers, for already one of his enemies is kneeling on his breast with the red-hot iron to blind him.

'Now –' said Wanda. 'Why, you are all lost in thought. What is the matter with you, everything will remain just as it was, even after you have signed, don't you know me yet, dear heart?'

I looked at the agreement. Her name was written there in bold letters. I peered once more into her eyes with their potent magic, then I took the pen and quickly signed the agreement.

'You are trembling,' said Wanda calmly, 'shall I help you?'

She gently took hold of my hand, and my name appeared at the bottom of the second paper. Wanda looked once more at the two documents, and then locked them in the desk which stood at the head of the ottoman.

'Now then, give me your passport and money.'

I took out my wallet and handed it to her. She inspected it, nodded, and put it with the other things while in a sweet drunkenness I kneeled before her leaning my head against her breast.

Suddenly she thrusts me away with her foot, leaps up, and pulls the bell-rope. In answer to its sound three young, slender negresses enter; they are as if carved of ebony, and are dressed from head to foot in red satin; each one has a rope in her hand.

Suddenly I realise my position, and am about to rise. Wanda stands proudly erect, her cold beautiful face with its sombre brows and contemptuous eyes is turned towards me. She stands before me as mistress, commanding, gives a sign with her hand, and before I really know what has happened to me the negresses have dragged me to the ground, and have tied me hand and foot. As in the case of one about to be executed my arms are bound behind my back, so that I can scarcely move.

'Give me the whip, Haydée,' commands Wanda, with unearthly calm.

The negress hands it to her mistress, kneeling.

'And now take off my heavy furs,' she continues, 'they impede me.'

The black woman obeyed.

'The jacket there!' Wanda commanded.

Haydée quickly brought her the *kazabaika*, trimmed with ermine, which lay on the bed, and Wanda slipped into it with two inimitably graceful movements.

'Now tie him to the pillar here!'

The black woman lifted me up, and twisting a heavy rope around my body, tied me standing against one of the massive pillars which supported the top of the wide Italian bed.

Then they suddenly disappeared, as if the earth had swallowed them.

Wanda swiftly approached me. Her white satin dress flowed behind her in a long train, like silver, like moonlight; her hair flared like flames against the white fur of her jacket. Now she stood in front of me with her left hand firmly planted on her hips; in her right hand she held the whip. She uttered an abrupt laugh.

'Now play has come to an end between us,' she said with heartless coldness. 'Now we will begin in deadly earnest. You fool, I laugh at you and despise you: you who in your insane infatuation have given yourself as a plaything to *me*, the frivolous and capricious woman. You are no longer the man I love, but *my slave*, at my mercy even unto life and death.

'You shall know me!

'First of all you shall have a taste of the whip in all seriousness, without having done anything to deserve it, so that you may understand what to expect if you are awkward, disobedient or refractory.'

With a wild grace she rolled back her fur-lined sleeve, and struck me across the back.

I winced, for the whip cut like a knife into my flesh.

'Well, how do you like that?' she exclaimed.

I was silent.

'Just wait, you will yet whine like a dog beneath my whip,' she threatened, and simultaneously began to strike me again.

The blows fell quickly, in rapid succession, with terrific force upon my back, arms, and neck; I had to grit my teeth not to scream aloud. Now she struck me in the face and warm blood ran down, but she laughed and continued her blows.

'It is only now I understand you,' she exclaimed. 'It really is a joy to have someone so completely in one's power, and a man at that, who loves you – you do love me? – No – Oh! I'll tear you to shreds yet, and with each blow my pleasure will grow. Now, twist like a worm, scream, whine! You will find no mercy in me!'

Finally, she seemed tired.

She tossed the whip aside, stretched out on the ottoman, and rang.

The negresses entered.

'Untie him!'

As they loosened the rope, I fell to the floor like a lump of wood. The black women grinned, showing their white teeth.

'Untie the rope around his feet.'

They did it, and at first I was unable to rise.

'Come over here, Gregor.'

I approached the beautiful woman. Never did she seem more seductive to me than today in spite of all her cruelty and contempt.

'One step further,' Wanda commanded. 'Now kneel down, and kiss my foot.'

She extended her foot beyond the hem of white satin, and I, the supersensual fool, pressed my lips upon it.

'Now, you won't lay eyes on me for an entire month, Gregor,' she said seriously. 'I want to become a stranger to you, so you will more easily adjust yourself to our new relationship. In the meantime, you will work in the garden, and await my orders. Now, off with you, slave!'

* * *

A month has passed with monotonous regularity, heavy work, and a melancholy hunger, hunger for her, who is inflicting all these torments on me. I am under the gardener's orders; I help him lop the trees and prune the hedges, transplant flowers, turn over the flower beds, sweep the gravel paths; I share his coarse food and his hard cot; I rise and go to bed with the chickens. Now and then I hear that our mistress is amusing herself, surrounded by admirers. Once I heard her gay laughter even down here in the garden.

I seem awfully stupid to myself. Was it the result of my present life, or was I so before? The month is drawing to a close – the day after tomorrow. What will she do with me now, or has she forgotten me, and left me to trim hedges and bind bouquets till my dying day?

A written order.

The slave Gregor is herewith ordered to my personal service.

WANDA DUNAJEW

With a beating heart I draw aside the damask curtain on the following morning, and enter the bedroom of my divinity. It is still filled with a pleasant half-darkness.

'Is it you, Gregor?' she asked, while I kneel before the fireplace, building a fire. I tremble at the sound of the beloved voice. I cannot see her; she is invisible behind the curtains of the four-poster bed.

'Yes, my mistress,' I reply.

'How late is it?'

'Past nine o'clock.'

'Breakfast.'

I hasten to get it, and then kneel down with the tray beside her bed.

'Here is breakfast, my mistress.'

Wanda draws back the curtains, and curiously enough at the first glance when I see her among the pillows with loosened flowing hair, she seems an absolute stranger, a beautiful woman, but the beloved soft lines are gone. This face is hard and has an expression of weariness and satiety.

Or is it simply that formerly my eye did not see this?

She fixes her green eyes upon me, more with curiosity than with menace, perhaps even somewhat pityingly, and lazily pulls the dark sleeping fur on which she lies over the bared shoulder.

At this moment she is very charming, very maddening, and I feel my blood rising to my head and heart. The tray in my hands begins to sway. She notices it and reaches out for the whip which is lying on the toilet-table.

'You are awkward, slave,' she says furrowing her brow.

I lower my looks to the ground, and hold the tray as steadily as possible. She eats her breakfast, yawns, and stretches her opulent limbs in the magnificent furs.

She has rung. I enter.

'Take this letter to Prince Corsini.'

I hurry into the city, and hand the letter to the prince. He is a handsome young man with glowing back eyes. Consumed with jealousy, I take his answer to her.

'What is the matter with you?' she asks with lurking spitefulness. 'You are very pale.'

'Nothing, mistress, I merely walked rather fast.'

At luncheon the prince is at her side, and I am condemned to serve both her and him. They joke, and I am as if non-existent for both. For a brief moment I see red; I was just pouring some Bordeaux in his glass, and spilled it over the tablecloth and her gown.

'How awkward,' Wanda exclaimed and slapped my face. The prince laughed, and she also, but I felt the blood rising to my face.

After luncheon she drove in the Cascine. She has a little carriage with a handsome, brown English horse, and holds the reins herself. I sit behind and notice how coquettishly she acts and nods with a smile when one of the distinguished gentlemen bows to her.

As I help her out of the carriage, she leans lightly on my arm; the contact runs through me like an electric shock. She *is* a wonderful woman, and I love her more than ever.

* * *

For dinner at six she has invited a small group of men and women. I serve, but this time I do not spill any wine over the tablecloth.

A slap in the face is more effective than ten lectures. It makes you understand very quickly, especially when the instruction is by way of a small woman's hand.

After dinner she drives to the Pergola Theatre. As she descends the stairs in her black velvet dress with its large collar of ermine and with a diadem of white roses on her hair, she is literally stunning. I open the carriage-door, and help her in. In front of the theatre I leap from the driver's seat; in alighting she leans on my arm, which trembles under the sweet burden. I open the door of her box, and then wait in the vestibule. The performance lasts four hours; she receives visits from her cavaliers, the while I grit my teeth with rage.

It is long after midnight when my mistress's bell sounds for the last time.

'Fire!' she orders abruptly, and when the fireplace crackles, 'Tea!'

When I return with the samovar, she has already undressed, and with the aid of the negress Haydée slips into a white négligé.

Haydée thereupon leaves.

'Hand me the sleeping-furs,' says Wanda, sleepily stretching her lovely limbs. I take them from the armchair, and hold them while she slowly and lazily slides into the sleeves. She then throws herself down on the cushions of the ottoman.

'Take off my shoes, and put on my velvet slippers.'

I kneel down and tug at the little shoe which resists my efforts. 'Hurry, hurry!' Wanda exclaims, 'you are hurting me! Just you wait – I will teach you.' She strikes me with the whip, but now the shoe is off.

'Now get out!' A final kick – and then I can go to bed.

Tonight I accompanied her to a soirée. In the entrance hall she ordered me to help her out of her furs; then with a proud smile, confident of victory, she entered the brilliantly illuminated room. I again waited with gloomy and monotonous thoughts, watching hour after hour run by. From time to time the sounds of music reached me, when the door remained open for a moment. Several servants tried to start a conversation with me, but soon desisted, since I know only a few words of Italian.

Finally I fell asleep, and dreamed that I murdered Wanda in a violent attack of jealousy. I was condemned to death, and saw myself strapped on the board; the knife fell, I felt it on my neck, but I was still alive –

Then the executioner slapped my face.

No, it wasn't the executioner; it was Wanda who stood wrathfully before me demanding her furs. I am at her side in a moment, and help her on with them.

There is a deep joy in wrapping a beautiful woman into her furs, and in seeing and feeling how her neck and magnificent limbs nestle in the precious soft furs, and to lift the flowing hair over the collar. When she throws it off a soft warmth and the faint fragrance of her body still clings to the ends of the hairs of sable. It is enough to drive one mad.

Finally a day came when there were neither guests, nor theatre, nor other company. I breathed a sigh of relief. Wanda sat in the gallery, reading, and apparently had no orders for me. At dusk when the silvery evening mists fell she withdrew. I served her at dinner, she ate by herself, but had not a look, not a syllable for me, not even a slap in the face.

I actually desire a slap from her hand.

Tears fill my eyes, and I feel that she has humiliated me so deeply, that she doesn't even find it worthwhile to torture or maltreat me any further.

Before she goes to bed, her bell calls me.

'You will sleep here tonight. I had horrible dreams last night, and am afraid of being alone. Take one of the cushions from the ottoman, and lie down on the bearskin at my feet.'

Then Wanda put out the lights. The only illumination in the room was from a small lamp suspended from the ceiling. She herself got into bed. 'Don't stir, so as not to wake me.'

I did as she had commanded, but could not fall asleep for a long time. I saw the beautiful woman, beautiful as a goddess, lying on her back on the dark sleeping-furs, her arms beneath her neck, with a flood of red hair over them. Her magnificent breast rose in deep regular breathing, and whenever she moved ever so slightly I woke up and listened to see whether she needed me.

But she did not require me.

No task was required of me; I meant no more to her than a night-lamp, or a revolver which one places under one's pillow.

Am I mad or is she? Does all this arise out of an inventive, wanton woman's brain with the intention of surpassing my supersensual fantasies, or is this woman really one of those Neronian characters who take a diabolical pleasure in treading underfoot, like worms, human beings who have thoughts and feelings and a will like theirs?

What have I experienced?

When I knelt with the coffee-tray beside her bed, Wanda suddenly placed her hand on my shoulder and her eyes plunged deep into mine.

'What beautiful eyes you have,' she said softly, 'and especially now since you suffer. Are you very unhappy?'

I bowed my head, and kept silent.

'Severin, do you still love me,' she suddenly exclaimed passionately, 'can you still love me?'

She drew me close with such vehemence that the coffee-tray upset, the jug and cups fell to the floor, and the coffee ran over the carpet.

'Wanda – my Wanda,' I cried out and held her passionately against me; I covered her mouth, face and breast with kisses.

'It is my unhappiness that I love you more and more madly the worse you treat me, the more frequently you betray me. Oh, I shall die of pain and love and jealousy.'

'But I haven't betrayed you, as yet, Severin,' replied Wanda smiling.

'Not? Wanda! Don't jest so mercilessly with me,' I cried. 'Haven't I myself taken the letter to the prince –'

'Of course, it was an invitation for luncheon.'

'You have, since we have been in Florence –'

'I have been absolutely faithful to you,' replied Wanda, 'I swear it by all that is holy to me. All that I have done was merely to fulfil your dream and it was done for your sake.

'However, I shall take a lover, otherwise things will be only half accomplished, and in the end you will yet reproach me with not having treated you cruelly enough, my dear beautiful slave! But today you shall be Severin again, the only one I love. I haven't given away your clothes. They are here in the chest. Go and dress as you used to in the little Carpathian health-resort when our love was so intimate. Forget everything that has happened since; oh, you will forget it easily in my arms; I shall kiss away all your sorrows.'

She began to treat me tenderly like a child, to kiss me and caress me. Finally she said with a gracious smile, 'Go now and dress. I too will dress. Shall I put on my fur jacket? Oh yes, I know, now run along!'

When I returned she was standing in the centre of the room in her white satin dress, and the red *kazabaika* edged with ermine; her hair was white with powder and over her forehead she wore a small diamond diadem. For a moment she reminded me in an uncanny way of Catherine the Great, but she did not give me much time for reminiscences. She drew me down on the ottoman beside her and we enjoyed two blissful hours. She was no longer the stern capricious mistress, she was entirely a fine lady, a tender sweetheart. She showed me photographs and books which had just appeared, and talked about them with so much intelligence, clarity and good taste, that I more than once carried her hand to my lips, enraptured. She then had me recite several of Lermontov's poems, and when I was all afire with enthusiasm, she placed her small hand gently on mine. Her expression was soft, and her eyes were filled with tender pleasure.

'Are you happy?'

'Not yet.'

She then leaned back on the cushions, and slowly opened her *kazabaika.*

But I quickly covered the half-bared breast again with the ermine. 'You are driving me mad,' I stammered.

'Come!'

I was already lying in her arms, and like a serpent she was kissing me with her tongue, when again she whispered, 'Are you happy?'

'Infinitely!' I exclaimed.

She laughed aloud. It was an evil, shrill laugh which made cold shivers run down my back.

'You used to dream of being the slave, the plaything of a beautiful woman, and now you imagine you are a free human being, a man, my lover – you fool! A sign from me, and you are a slave again. Down on your knees!'

I sank down from the ottoman to her feet, but my eye still clung doubtingly on hers.

'You can't believe it,' she said, looking at me with her arms folded across her breasts. 'I am bored, and you will just do to while away a couple of hours of time. Don't look at me like that –'

She kicked me with her foot.

'You are just what I want, a human being, a thing, an animal –'

She rang. The three black woman entered.

'Tie his hands behind his back.'

I remained kneeling and unresistingly let them do this. They led me into the garden, down to the little vineyard, which forms the southern boundary. Corn had been planted between the espaliers, and here and there a few dead stalks still stood. To one side was a plough.

The negresses tied me to a post, and amused themselves sticking me with their golden hairpins. But this did not last long, before Wanda appeared with her ermine cap on her head, and with her hands in the pockets of her jacket. She had me untied, and then my hands were fastened together behind my back. She finally had a yoke put around my neck, and harnessed me to the plough.

Then her black women drove me out into the field. One of them held the plough, another led me by a line, the third applied the whip, and Venus in Furs stood to one side and looked on.

Algernon Charles Swinburne (1837–1909)

Swish Fulfilment

Swinburne was a blue-blood through and through. His effete aesthete's outlook was no doubt influenced by his paternal grandfather, who continued to dress as a French nobleman of the *ancien regime* throughout the 1840s. His own father, by contrast, was an upright naval man and his family observed the rituals of High Anglicanism common among its class. On coming down from Oxford, where he always knew his own mind with regard to the many disputes he engaged in, Swinburne associated with the pre-Raphaelites Burne-Jones and Rossetti, and with William Morris. His passion was Italian culture, and he held ambivalent, but always opinionated, views on religion.

Excitable, by all accounts amiable, but with an addictive personality and prone to hysterical moods and drunken binges, he would continually disturb Rossetti, with whom he lived, sliding down banisters and raising his own brand of unthreatening hell with his rakish friends. He was mostly gay, although he'd had a heartbreaking relationship with a female cousin when young. During his bohemian years he was a great self-mythologiser, and loved to play with gossip. His opinions of others were by all accounts manic, sliding from wild endorsement to wild disdain. Putting it unkindly, he was something of a Walter Mitty. Putting it kindly, he loved the romance of the imagination.

Oscar Wilde called him 'a braggart in matters of vice, who had done everything he could to convince his fellow citizens of his homosexuality and bestiality without being in the slightest degree a homosexual or a bestialiser'.

Worn out with dissolution, he repaired to the house of his financial adviser, where he lived quietly for many years and made a second career as a literary critic until his death from influenza in 1909. His poetry is considered vapid and lightweight today perhaps, but academics who championed his collections such as *Poems and Ballads* and *A Channel Passage* chose to gloss over the number of unpublished works which eulogise flagellation, in which his passion is plain. In the metre of 'Arthur's Flogging', there are echoes of 'All Things Bright and Beautiful'. It's a worshipful paean to corporal punishment in which, hamming up the extent to which he believes in the innate wisdom of the practice, Swinburne clearly hopes to increase the volume of opprobrium incurred. Irrevocably damaged perhaps, Swinburne was also a supreme wind-up merchant, and there's something satirical in his elevation of the birch to a godhead. Nonetheless, it's clear that CP also gave the poet a rustle in his trousers.

One can't responsibly present poems like this and 'Reginald's Flogging' without a word of clarification. 'Arthur's Flogging' in particular contains offputtingly vivid scenes of the chastisement of a young man who is sexually underage. While, from the excited chatter of the youths who flock around poor Reginald, we can imagine the barbarity and severity of his punishment and the abject ignominy of *his* position. Given the widespread disciplinary use of CP throughout the world – and legendarily the English public school system – in the Victorian age, it would be anachronistic and unnecessarily revisionist to ignore these works altogether. For the poet's peers, as for Sacher-Masoch's readership, the application of discipline was not in itself seen as automatically sexual. But it is today, and Nexus would never condone sexual activity with anyone the laws of responsible nations deem incapable of giving consent. And the issue of consent is at the heart of the sickening mind games and methods of persuasion that are a feature of paedophilia: informed consent is the only kind of consent there can be. These two poems are excerpted here for historical interest. If they sexually excite you on account of the age of their characters, instead of making you squirm uneasily, you would do well to talk to a mental health professional. The poet himself did not take these all that seriously.

Swinburne wants to take, not give, CP, and he's laughing at himself for looking through the rose-tinted spectacles of nostalgia at his own rosy buttocks. It's arguable that the gender of the one wielding the instrument of chastisement is ultimately irrelevant for him, for in his non-flagellatory work he shared Blake's idea of an androgynous soul, 'male and female, who from of old was neither female nor male, but perfect man [human] without division of flesh, until the setting of sex against sex by the malignity of animal creation'. Unlike the decadents and fetishists of an atheistic or nihilistic turn of mind, then, Swinburne is a believer in a life beyond our corporeal one.

One wonders what trials Swinburne himself endured at Eton, but suffice to say that every pupil in the mid-nineteenth century would have known a severe beating. According to the historian Ian Gibson,[1] flogging blocks were located throughout the school, and a birching was carried out in public, the 'miscreant' given plenty of advance notice in which to contemplate forthcoming events. Boys readily witnessed each others' humiliations, and yet all were subject to them. Swinburne thought this democratic; to us it's basic divide-and-rule. And all the while their fathers in the City were enjoying the constitutional invigorations of the Berkeley Horse.

Whatever the degree of humiliating and painful punishment Swinburne himself endured, it seems his response was to glory in it. It's one survival mechanism. In being past caring, beyond the shame of writing a poem like 'Arthur's Flogging', Swinburne makes the sexual power that the

---

[1] *The English Vice*, Duckworth (1978).

situation has for him explicit. Corporal punishment was seldom written about in such acknowledged terms in the nineteenth century. One problem for humanitarians of the time was the difficulty in speaking plainly about the practice. Henry Salt, a reformer, himself complained that 'One cannot speak in detail on this unpleasant subject.' He went on to manage, 'Anyone who can be disgusted by anything would have been disgusted by *that* spectacle.'[2]

It's highly likely that the poet, or at least one of his flagellant friends, was the author of a letter to the *Morning Post* which sent up the bluff 'never did me any harm' opinions on corporal punishment in schools prevalent at the time:

> Now I can vouch that, from the earliest days to the days of the immortal [headmaster] Keate . . . they have, one and all, appealed to the very *seat* of honour . . . And, mark me, flogging, used with sound judgement, is the only *fundamental* principle upon which our large schools can be conducted. I am all the better of it and am therefore,
>
> One who has been well swished.[3]

Whether he was the author of this letter or not, it seems that Swinburne, for all his irritating traits and drink problems, was sufficiently at ease with himself in his adult life to enjoy the flagellant aspect of his sexuality, however it got there. In this perhaps he was ahead of the majority of public school alumni of the time. The universality of corporal punishment at public schools of the nineteenth century was nothing short of a psychological holocaust among the children of the aristocracy. One can see something of its brutalising hopelessness in 'Reginald's Flogging', where even an appeal to the supreme authority represented by the poor lad's father fails to win sympathy. This must be a worm in the bud even for apologists of the

---

[2] Ibid..
[3] Ibid..

British Empire, for we have to add its diplomats, administrators and soldiers to the ranks of its victims, even though they'd have belly-laughed at being considered such. For the Empire was built not on the playing fields, but on the flogging blocks, of Eton.

Arthur's Flogging

Oh Birch! thou common dread and doom of all boys,
  Who found out first thy properties of pain?
Who gave thy tough lithe twigs their power to appal
    boys?
  Who laid the red foundations of thy reign?
Who made thee haunt by night the dreams of small boys?
  Who gave thee power o'er us thy trembling train?
Who made thee master of our bums, and lord?
Who flogged boys first? and what flogged boy first
    roared?

No tongue there is to say, no soul to know it;
  In blood and tears were laid thy first foundations,
But by whose hand who knows, and who can show it?
  So long the rod has ruled boys of all nations.
Oh, Birch! accept a schoolboy for thy poet,
  Whose bum has blushed from frequent flagellations
These three years past; thou knowest it, Birch, and more;
And while I write is not my bottom sore?

Oh, Birch! whose mouth should sing thee if not mine?
  Is there a schoolboy oftener flogged than I am?
Have I not marks upon me still of thine?
  Is there a boy, I say, from here to Siam,
Between the ages of eighteen and nine,
  Or has there been a boy since the age of Priam,
In days unknown of or in years unsearched,
Who has been oftener or more soundly birched?

Right well thou knowest the voice that now invokes
  Thine oft experienced aid and inspiration;

by all the rods I have felt, and all their strokes,
By all the burning pangs of my probation;
By the salt brine in which thy keeper soaks
Thy twigs to make them fit for flagellation,
By their green buds that make one hate the spring,
By all their suppleness and all their sting;

By all the scars I ever took behind,
By all the cuts thou has ever given me, since
At my first flogging, still I keep in mind,
The first cut made my young posteriors wince;
By thy full power on boys of every kind,
Alike on smarting page and tingling prince;
By all my floggings, whereso'er I got 'em;
By all the weals upon my naked bottom;

By all the blood of mine that thou hast shed,
And all the blood of all my schoolfellows,
And all that ever made the birch twigs red,
From tender bottoms blushing like a rose;
By all the boyish bums that ever bled,
Or ever will bleed from thy backside blows,
As long as supple twig and swelling bud
Make high-born bottoms 'blush with noble blood'.

For, as all schoolboys know, the birch, like God,
Has no respect of persons; all that come
Within the rule and reach of the red rod,
Are equal in the rod's sight, all and some;
Down go all breeches at the master's nod,
No preference shown of bum to blushing bum;
The birch still red with blood of his inferiors,
May flog the far descended boys posteriors.

Yes, birch is democratic; for my part,
When on the flogging block, I've often wished
To be a boy that drives a plough or cart
By fields and streams where once I rode and fished;
If when we're flogged birch did not make us smart

As it makes me smart every time I'm swished,
It were worth while to boast of long descent
If it could save our skins from detriment.

But crests and arms and quarterings and supporters,
And all emblazoned flourishes her field,
Are no defence for a boy's hinder quarters,
Nor will he find his coat of arms a shield
For his bare bottom, when, like other martyrs,
He writhes beneath the birch that leaves him wealed
All over his red quivering nether parts,
And smarts and roars, or only sobs and smarts.

His coat is birch *per fesse*, and total gules,
Poor fellow! 'tis an ancient coat, and good;
And, from of old, was borne in all boys' schools
Since the first flogging block was made of wood;
All dunces, truants, rebels, idlers, fools,
That e'er were birched have dyed it with their blood;
I too have often borne it. I, thy poet,
Thou knowest, Oh, Birch! and my posteriors know it.

Thou knowest my floggings, when and where I got 'em,
How I was flogged, how often, and what for;
Though I myself have in great part forgot 'em,
Now that the marks are on my flesh no more;
Thou knowest the new marks fresh upon my bottom,
All the scars, cuts, and weals that make it sore,
All the red ridges, all the parts half healed,
Since last my bottom gave thee a fair field.

By all these tokens, and each smarting sign,
Birch! hear once more a flogged boy's invocation,
Who never in his life had less than nine,
And never skulked or shirked his flagellation,
And never came off without marks of thine
To show for days in written indication;
He must have been well swished the day he got 'em,
To bear in sign of birch on his bare bottom.

I sing of Arthur's Flogging; I, who heard
  The boy himself sing out beneath the birch,
Louder and shriller than a singing bird,
  Or screaming parrot on its gilded perch;
He has had this week three floggings; this, the third,
  A good sound swishing, was for missing church.
And on this point no two boys ever differed,
That no boy gets more flogged than Arthur Clifford.

The time was noon; the flogging room the scene;
  And all the boys in Arthur's form were there;
And in they brought the culprit of thirteen,
  A boy with bright dark eyes and bright gold hair,
Of slender figure and of careless mien,
  Though now his flushed face wore a cloud of care,
And with eyes downcast like a shrinking girl's,
He came on blushing right up to his curls.

To him the doctor, in judicial wise,
  'What kept you, Clifford Minor, out of church?'
Then the boy lifted his dark violet eyes,
  And saw the flogging block, and saw the birch,
And felt the blood to cheeks and forehead rise,
  And wistfully looked round him as in search
Of any pretext to ward off his fate,
And answered boldly, 'Please, sir, I was late.'

'What made you late, sir?' with a smile and frown
  Of outward wrath and cruel inward joy,
Replied the master, 'Were you not up town
  On some vain errand for some foolish boy?'
No answer. 'Clifford, take your trousers down.'
  With piteous eyes uplifted, the poor boy
Just faltered, 'Please, sir,' and could get no farther.
Again, that voice, 'Take down your trousers, Arthur.'

Then smiles were seen on many small boys' faces,
  And smothered laughs on many a big boy's lips,

With stifled whispers and subdued grimaces,
  While Arthur, with cold trembling finger tips,
Stood fumbling at his waistband and his braces,
  Then bared the fleshy parts about his hips,
And let his trousers fall about his heels,
And showed a pair of buttocks full of weals.

So with his parti-coloured bottom bare,
  With all its wounds for all the school to mock,
With naked haunches delicately fair,
  The parts unscarred as white as lady's smock,
A boy with violet eyes and yellow hair
  Knelt, with his shirt up, on the flogging block;
And o'er him stood his master, fresh from church,
With a long, strong, lithe, new, green, sappy birch.

Once – twice – he whirled it whistling round his head,
  Then struck with all a strong man's utmost might,
And Arthur's bottom blushed one burning red
  All over, not an inch was left of white,
And from a score of weals at once it bled,
  Great tingling weals that sprang up left and right
Under the birch, and from them every one
The drops of blood as thick as raindrops spun.

And all the cuts his bottom had before,
  The parts where bits of birch were sticking still
Like spearheads in the wounds they had made of yore,
  When last the birch had all its cruel will,
Began to bleed afresh and smart once more
  As sheer through the air the whistling twigs swept
    shrill,
There, they're very sharp and straight, and smote afresh
The tingling space of naked quivering flesh.

The first cut made the flogged boy flinch and start,
  And from his lips pain forced a short sharp cry,
So hard it fell on such a tender part,
  Still sore from floggings felt so recently;

Right through his flesh he felt the bitter smart,
  Like a snake's sting down darted from on high,
And writhed, and roared out at the second blow –
'Oh! please, sir; oh! sir! Oh! oh! oh! oh! oh!

Swift as the birch on Arthur's bottom fell,
  Hard as the birch on Arthur's bottom rung,
Like the deep notes of a funeral bell,
  The master's words of keen rebuke were flung,
'I'll flog you well for crying – flog you well;
  I'll have no crying here, boy; hold your tongue;
I'll give you more to cry for, you young dog, you!
I'll flog you – flog you – flog, flog, flog, flog,
    flog you.'

At every pause, at every word, a blow
  Fell, and made Arthur's bottom smart and bleed.
'Take that, sir,' 'Oh! sir, please, it hurts me so;
  You don't know how you hurt me, sir, indeed;
Oh! sir, I'll never – Oh! sir, please, sir, Oh!'
  And many a blood flake like a crimson bead,
At each fresh cut showed where each twig or bud
Had fallen, and drawn its one drop more of blood.

At each cut, Arthur, while his hands were free,
  Pulled down his shirt and rubbed his bottom; but
Though some relief from torture it might be,
  The gate of mercy was that instant shut;
And Arthur felt all through, but could not see,
  How hard the doctor laid on the next cut,
And as the sharp twigs were afresh applied,
Fresh blood ran from fresh weals on his backside.

And over him in front stood Philip Shirley
  And Edward Beauchamp, holding up his shirt;
And if he plucked it from them, they looked surly,
  As they drew up again the blood-stained skirt,
And shook their fists aside at Arthur's curly
  Head, or else grinned, and whispered, 'Does it hurt?'

And only held the spotted shirt up higher,
Till the birch seemed to set his bum on fire.

He clapped his hands behind – the birch twigs caught
'em
  Across, and made them tingle too and bleed;
And harder still the birch fell on his bottom,
  And left some fresh red letters there to read;
Weeks passed before the part inscribed forgot 'em,
  The fleshy tablets, where the master's creed
Is written on boy's skin with birchen pen,
At each re-issue copied fair again.

This was the third edition, not the first,
  Printed on Arthur's bottom in red text
That very week, with comments interspersed,
  And cuts that left the student's eye perplexed,
Though in the love of flagellation versed,
  You hardly could tell one cut from the next;
All the smooth creamy paper, white and pink,
Was crossed and scored and blotted with red ink.

All down the cream white margins, line on line,
  Ran the red tracery of the engraver's tool,
With many a capital and flourish fine,
  And ere the characters had time to cool
The well-soaked birch, still supple from the brine,
  Made a fresh score in sight of the whole school,
Who saw the inscription on the bare flesh scored,
While Arthur writhed with agony, and roared.

Like a large crimson flower of tropic lands
  That opens to the morning sun, and shuts
Again, at evening, and again expands,
  So Arthur's bottom seems, between the cuts,
To vibrate under his tormentor's hands,
  Who, gloating on it, as he flogs it, gluts
His eyes with the full prospect, while these great
Red cheeks contract at each cut, and dilate.

Then faster still the next few cuts are plied
  On those round naked fleshy hemispheres,
The rosy globes of Arthur's bare backside,
  The glowing cheeks that stream with crimson tears;
Cut after cut on Arthur's naked hide,
  And at each cut a fresh red streak appears,
And a fresh weal for each tough knotty bud,
And for each weal a fresh great flake of blood.

'By Jove! I say, he's getting peppered, ain't he?'
  Thus Philip Shirley whispers Edward Beauchamp,
'And still the old one seems as fresh as paint, he
  Swore he'd show all the school a sight to teach 'em
Next time; look there! the boy may well cry, mayn't he?
  He thinks our bums were made for him to switch 'em,
Made to bear all the cuts he's pleased to allot 'em,
By Jove! just look at Clifford Minor's bottom!

All seamed with bloody weals and streaks vermilion,
  That each cut makes blood run from in small streams,
He's got more cuts to show than Frank Tressilion,
  And Frank's all scored behind with crimson seams.
I wouldn't have his bottom for a million,
  There, the birch caught him nicely – how he screams!
Well, it's a shame to try the poor lad farther.
I say, that stings, eh? How's your bottom, Arthur?'

He grins and whispers, but the boy scarce hears;
  He struggles with the rising sobs, and chokes,
Striving in vain to swallow down his tears
  And not cry out, since every cry provokes
Fresh punishment, and for each sob he fears
  A fresh instalment of still sharper strokes;
And then the fresh cuts wring fresh tears and cries
From Arthur's quivering lips and streaming eyes.

His dark blue eyes look up, all dimd with pain,
  From under his rough tangled yellow hair,
And plead for mercy piteously, in vain;

The master never yet was known to spare;
Again his sinewy arm is raised, – again
The rod comes whistling down on Arthur there,
And his bare haunches quiver from the blow.
'Oh! oh! oh! don't, please don't, sir! Oh! sir, oh!

Oh! let me off now, please, sir – please, sir, do, sir!
I'll never – oh! – be late nor – oh! – miss church;
Oh; please, sir – Oh! sir, if you only knew, sir,'
Cries Arthur, while the burning tears besmirch
His fair flushed cheeks, 'You'll cut my bottom through, sir,
Oh! please, do stop, sir – do put down the birch –
Do, do, sir! please, sir! please, it cuts me so, sir!
I will take care, if you won't flog me – oh, sir!

I will, indeed I will, sir, try and mind–
I won't, indeed I won't, be late again.'
But still the same birch lashed the boy behind,
And the same cuts fell on him thick as rain,
And with arm raised and body half inclined
To hit more hard and give more stinging pain
Through all the smarting bottom's breadth and length,
The master flogged the boy with all his strength.

As vigorously as his right hand could wield it,
He plied the birch, till many a fragment broke
On the bare bottom with no shirt to shield it,
The sensitive soft flesh without a cloak
All swollen and sore with crimson stripes that wealed it,
All blood bespotted from the tingling stroke;
Till Arthur with clenched teeth began to suck
His rosy lips in, and get up his pluck.

Down came the birch; this time he did not squeak;
Down came the birch; he hardly flinched from it;
Down came the birch; the blood rose to his cheek;
Down came the birch; blood followed where it hit;
Down came the birch; he'll not sit down this week;

Down came the birch; he didn't wince one bit;
Down came the birch; it cut him to the quick;
Down came the birch; he bore it like a brick.

He had cried at first as if he could not bear it,
With eyes o'erflowing and imploring mien;
But as the strokes went on he plucked up spirit
And smarting silently drew breath between,
As one who knows birch and won't seem to fear it,
With all the cheek of schoolboys of thirteen;
As each cut fell he seemed to draw his bum tight
To bear the smart, with muscles braced up drum tight.

Though when he cried he had been well flogged for crying,
He was flogged more now that he held his tongue;
He tried to hold out, and was flogged for trying;
He was like some boys who seem always wrong,
Who are flogged for telling truth, and flogged for lying;
It moved his master's bile that such a young
Boy should have cheek enough, even while he thrashed him,
Not to cry out beneath the twigs that lashed him.

This is the way with schoolmasters; their fashion
Is to flog boys for silence as for speech;
If a boy blubbers while they lay the lash on
They dry his tears with a fresh cut for each;
If he won't cry, it puts them in a passion,
And they lay twice as much upon his breech;
So, if you cry, you're flogged; and if you don't,
You're flogged for impudence because you won't.

So was it with young Clifford; for his master
First, for his first fault, flogged him till he cried,
And then because he cried, he flogged the faster,
Till the weals grew as thick on his bare hide
As grains one shakes out of a pepper caster,

Grains of red pepper on his red backside;
So that each cut drew down a fresh tear; but
Each tear as surely drew down a fresh cut.

So Arthur stopped; but when he left off crying,
The doctor flogged him harder than before
Because he sulked beneath the birch, defying
The hand that flogged him, and the strokes he bore;
With all his might he laid each lash on, trying
To increase the smart as he increased the score,
That each cut singly might give double pain,
And flogged the more because he flogged in vain.

For all the boys who saw him flogged would swear
That Arthur took his flogging like a trump
After the first cuts; and it wasn't fair
To lay so many on such a youngster's rump;
A pretty boy, too, with his white limbs bare,
Round, rosy, naked haunches, fair and plump,
As ever served a school for laughing stock,
Was Arthur Clifford on the flogging block.

A pretty boy with fair flushed upturned face,
Dark eyebrows and dark eyes, and yellow hair,
With breeches down for flogging, in disgrace;
With the birch hanging over him in air,
With scar on scar and bloody trace on trace
Of flogging all across the parts laid bare,
All his fair limbs and features drawn with pain,
As the birch showered its strokes on him like rain.

The bright tears on his long dark lashes hung,
And on his soft cheeks stood like dew on peaches;
But though the birch twigs bit his flesh and stung,
And at each following stroke drew blood like leeches.
No word of plaint now fell from Arthur's tongue,
Though spots of red were on his shirt and breeches,
As the blood spun from his bare haunches, quivering
With pain that left his slender body shivering.

Till pausing, with an eye of sharp research,
The master scanned the boy's round plump backside,
To see where best to apply the impending birch,
Where to sting most, and mark the naked hide.
'Now, see, boys, what one gets for shirking church,'
With eyes that glanced round all the school, he cried,
And raised the rod. 'You know now if you wish
For a good flogging, how to get it.' Swish!

Just where the broad bare bottom, smooth and plump,
Flaked with red drops like rose leaf fallen on snow,
Sloped toward the tender thighs – there, worn to a
stump,
The frayed birch dealt its last and sharpest blow;
On either swelling cheek the whipped boy's rump
Had fresh red lines and starting blood to show,
Even where the round cheeks gradually divide,
The specks of blood sprang bright on either side.

'That's all, for this time; now get up, boy.' As
These words fell from the master's lips at last,
And Arthur heard, and rose, his bottom was
A map of bloody lines, where lashes part
Had left the fair flesh one red quivering mass
Of stripes and cuts and sores; so hard and fast
The birch had laid its strokes on, that his bottom
Not for a fortnight or a month forgot 'em.

He rose, and drew his trousers up, and turned
Back to his place; tears on his face were yet,
And still his smarting bottom throbbed and burned,
As he sat down with cheeks all flushed and wet,
And flinched, and then tried to seem unconcerned
As far as pain would let him, when he met
The next boy's laughing eyes, and felt him jogging
His arm, 'Well, Arthur, how d'ye like your flogging?'

Reginald's Flogging

Part II

Now Reggie Fane stands at his master's desk,
Watching his master's frown,
And out then spake his auld master,
'Now take your breeches down, Reggie, now take your breeches down.'

Oh, curly and fair was his thick soft hair,
And bright his bonny blue 'ee,
But the marks that were on his bottom
Were a piteous sight to see, my boys, were a piteous sight to see.

'Now give me here my good birch rod,
That is both stout and tough,
And take up his shirt now, two of you boys,
And you shall have cuts enough, Reggie, your bum shall have cuts enough.'

They set him on the flogging block,
They set him on his knee;
And the flush on his face and the flush on his bum
Was a stunning sight to see, my boys, was a stunning sight to see.

Charlie and Fred stood at Reginald's head,
And Algernon stood at his feet;
And Hugh stood by, and Willie was nigh,
And Arthur and Frank as was meet, my boys, to take their turn as was meet.

Up then stood that proud master,
His birch in hand he's ta'en,
He's laid it well into Reggie's bottom,
'Take that to begin with, Fane,' he says, 'take that to begin with, Fane.'

Never a word spoke Reginald then,
But he winced and flushed with pain;
The next good cut on Reginald's bottom,
'And how do you like it, Fane?' he says, 'does it sting? does it sting you, Fane?'

Oh, fain was Reggie to rub his bottom,
To rub it with his shirt;
As he laid the rod on Reginald's bottom,
'Does it hurt, my boy, does it hurt?' he says, 'Eh, Reggie, my boy, does it hurt?'

The first six cuts on Reggie's bottom
He hardly winced at all;
But at every cut on Reggie's bottom
You could see the salt tears fall, my boys, the thick tears gather and fall.

But wae's my heart for Reggie's bottom,
When the seventh and eighth cuts fell,
The red blood ran from Reggie's bottom,
For Reggie was flogged right well, my boys, for his bottom was flogged right well.

The next three cuts on Reggie's bottom,
They made it very sore,
But at the twelfth it was bloody and wealed,
And he could not choose but roar, poor boy, he could not choose but roar.

The next few cuts on Reggie's bottom,
It reddened more and more,
As the red rod fell on his tender flesh,
On the weals that it made before, poor boy, on the weals that it raised before.

'Oh, look at his bottom, Algernon!
Oh, isn't it jolly and red!
Oh, Reggie, I wouldn't be you, my boy;

Oh, look at the weals there, Fred, by Jove! the stripes, and the blood, then, Fred.

'Oh, look at his weals, and guess what he feels,
Oh, isn't his bottom sore!
Oh, look at the cuts in his flesh, what nuts!
Oh, doesn't the pain make him roar, by Jove! Oh, doesn't he cry and roar.

'Oh, hold his shirt up, Algernon,
Hold the boy's shirt up high;
Let us all have a view of his bottom, Hugh,
Oh, doesn't the pain make him cry, by Jove! Oh, doesn't the pain make him cry.

'Oh, isn't it nuts to see so many cuts,
And think it's young Reggie who's got 'em!
It won't be done this hour, what fun!
Oh, look at his jolly red bottom, by Jove! Oh, I say, what a stunning red bottom!

'Oh, isn't it ruddy, and ridgy and bloody!
Oh, don't I know what he feels!
How he yells with the pain; well, I wouldn't be Fane,
Oh, isn't it covered with weals, I say! and ain't they jolly big weals!

'Look, by Jove, though he's trying, he is, to stop crying,
You'll catch it, by Jove, Reggie Fane!
Ah, my boy, it won't do – well. I wouldn't be you!
How his bottom goes in with the pain, by Jove! how it winces and shrinks with the pain.

'Oh, haven't I wished to see Reginald swished,
And count up the cuts as he got 'em?
But, by Jove, you can't count such an awful amount,
You can only look at his bottom, by Jove! at the weals that are on his bottom.

'There are six – what nuts! no, seven more cuts –
Nine cuts in a breath, by God!
Oh, look at him, do! is he blubbering, Hugh?
Oh, they're bringing another good rod, by Jove! a jolly good stinging new rod.

'There, there now, swish! as a fellow could wish!
Well this is a swishing to see!
You remember I said to the boy's brother Fred,
What a sight for a school it would be, my boys, what a stunning good sight it would be!

'There, swish! swish! swish! Well, I almost could wish . . .
By Jove, though isn't it nuts?
Well, I give you joy of it, Reggie, my boy!
Ah, there were two sharp fleshy cuts, by Jove! two right down stinging good cuts.

'Oh, Algernon – do let me see there, Hugh!
I want a good sight of his bottom;
Have you got a good view of the cuts on it, too?
And to think it's young Reggie who's got 'em, by Jove, that curly-haired youngster who's got 'em.

'Who's as sorry and fair if you look at him there,
Well, this really is more than I wished!
Aye, well may he roar! Yes, it really is more,
But isn't he getting well swished! my eyes; Ah, isn't he getting well swished!

' "Bring a rod!" What, a third? Come, I say, on my word,
It's a chouse – it's a thundering shame!
' "Bring a rod there!" I wish – there – swish! swish! swish!
I say though, ain't it a game, my boys? I say, Frank, ain't it a game?

'Oh, many's the bum I've seen swished since I've come,
And many's the swishing I've had,
But I never saw yet, and I ne'er shall forget
Such a swishing as that of this lad, I trow, this yellow-haired, rosy-cheeked lad.

'Stand aside again, Hugh, and let's look at him, do!
Do, Algernon, let me see!
The weals and cuts are like ridges and ruts,
Oh, ain't his bottom a spree, Willie, his bloody wealed bottom a spree?

'Left cheek and right, it is all the same sight,
It's all one blossom of red,
Of red wetted flesh, with the cuts in it fresh,
And the sores where his bottom has bled, Will, where his poor little bottom has bled.

'Oh, by Jove! how he squeaks! and his broad hinder cheeks
How they quiver afresh at each blow!
If he's rosy above as a little boy love,
I'll swear he's rosier below, my boys, the rod's made him rosier below.

'See the master there, Will, how he's flogging him still,
At each cut how he does lay the lash on,
I can tell you, young Fane, you may roar out with pain,
But you won't move the master's compassion, my boy, though you may move your comrades' compassion.

'There! hush! did you hear him? I say, boys near him,
Is his bottom cut right to the bone?
Has his birch cut him through? has it cut him in two?
Why can't he let him alone, I trow, let the poor naked bottom alone?

'It's worth while though to see what a flogging can be–
Reggie Fane knows by this time, I'll swear!
And its written, I think, pretty broad in red ink,
On his bottom so broad and so bare, my boys, on his red flesh naked and bare.

'Swish! swish! what, another? he looks at his brother,
And Freddy begins to cry;
He begins to blub, too – Fred, if I were you,
I'd rather my brother than I, by Jove! I'd rather he smarted than I.

'Oh, hark, you fellows, by Jove, how he bellows!
Oh, hark to Reginald, hark!
"Oh, sir, I can't bear it. Oh, spare me, do spare."
Oh, ain't Reggie's flogging a lark, my boys, and ain't Reggie Fane a good lark?

'What again and again! Well done, Reggie Fane!
Swish! oh, swish! Hark to him! Oh!
Now, Reggie! now, Rod! It's a chorus, by God –
And each cut makes the red drops flow, my boys, and Reginald roars as they flow.

'There, it's over at last, never mind, man, it's past;
It isn't, by Jupiter, no!
It's a chouse then – I wish he was Reggie there – swish!
There, didn't he just sing out, oh, my boys? ah, didn't the boy sing out, oh?'

Reggie Fane gets up sobbing, with all his stripes throbbing,
He roars as he rises, hark,
With the tears in his eyes, from the block see him rise –
'Oh, ain't a good flogging a lark, my boys, and ain't Reggie Fane a good lark?'

Now Reggie Fane stands in his schoolfellows' midst,
Crying and roaring with pain;

And out then spake his schoolmaster,
'Let me hear no more noise there, Fane,' he says, 'stop crying this instant, Fane.

'Stop crying, you dunce, when I tell you, at once –
Very well then, come hither to me.'
Oh, look how he's trying in vain to stop crying,
And ain't a good flogging a spree, my boys, and ain't Reggie Fane a good spree?

Oh, doesn't he try in his funk not to cry?
But Reginald tried in vain,
For again Dr Church takes up a long birch,
'Come here and kneel down, Reggie Fane,' he says, 'go down on the block, Reggie Fane.'

'Oh, please sir, no! I can't help, you know,
If the birch makes me cry with the pain.'
'I'll have no crying here – not a cry – not a tear,
So unbutton your trousers again, Reggie, and down with your trousers again.'

Now Reggie Fane kneels at his master's feet,
With his backside naked again,
And the birch falls afresh on his red-wealed flesh –
'Take that now, and that, young Fane,' it says, 'take that Master Reginald Fane.'

At the torture he feels from these fresh bloody weals,
He bellows with all his young might,
And the blood lies in streaks on his bare nether cheeks,
And ain't a good switching a sight, my boys? and ain't Reggie's bottom a sight?

And the blood runs in streams down his bottom, it seems,
And the tears down his rosy face pouring;
And his naked hind part, how each stroke makes it smart,

And how can the poor fellow stop roaring, my boys?
and how *is* Reggie Fane to stop roaring?

He's half bit through his red lips, too,
To stifle the cries of pain;
Well, I do think, I do, it's hard lines on him, too –
Hard lines on your brother Fred Fane, my boy, he's a plucky boy, too, Reggie Fane.

But it is a good lark – there, swish! again, hark –
Swish! What a cut! What a cry!
Why he'll wear out the birch, and he'll tire out old Church;
Well, rather Reggie than I, my boys, by Jove! I'm glad it's not I.

'Though your bottom by flayed, sir, I will be obeyed,'
Thus Reginald's schoolmaster speaks,
And by dint of hard trying, at least he stops crying,
And rises with burning cheeks, poor boy, with swollen and crimson cheeks.

The master stops – the birch rod drops,
The boys still gaze in doubt;
But they see Reggie Fane with his clothes on again,
As with tears in his eyes he goes out, poor boy, as with bottom well flayed he goes out.

Who ever yet saw a boy's bottom so raw
As Fane's, now his flogging is done?
With his bottom all bloody, his face fair and ruddy,
Oh! ain't a good flogging good fun, my boys, and ain't Reggie's flogging good fun.

Now Reggie Fane stands at his father's knee,
Trembling and wincing with pain,
And its, 'Well, have you had a good flogging, my lad?
Speak up now, Reggie Fane,' he says, 'speak up now, Reggie Fane.'

‘Oh! I’ve had such a flogging dear father,’ he says,
‘My bottom is so sore,
I shall never sit down again,
My cuts will heal no more, father, my bum will heal no more.’

‘The man that whipped your bottom, my boy,
O blest may his right hand be;
And were you stripped in school and whipped?
And did your schoolfellows see, Reggie, and did your schoolfellows see?’

‘They stripped me bare in the high school hall,
And all the boys were by;
And they saw the weals on my bare bottom,
And laughed to hear me cry, father, when the birch had made me cry.’

‘And did ye cry for pardon, Reggie?
And did ye cry in vain?
And did ye cry as the birch came down?
Oh! my boy, Reggie Fane,’ he says, ‘you bad boy, Reggie Fane.

‘And did ye howl for mercy, Reggie?
And did ye roar with pain?
And is it so bad to be whipped, my lad?
And must ye be whipped again, Reggie? and must ye taste birch twigs again?

‘Had I been there while your bottom was bare,
Oh! my boy, Reggie Fane,
For each cut of the birch from Dr Church
From me ye should have had twain, Reggie, I’d have given your bare breech twain.

‘Had I here the rod in my hand, by God,
Oh, my son, Reggie Fane,
You’d think no more of your switching before,

When your breeches were down again, Reggie, when your bottom was tingling again.

'Had I here the school birch, like Dr Church,
My young son, Reggie Fane,
I'd lay the lash on in such sharp fashion,
I'd make you roar with the pain, Reggie, while your bottom could bear the pain.'

'There's no room for the birch on my bottom, father,
My bottom is far too sore;
There's no room on my flesh, while these marks are fresh,
For a single flesh wound more, father, for one cut or for one weal more.

'For the master's stripes were so hard, father,
And the twigs of birch so lithe,
That each twig and each bud as it fell drew blood,
And oh! how it made me writhe, father. Oh, sir, how it made me writhe.

'Each cut laid afresh on my quivering flesh,
Hurt the same tender part,
Each hard birchen bud drew a drop of my blood,
And oh! how it made me smart, father, by Jove! how it made me smart!

'And Dr Church, as he 'plied the birch,
Till he made the fragments fly,
Took aim with each blow where to hurt, you know,
And oh! how he made me cry, father, how the birch in his hand made me cry!

'And the other boys there, what a lot they were,
And that was worst of all,
They could see my bare bum, they could see the blood come,

They could see the birch used on me fall, father, they
could look on and see the birch fall.

'They could see the blood spin from the weals on my
skin,
They could see the birch fall and stand by;
And I heard them laughing, and knew they were
chaffing,
And they laughed if they saw me cry, father, and I
heard and it made me cry.

'And the rods were there that he used on me.
And he's promised to flog me again.'
'And as long as he's got 'em to use on your bottom,
May he give you as good, Reggie Fane, my boy; may
he flog you as well, Reggie Fane.'

Aubrey Beardsley (1872–1898)

Cruelly Trimmed

Poor Beardsley. Facing an untimely death, he desired *Venus and Tannhäuser*, among other things, to be destroyed, seemingly aware that art and literary history would view such works as a dilettante's confection of fripperies, a footnote. He hadn't had the opportunity to produce work of greater gravitas, of which he felt himself capable.

Venus and Tannhäuser is primarily a text for a series of genuinely saturnalian illustrations, and, like them, it is heavily drawn and a magnificent exercise in style that displays flashes of the talent that may indeed have made him the great man of letters he so wanted to be. Perhaps he needn't have worried. His rehabilitation, begun thanks to the unwelcome press attention generated by an attempt to ban a London exhibition in the late 1960s, is now complete. In *Venus*, he takes a conspiratorial tone with the reader, inviting you into his created world of delights. For example, he permits himself some Frenchified-English euphemism on occasion, to add some covertness to his filth, like Pepys almost, except with none of the latter's puffed-up sexual hypocrisy. His parade of satyrs and unicorns are worthy of sci-fi fantasy, but don't let that put you off. Even when they're doing nothing more than waiting on Venus and Tannhäuser with salvers of asparagus, one is always left aware of their sexual potency. For the novella is suffused with a tender eroticism, always with the twist of cruelty that betrays a true perv's understanding – that for some, passion is often most satisfyingly expressed with precision, the devil in the detail.

Venus and Tannhäuser is permeated with the ripe and rank fruits of a genuinely filthy mind. Mincingly powerful, Beardsley's work, sadly unfinished at the time of his death (it only runs to around eighty typeset pages), speaks softly, but carries a big stick.

The Story of Venus and Tannhäuser

As the toilet was in progress, Mrs Marsuple, the fat manicure and fardeuse, strode in and seated herself by the side of the dressing-table, greeting Venus with an intimate nod. She wore a gown of white watered silk with gold lace trimmings, and a velvet necklet of false vermilion. Her hair hung in bandeaux over her ears, passing into a huge chignon at the back of her head, and the hat, wide-brimmed and hung with a vallance of pink muslin, was floral with red roses.

Mrs Marsuple's voice was full of salacious unction; she had terrible little gestures with the hands, strange movements with the shoulders, a short respiration that made surprising wrinkles in her bodice, a corrupt skin, large horny eyes, a parrot's nose, a small loose mouth, great flaccid cheeks, and chin after chin. She was a wise person, and Helen loved her more than any of her servants, and had a hundred pet names for her, such as Dear Toad, Pretty Poll, Cock Robin, Dearest Lip, Touchstone, Little Cough Drop, Bijou, Buttons, Dear Heart, Dick-Dock, Mrs Manly, Little Nipper, Cochon-de-lait, Naughty-naughty, Blessed Thing, and Trump. The talk that passed between Mrs Marsuple and her mistress was of that excellent kind that passes between old friends, a perfect understanding giving to scraps of phrases their full meaning, and to the merest reference a point. Naturally Tannhäuser the new-comer was discussed a little. Venus had not seen him yet, and asked a score of questions on his account that were delightfully to the point. Mrs Marsuple told the story of his arrival, his curious wandering in the gardens, and calm satisfaction with all he saw there, his impromptu affection for a slender girl upon the first terrace, of the crowd of frocks that gathered round and pelted him with roses, of the graceful way he defended himself with his mask, and of the queer reverence he made to the God of all gardens, kissing that deity with a pilgrim's devotion. Just then Tannhäuser was at the baths, and was creating a favourable impression.

The report and the coiffing were completed at the same moment.

'Cosmé,' said Venus, 'you have been quite sweet and quite brilliant, you have surpassed yourself tonight.'

'Madam flatters me,' replied the antique old thing, with a girlish giggle under his black satin mask. 'Gad, Madam; sometimes I believe I have no talent in the world, but tonight I must confess to a touch of the vain mood.'

It would pain me horribly to tell you about the painting of her face; suffice it that the sorrowful work was accomplished; frankly, magnificently, and without a shadow of deception.

Venus slipped away the dressing-gown, and rose before the mirror in a flutter of frilled things. She was adorably tall and slender. Her neck and shoulders were wonderfully drawn, and the little malicious breasts were full of the irritation of loveliness that can never be entirely comprehended, or ever enjoyed to the utmost. Her arms and hands were loosely, but delicately articulated, and her legs were divinely long. From the hip to the knee, twenty-two inches; from the knee to the heel, twenty-two inches, as befitted a goddess.

I should like to speak more particularly about her, for generalities are not of the slightest service in a description. But I am afraid that an enforced silence here and there would leave such numerous gaps in the picture that it had better not be begun at all than left unfinished. Those who have seen Venus only in the Vatican, in the Louvre, in the Uffizi, or in the British Museum, can have no idea of how very beautiful and sweet she looked. Not at all like the lady in 'Lemprière.'

Mrs Marsuple grew quite lyrical over the dear little person, and pecked at her arms with kisses.

'Dear Tongue, you must really behave yourself,' said Venus, and called Millamant to bring her the slippers.

The tray was freighted with the most exquisite and shapely pantoufles, sufficient to make Cluny a place of naught. There were shoes of grey and black and brown suède, of white silk and rose satin, and velvet and sarcenet; there were some of sea-green sewn with cherry blossoms, some of red with willow branches, and some of grey with bright-winged birds. There were heels of silver, of ivory, and of gilt; there were buckles of very precious stones set in most strange and esoteric devices; there were ribbons tied and twisted into cunning forms; there were buttons so beautiful that the buttonholes might have no pleasure till they closed upon them; there were soles of delicate leathers scented with maréchale, and linings of soft stuffs scented with the juice of July flowers. But Venus, finding none of them to her mind, called for a discarded pair of blood-red maroquin, diapered with pearls. They looked very distinguished over her white silk stockings. As the tray was being carried away, the capricious Florizel snatched as usual a slipper from it, and fitted the foot over his penis, and made the necessary movements. That was Florizel's little caprice. Meantime, La Popelinière stepped forward with the frock.

'I shan't wear one tonight,' said Venus. Then she slipped on her gloves.

When the toilet was at an end all her doves clustered round her feet loving to *frôler* her ankles with their plumes, and the dwarfs clapped their hands, and put their fingers between their lips and whistled. Never before had Venus been so radiant and compelling. Spiridion, in the corner, looked up from his game of Spellicans and trembled. Claude and Clair, pale with pleasure, stroked and touched her with their delicate hands, and wrinkled her stockings with their nervous lips, and smoothed them with their thin fingers; and Sarrasine undid her garters and kissed them inside and put them on again, pressing her thighs with his mouth. The dwarfs grew very daring, I can tell you. There was almost a mêlée. They illustrated pages 72 and 73 of Delvau's *Dictionary*.

In the middle of it all, Pranzmungel announced that supper was ready upon the fifth terrace. 'Ah!' cried Venus, 'I'm famished!'

As the courses advanced, the conversation grew bustling and more personal. Pulex and Cyril, and Marisca and Cathelin, opened a fire of raillery. The infidelities of Cerise, the difficulties of Brancas, Sarmean's caprices that morning in the lily garden, Thorillière's declining strength, Astarte's affection for Roseola, Felix's impossible member, Cathelin's passion for Sulpilia's poodle, Sola's passion for herself, the nasty bite that Marisca gave Chloe, the *epilatière* of Pulex, Cyril's diseases, Butor's illness, Maryx's tiny cemetery, Lesbia's profound fourth letter, and a thousand amatory follies of the day were discussed.

From harsh and shrill and clamant, the voices grew blurred and inarticulate. Bad sentences were helped out by worse gestures, and at one table Scabius expressed himself like the famous old knight in the first part of the *Soldier's Fortune* of Otway. Bassalissa and Lysistrata tried to pronounce each other's names, and became very affectionate in the attempt; and Tala, the tragedian, robed in roomy purple, and wearing plume and buskin, rose to his feet, and, with swaying gestures, began to recite one of his favourite parts. He got no further than the first line, but repeated it again and again, with fresh accents and intonations each time, and was only silenced by the approach of the asparagus that was being served by satyrs dressed in white. Clitor and Sodon had a violent struggle over the beautiful Pella, and nearly upset a chandelier. Sophie became very intimate with an empty champagne bottle, swore it had made her enceinte, and ended by having a mock *accouchement* on the top of the table; and Belamour pretended to be a dog, and pranced from couch to couch on all fours, biting and barking and licking.

Mellefont crept about dropping love philtres into glasses. Juventus and Ruella stripped and put on each other's things, Spelto offered a prize for whoever should come first, and Spelto won it! Tannhäuser, just a little grisé, lay down on the cushions and let Julia do whatever she liked.

I wish I coud be allowed to tell you what occurred round table fifteen, just at this moment. It would amuse you very much, and would give you a capital idea of the habits of Venus' retinue. Indeed, for deplorable reasons, by far the greater part of what was said and done at this supper must remain unrecorded and even unsuggested.

Venus allowed most of the dishes to pass untasted, she was so engaged with the beauty of Tannhäuser. She laid her head many times on his robe, kissing him passionately; and his skin at once firm and yielding, seemed to those exquisite little teeth of hers, the most incomparable pasture. Her upper lip curled and trembled with excitement, showing the gums. Tannhäuser, on his side, was no less devoted. He adored her all over and all the things she had on, and buried his face in the folds and flounces of her linen, and ravished away a score of frills in his excess. He found her exasperating, and crushed her in his arms, and slaked his parched lips at her mouth. He caressed her eyelids softly with his finger tips, and pushed aside the curls from her forehead, and did a thousand gracious things, tuning her body as a violinist tunes his instrument before playing upon it.

Mrs Marsuple snorted like an old war horse at the sniff of powder, and tickled Tannhäuser and Venus by turns, and slipped her tongue down their throats, and refused to be quiet at all until she had had a mouthful of the Chevalier. Claude, seizing his chance, dived under the table and came up on the other side just under Venus' couch, and before she could say 'One!' he was taking his coffee 'aux deux colonnes.' Clair was furious at his friend's success, and sulked for the rest of the evening.

[Tannhäuser] thought of . . . a strange pamphlet he had found in Venus' library, called *A Plea for the Domestication of the Unicorn*.

Of the *Bacchanals of Sporion.*

Of love, and of a hundred other things.

Then his half-closed eyes wandered among the prints that hung upon the rose-striped walls. Within the delicate curved frames lived the corrupt and gracious creatures of Dorat and his school, slender children in masque and domino smiling horribly, exquisite lechers leaning over the shoulders of smooth doll-like girls and doing nothing in particular, terrible little Pierrots posing as lady lovers and pointing at something outside the picture, and unearthly fops and huge birdlike women mingling in some rococo room, lighted mysteriously by the flicker of a dying fire that throws great shadows upon wall and ceiling. One of the prints showing how an old marquis practised the five-finger exercise, while in front of him his mistress offered her warm fesses to a panting poodle, made the Chevalier stroke himself a little.

Tannhäuser had taken some books to bed with him. One was the witty, extravagant *Tuesday and Josephine*, another was the score of *The Rheingold.* Making a pulpit of his knees he propped up the opera before him and turned over the pages with a loving hand, and found it delicious to attack Wagner's brilliant comedy with the cool head of the morning.[1] Once more he was ravished with the beauty and wit of the opening scene; the mystery of its prelude that seems to come up from the very mud of the Rhine, and to be as ancient, the abominable primitive wantonness of the music that follows the talk and movements of the Rhine-maidens, the black, hateful sounds in Alberich's love-making, and the flowing melody of the river of legends.

But it was the third tableau that he applauded most that morning, the scene where Loge, like some flamboyant primeval Scapin, practises his cunning upon Alberich. The

---

[1] It is a thousand pities that concerts should only be given either in the afternoon, when you are torpid, or in the evening, when you are nervous. Surely you should assist at fine music as you assist at the Mass – before noon – when your brain and heart are not too troubled and tired with the secular influences of the growing day.

feverish insistent ringing of the hammers at the forge, the dry staccato restlessness of Mime, the ceaseless coming and going of the troup of Nibelungs, drawn hither and thither like a flock of terror-stricken and infernal sheep, Alberich's savage activity and metamorphoses, and Loge's rapid, flaming, tonguelike movements, make the tableau the lease reposeful, most troubled and confusing thing in the whole range of opera. How the Chevalier rejoiced in the extravagant monstrous poetry, the heated melodrama, and splendid agitation of it all!

At eleven o'clock Tannhäuser got up and slipped off his dainty night-dress, and postured elegantly before a long mirror, making much of himself. Now he would bend forward, now lie upon the floor, now stand upright, and now rest upon one leg and let the other hang loosely till he looked as if he might have been drawn by some early Italian master. Anon he would lie upon the floor with his back to the glass, and glance amorously over his shoulder. Then with a white silk sash he draped himself in a hundred charming ways. So engrossed was he with his mirrored shape that he had not noticed the entrance of a troop of serving boys, who stood admiringly but respectfully at a distance, ready to receive his waking orders. As soon as the Chevalier observed them he smiled sweetly, and bade them prepare his bath.

The bathroom was the largest and perhaps the most beautiful apartment in his splendid suite. The well-known engraving by Lorette that forms the frontispiece to Millevoye's *Architecture du* XVIII *siècle* will give you a better idea than any words of mine of the construction and decoration of the room. Only in Lorette's engraving the bath sunk into the middle of the floor is a little too small.

Tannhäuser stood for a moment like Narcissus gazing at his reflection in the still scented water, and then just ruffling its smooth surface with one foot, stepped elegantly into the cool basin and swam round it twice very gracefully.

'Won't you join me?' he said, turning to those beautiful boys who stood ready with warm towels and perfume. In a moment they were free of their light morning dress, and jumped into the water and joined hands, and surrounded the Chevalier with a laughing chain.

'Splash me a little,' he cried, and the boys teased him with water and quite excited him. He chased the prettiest of them and bit his fesses, and kissed him upon the perineum till the dear fellow banded like a carmelite, and its little bald top-knot looked like a great pink pearl under the water. As the boy seemed anxious to take up the active attitude, Tannhäuser graciously descended to the passive – a generous trait that won him the complete affections of his *valets de bain*, or pretty fish, as he liked to call them, because they loved to swim between his legs.

However, it is not so much at the very bath itself as in the drying and delicious frictions that a bather finds his chiefest joys, and Venus had appointed her most tried attendants to wait upon Tannhäuser. He was more than satisfied with their skill, and the delicate attention they paid his loving parts aroused feelings within him almost amounting to gratitude, and when the rites were ended any touch of home-sickness he might have felt was utterly dispelled. After he had rested a little, and sipped his chocolate, he wandered into the dressing-room. Daucourt, his *valet de chambre*, Chenille, the perruquier and barber, and two charming young dressers, were awaiting him and ready with suggestions for the morning toilet. The shaving over, Daucourt commanded his underlings to step forward with the suite of suits from which he proposed Tannhäuser should make a choice. The final selection was a happy one. A dear little coat of pigeon rose silk that hung loosely about his hips, and showed off the jut of his behind to perfection; trousers of black lace in flounces, falling – almost like a petticoat – as far as the knee; and a delicate chemise of white muslin, spangled with gold and profusely pleated.

The two dressers, under Daucourt's direction, did their work superbly, beautifully, leisurely, with an exquisite deference for the nude, and a really sensitive appreciation of the Chevalier's scrumptious torso.

* * *

As pleased as Lord Foppington with his appearance, the Chevalier tripped off to bid good-morning to Venus. He found her in a sweet muslin frock, wandering upon the lawn, and plucking flowers to deck her breakfast table. He kissed her lightly upon the neck.

'I'm just going to feed Adolphe,' she said, pointing to a little reticule of buns that hung from her arm. Adolphe was her pet unicorn. 'He is such a dear,' she continued; 'milk white all over excepting his nose, mouth, nostrils and John. *This* way.' The unicorn had a very pretty palace of its own, made of green foliage and golden bars, a fitting home for such a delicate and dainty beast. Ah, it was a splendid thing to watch the white creature roaming in its artful cage, proud and beautiful, knowing no mate, and coming to no hand except the Queen's itself. As Tannhäuser and Venus approached, Adolphe began prancing and curveting, pawing the soft turf with his ivory hoofs and flaunting his tail like a gonfalon. Venus raised the latch and entered.

'You mustn't come in with me: Adolphe is so jealous,' she said, turning to the Chevalier, who was following her, 'but you can stand outside and look on; Adolphe likes an audience.' Then in her delicious fingers she broke the spicy buns and with affectionate niceness breakfasted her snowy pet. When the last crumbs had been scattered, Venus brushed her hands together and pretended to leave the cage without taking any further notice of Adolphe. Every morning she went through this piece of play, and every morning the amorous unicorn was cheated into a distressing agony lest that day should have proved the last of Venus' love. Not for long, though, would she leave him in that doubtful, piteous state, but running back passionately to where he stood, made adorable amends for her unkindness.

Poor Adolphe! How happy he was, touching the Queen's breasts with his quick tongue-tip. I have no doubt that the keener scent of animals must make women much more attractive to them than to men; for the gorgeous odour that but faintly fills our nostrils must be revealed to the brute creation in divine fullness. Anyhow, Adolphe sniffed as never a man did around the skirts of Venus. After the first charming interchange of affectionate delicacies was over, the unicorn lay down upon his side, and, closing his eyes, beat his stomach wildly with the mark of manhood.

Venus caught that stunning member in her hands and laid her cheek along it; but few touches were wanted to consummate the creature's pleasure. The Queen bared her left arm to the elbow, and with the soft underneath of it made amazing movements upon the tightly-strung instrument. When the melody began to flow, the unicorn offered up an astonishing vocal accompaniment. Tannhäuser was amused to learn that the etiquette of the Venus-berg compelled everybody to await the outburst of these venereal sounds before they could sit down to déjeuner.

Adolphe had been quite profuse that morning.

Venus knelt where it had fallen, and lapped her little apéritif.

At the further end of the lawn, and a little hidden by a rose-tree, a young man was breakfasting alone. He toyed nervously with his food now and then, but for the most part leant back in his chair with unemployed hands, and gazed stupidly at Venus.

'That's Felix,' said the Goddess, in answer to an enquiry from the Chevalier; and she went on to explain his attitude. Felix always attended Venus upon her little latrinal excursions, holding her, serving her, and making much of all she did. To undo her things, lift her skirts, to wait and watch the coming, to dip a lip or finger in the royal output, to stain himself deliciously with it, to lie beneath her as the favours fell, to carry off the crumpled, crotted paper – these were the pleasures of that young man's life.

Truly there never was a queen so beloved by her subjects as Venus. Everything she wore had its lover. Heavens! how her handkerchiefs were filched, her stockings stolen! Daily, what intrigues, what countless ruses to possess her merest frippery? Every scrap of her body was adored. Never, for Savaral, could her ear yield sufficient wax! Never, for Pradon, could she spit prodigally enough! And Saphius found a month an intolerable time.

After breakfast was over, and Felix's fears lest Tannhäuser should have robbed him of his capricious rights had been dispelled, Venus invited the Chevalier to take a more extensive view of the gardens, parks, pavilions, and ornamental waters. The carriage was ordered. It was a delicate, shell-like affair, with billowy cushions and a light canopy, and was drawn by ten satyrs, dressed as finely as the coachmen of the Empress Pauline the First.

The drive proved interesting and various, and Tannhäuser was quite delighted with almost everything he saw.

And who is not pleased when on either side of him rich lawns are spread with lovely frocks and white limbs – and upon flower-beds the dearest ladies are implicated in a glory of underclothing – when he can see in the deep cool shadow of the trees warm boys entwined, here at the base, there at the branch – when in the fountain's wave Love holds his court, and the insistent water burrows in every delicious crease and crevice?

A pretty sight, too, was little Rosalie, perched like a postilion upon the painted phallus god of all gardens. Her eyes were closed and she was smiling as the carriage passed. Round her neck and slender girlish shoulders there was a cloud of complex dress, over which bulged her wig-like flaxen tresses. Her legs and feet were bare, and the toes twisted in an amorous style. At the foot of the statue lay her shoes and stockings and a few other things.

Tannhäuser was singularly moved at this spectacle, and rose out of all proportion. Venus slipped the fingers of comfort under the lace flounces of his trousers, saying, 'Is it all mine? Is it all mine?' and doing fascinating things. In the end, the carriage was only prevented from being overturned by the happy intervention of Mrs Marsuple, who stepped out from somewhere or other just in time to preserve its balance.

How the old lady's eye glistened as Tannhäuser withdrew his panting blade! In her sincere admiration for fine things, she quite forgot and forgave the shock she had received from the falling of the gay equipage. Venus and Tannhäuser were profuse with apology and thanks, and quite a crowd of loving courtiers gathered round, consoling and congratulating in a breath.

The Chevalier vowed he would never go in the carriage again, and was really quite upset about it. However, after he had had a little support from the smelling-salts, he recovered his self-possession, and consented to drive on further.

Joris-Karl Huysmans (1848–1907)

Decadent Days

> . . . each liquor corresponded in taste, he fancied, with the sound of a particular instrument. Dry curaçao, for example, resembled the clarinet in its shrill, velvety tone; kümmel was like the oboe, whose timbre is sonorous and nasal; crème de menthe and anisette were like the flute, both sweet and poignant, whining and soft. Then to complete the orchestra came kirsch, blowing a wild trumpet blast; gin and whisky, deafening the palate with their harsh eruptions of cornets and trombones; liqueur brandy, blaring with the overwhelming crash of tubas, while the thundering of cymbals and the big drum, beaten hard, evoked . . . rakis.

This passage from *À Rebours* is typical of the decadent's heightened awareness of sensation, with which Huysmans is chiefly associated today. But unlike the legion of decadent poets that includes Rimbaud, Verlaine and Baudelaire, he was hardly a nihilist, craving the green anaesthetic fog of absinthe and seeking welcome oblivion through dissipation. On the contrary, by the end of his life, he was an arch-Catholic and a leading light of France's Academie Goncourt, having spent thirty-two years holding down his civil service day job, for which he was awarded the Legion d'Honneur (beats a gold watch). Although fascinated by alienation, he didn't feel alienated himself. In fact, despite being half-Dutch, he managed to be both independent-minded and an establishment figure, in the admirable way that French thinkers occasionally can.

In moving on from naturalism, through decadence, to *super*-natural belief, Huysmans was a man of his time. *À Rebours* is the fulcrum of this intellectual transition, the tipping point away from nature. A wealthy aesthete, the Duc Jean des Essientes, flirts with erotic and sensual pleasure, eventually sealing himself so well into his bubble of sensation that he does not dare to leave his home in case reality disappoints. 'The age of nature', says Des Esseintes, 'is past; it has finally exhausted the patience of all sensitive minds by the loathsome monotony of its landscapes and skies.' Finally, he is welcomed into the embrace of a woman whose genitals are featured like a Venus Flytrap. *À Rebours* is the 'poisonous book' referred to in *The Picture of Dorian Grey.* All in all then, one for a future volume of *Saturnalia.*

It's almost paradoxical to talk about the decadents as a movement, but, in the Paris of Lautrec and the *Moulin Rouge*, they were. Modern-day pagans and nature-worshippers who complain about being spoken of in the same breath as Satanists will be heartened that Huysmans, for one, understood the distinction. In fact, although he began his literary career in thrall to Zola's naturalism, and then to the sensual world of the decadents, it was this very study of Satanism – which of course requires belief in the Christian creed in order to see a point in inverting it – which started Huysmans on the road to Catholic mysticism.

Là Bas, or *Down There* was Huysmans' first commercially successful novel, no doubt due to its controversial depictions of a Black Mass – sensational in the other sense of the word – and the one extracted here. In the novel the hero, Durtal, who has much in common with Huysmans, becomes enmeshed in the Satanism of contemporary Paris while researching a book about the fifteenth-century child-murderer, Gilles de Rais (1404–1440). Huysmans actually visited Bluebeard's castle and charnel house, Chateau Tiffauges, in researching the novel, and then wrote about a writer writing about it – a process more appropriate in its self-referential quality to the end of the last century than to the one before.

Huysmans, like Sacher-Masoch, was a highly autobiographical writer of fiction, and his own love life weaves in and out of *Down There*. Berthe Courrière was the lover who introduced him to the occult, and Henriette Maillat, with whom he had a brief affair, wrote letters to him which appear almost verbatim in the novel. The character of Hyacinthe Chantelouve is a composite of both women. Later, in the early 1890s, he had to commit his long-term mistress to an insane asylum. Following which, tired and disillusioned, Huysmans retreated for a brief time to a Trappist monastery, where he converted fully to Catholicism and began work on *En Route*, the 'white' sequel to the 'black' *Là Bas*, which chronicles Durtal's conversion, and his longing for a monastic life, devoted to spiritual contemplation. He was by now far from Zola's view of art as 'a corner of nature observed by a temperament', and far, too, from the sensualism of the decadents. And yet hints of his ultimate intellectual destination were always there, with hindsight, in his earlier work: in his authorial ambivalence towards des Essientes in *À Rebours*, and in Durtal's unfulfilment in *Là Bas*.

Some of this spiritual unfulfilment can be seen in the following extract, from chapters 13 and 14 of *Down There*. Certainly Durtal could, in one way, benefit from a degree more self-knowledge, and from pulling his head, proverbially speaking, from his posterior with an almighty pop. And yet Durtal's *Weltschmertz* isn't simply spiritual, an empty chair that's waiting for God to sit on it, but sexual too. There's tragedy, not comedy, in the mistimings between Durtal and Hyacinthe Chantelouve, which produce not just bad sex but aching awkwardness and a sense of the awful void – the flatness of one's newfound freedom from desire – that follows when fragile enchantment has disappeared; the sense of loss experienced when we can only plead that we can't help our feelings. Durtal has a wicked crush on Mme Chantelouve, and has worked himself up to a pitch of obsession and expectation that – though he does not know it until too late – has become divorced from a reality that can't, by definition therefore, match it. There's a moral here for anyone with the kind of rich, saturnalian inner sexual life that can, by its own power, push reality away. That requires that life remain elsewhere, and therefore it's worthy of inclusion here.

Down There

He began again, as on the other evening, to clean house and establish a methodical disorder. He slipped a cushion under the false disarray of the armchair, then he made roaring fires to have the rooms good and warm when she came.

But he was without impatience. That silent promise which he had obtained, that Mme Chantelouve would not leave him panting this night, moderated him. Now that his uncertainty was at an end, he no longer vibrated with the almost painful acuity which hitherto her malignant delays had provoked. He soothed himself by poking the fire. His mind was still full of her, but plethoric, content. When his thoughts stirred at all it was, at the very most, to revolve the question, 'How shall I go about it, when the time comes, so as not to be ridiculous?' This question, which had so harassed him the other night, left him troubled but inert. He did not try to solve it, but decided to leave everything to chance, since the best planned strategy was almost always abortive.

Then he revolted against himself, accused himself of stagnation, and walked up and down to shake himself out of a torpor which might have been attributed to the hot fire. Well, well, was it because he had had to wait so long that his desires had left him, or at least quit bothering him – no, they had not, why, he was yearning now for the moment when he might crush that woman! He thought he had the explanation of his lack of enthusiasm in the stage fright inseparable from any beginning. 'It will not be really exquisite tonight until after the newness wears off and the grotesque with it. After I know her I shall be able to consort with her again without feeling solicitous about her and conscious of myself. I wish we were on that happy basis now.'

The cat, sitting on the table, cocked up its ears, gazed at the door with its black eyes, and fled. The bell rang and Durtal went to let her in.

Her costume pleased him. He took off her furs. Her skirt was of a plum colour so dark that it was almost black, the material thick and supple, outlining her figure, squeezing her arms, making an hourglass of her waist, accentuating the curve of her hips and the bulge of her corset.

'You are charming,' he said, kissing her wrists, and he was pleased to find that his lips had accelerated her pulse. She did not speak, could hardly breathe. She was agitated and very pale.

He sat down facing her. She looked at him with her mysterious, half sleepy eyes. He felt that he was falling in love all over again. He forgot his reasonings and his fears, and took acute pleasure in penetrating the mystery of these eyes and studying the vague smile of this dolorous mouth.

He enlaced her fingers in his, and for the first time, in a low voice, he called her Hyacinthe.

She listened, her breast heaving, her hands in a fever. Then in a supplicating voice, 'I implore you,' she said, 'let us have none of that. Only desire is good. Oh, I am rational, I mean what I say. I thought it all out on the way here. I left him very sad tonight. If you knew how I feel – I went to church today and was afraid and hid myself when I saw my confessor . . .'

These plaints he had heard before, and he said to himself, 'You may sing whatever tune you want to, but you shall dance tonight.' Aloud he answered in monosyllables as he continued to take possession of her.

He rose, thinking she would do the same, or that if she remained seated he could better reach her lips by bending over her.

'Your lips, your lips – the kiss you gave me last night –' he murmured, as his face came close to hers. She put up her lips and stood, and they embraced, but as his hands went seeking she recoiled.

'Think how ridiculous it all is,' she said in a low voice, 'to undress, put on night clothes – and that silly scene, getting into bed!'

He avoided declaring, but attempted, by an embrace which bent her over backward, to make her understand that she could spare herself those embarrassments. Tacitly, in his own turn, feeling her body stiffen under his fingers, he understood that she absolutely would not give herself in the room here, in front of the fire.

'Oh well,' she said, disengaging herself, 'if you will have it!'

He made way to allow her to go into the other room, and seeing that she desired to be alone he drew the portière.

Sitting before the fire he reflected. Perhaps he ought to have pulled down the bed covers, and not left her the task, but without doubt the action would have been too direct, too obvious a hint. Ah! and that water heater! He took it and, keeping away from the bedroom door, went to the bathroom, placed the heater on the toilet table, and then, swiftly, he set out the rice powder box, the perfumes, the combs and, returning into his study, he listened.

She was making as little noise as possible, walking on tiptoe as if in the presence of the dead. She blew out the candles, doubtless wishing no more light than the rosy glow of the hearth.

He felt positively annihilated. The irritating impression of the lips and eyes of Hyacinthe was far from him now. She was nothing but a woman, like any other, undressing in a man's room. Memories of similar scenes overwhelmed him. He remembered girls who like her had crept about on the carpet so as not to be heard, and who had stopped short, ashamed, for a whole second, if they bumped against the water pitcher. And then, what good was this going to do him? Now that she was yielding he no longer desired her! Disillusion had come even before possession, not waiting, as usual, till afterward. He was distressed to the point of tears.

The frightened cat glided under the curtain, ran from one room to the other, and finally came back to his master and jumped onto his knees. Caressing him, Durtal said to himself, 'Decidedly, she was right when she refused. It will be grotesque, atrocious. I was wrong to insist, but no, it's her fault, too. She must have wanted to do this or she wouldn't have come. What a fool to think she could aggravate passion by delay. She is fearfully clumsy. A moment ago when I was embracing her and really was aroused, it would perhaps have been delicious, but now! And what do I look like? A young bridegroom waiting – or a green country boy. Oh God, how stupid! Well,' he said, straining his ears and hearing no sound from the other room, 'she's in bed. I must go in.

'I suppose it took her all this time to unharness herself from her corset. She was a fool to wear one,' he concluded, when, drawing the curtain, he stepped into the other room.

Mme Chantelouve was buried under the thick coverlet, her mouth half-open and her eyes closed; but he saw that she was peering at him through the fringe of her blonde eyelashes. He sat down on the edge of the bed. She huddled up, drawing the cover over her chin.

'Cold, dear?'

'No,' and she opened wide her eyes, which flashed sparks.

He undressed, casting a rapid glance at Hyacinthe's face. It was hidden in the darkness, but was sometimes revealed by a flare of the red hot fire, as a stick, half consumed and smouldering, would suddenly burst into flame. Swiftly he slipped between the covers. He clasped a corpse; a body so cold that it froze him, but the woman's lips were burning as she silently gnawed his features. He lay stupified in the grip of this body wound around his own, supple as the . . . and hard! He could not move; he could not speak for the shower of kisses travelling over his face. Finally, he succeeded in disengaging himself, and, with his free arm he sought her; then suddenly, while she devoured his lips he felt a nervous inhibition and, naturally, without profit, he withdrew.

'I detest you!' she exclaimed.

'Why?'

'I detest you!'

He wanted to cry out, 'And I you!' He was exasperated, and would have given all he owned to get her to dress and go home.

The fire was burning low, unflickering. Appeased, now, he sat up and looked into the darkness. He would have liked to get up and find another nightshirt, because the one he had on was tearing and getting in his way. But Hyacinthe was lying on top of it – then he reflected that the bed was deranged and the thought affected him, because he liked to be snug in winter, and knowing himself incapable of respreading the covers, he foresaw a cold night.

Once more, he was enlaced; the gripe of the woman's on his own was renewed; rational, this time, he attended to her and crushed her with mighty caresses. In a changed voice, lower, more guttural, she uttered ignoble things and silly cries which gave him pain – My dear! – oh, hon! – oh I can't stand it!' – aroused nevertheless, he took this body which creaked as it writhed, and he experienced the extraordinary sensation of a spasmodic burning within a swaddle of ice-packs.

He finally jumped over her, out of bed, and lighted the candles. On the dresser the cat sat motionless, considering Durtal and Mme Chantelouve alternately. Durtal saw an inexpressible mockery in those black eyes and, irritated, chased the beast away.

He put some more wood on the fire, dressed, and started to leave the room. Hyacinthe called him gently, in her usual voice. He approached the bed. She threw her arms around his neck and hung there, kissing him hungrily. Then sinking back and putting her arms under the cover, she said, 'The deed is done. Now will you love me any better?'

He did not have the heart to answer. Ah, yes his disillusion was complete. The satiety following justified his lack of appetite preceding. She revolted him, horrified him.

Was it possible to have so desired a woman, only to come to – that? He had idealised her in his transports, he had dreamed in her eyes – he knew not what! He had wished to exalt himself with her, to rise higher than the delirious ravenings of the senses, to soar out of the world into joys supernal and unexplored. And his dream had been shattered. He remained fettered to earth. Was there no means of escaping out of one's self, out of earthly limitations, and attaining an upper ether where the soul, ravished, would glory in its giddy flight?

Ah, the lesson was hard and decisive. For having one time hoped so much, what regrets, what a tumble! Decidedly, Reality does not pardon him who despises her; she avenges herself by shattering the dream and trampling it and casting the fragments into a cesspool.

'Don't be vexed, dear, because it is taking me so long,' said Mme Chantelouve behind the curtain.

He thought crudely, 'I wish you would get to hell out of here,' and aloud he asked politely if she had need of his services.

'She was so mysterious, so enticing,' he resumed to himself. 'Her eyes, remote, deep as space, and reflecting cemeteries and festivals at the same time. And she has shown herself up for all she is, within an hour. I have seen a new Hyacinthe, talking like a silly little milliner in heat. All the nastinesses of women unite in her to exasperate me.'

After a thoughtful silence he concluded, 'I must be young indeed to have lost my head the way I did.'

As if echoing his thought, Mme Chantelouve, coming out through the portière, laughed nervously and said, 'A woman of my age doing a mad thing like that!' She looked at him, and though he forced a smile she understood.

'You will sleep tonight,' she said, sadly, alluding to Durtal's former complaints of sleeplessness on her account.

He begged her to sit down and warm herself, but she said she was not cold.

'Why, in spite of the warmth of the room you were cold as ice!'

'Oh, I am always that way. Winter and summer my flesh is chilly.'

He thought that in August this frigid body might be agreeable, but now!

He offered her some bonbons, which she refused, then she said she would take a sip of the alkermes, which he poured into a tiny silver goblet. She took just a drop, and amicably they discussed the taste of this preparation, in which she recognised an aroma of clove, tempered by flower of cinnamon moistened with distillate of rose water.

Then he became silent.

'My poor dear,' she said, 'how I should love him if he were more confiding and not always on his guard.'

He asked her to explain herself.

'Why, I mean that you can't forget yourself and simply let yourself be loved. Alas, you were reasoning all the time ...'

'I was not!'

She kissed him tenderly. 'You see I love you, anyway.' And he was surprised to see how sad and moved she looked, and he observed a sort of frightened gratitude in her eyes.

'She is easily satisfied,' he said to himself.

'What are you thinking about?'

'You!'

She sighed. Then, 'What time is it?'

'Half past ten.'

'I must go. He is waiting for me. No, don't say anything ...'

She passed her hands over her cheeks. He seized her gently by the waist and kissed her, holding her thus enlaced until they were at the door.

'You will come again soon, won't you?'

'Yes ... Yes.'

He returned to the fireside.

'Oof! it's done,' he thought, in a whirl of confused emotions. His vanity was satisfied, his self-esteem was no longer bleeding, he had attained his ends and possessed this woman. Moreover, her spell over him had lost its force. He was regaining his entire liberty of mind, but who could tell what trouble this liaison had yet in store for him? Then, in spite of everything, he softened.

After all, what could he reproach her with? She loved as well as she could. She was, indeed, ardent and plaintive. Even this dualism of a mistress who was a low cocotte in bed and a fine lady when dressed – or no, too intelligent to be called a fine lady – was a delectable pimento. Her carnal appetites were excessive and bizarre. What, then, was the matter with him?

And at last he quite justly accused himself. It was his own fault if everything was spoiled. He lacked appetite. He was not really tormented except by a cerebral erethism. He was used up in body, filed away in soul, inept at love, weary of tendernesses even before he received them and disgusted when he had. His heart was dead and could not be revived. And his mania for thinking, thinking! previsualising an incident so vividly that actual enactment was an anticlimax – but probably would not be if his mind would leave him alone and not be always jeering at his efforts. For a man in his state of spiritual impoverishment all, save art, was but a recreation more or less boring, a diversion more or less vain. 'Ah, poor woman, I am afraid she is going to get pretty sick of me. If only she would consent to come no more! But no, she doesn't deserve to be treated in that fashion,' and, seized by pity, he swore to himself that the next time she visited him he would caress her and try to persuade her that the disillusion which he had so ill concealed did not exist.

He tried to spread up the bed, get the tousled blankets together, and plump the pillows, then he lay down.

He put out his lamp. In the darkness his distress increased. With death in his heart he said to himself, 'Yes, I was right in declaring that the only women you can continue to love are those you lose.

'To learn, three years later, when the woman is inaccessible, chaste and married, dead, perhaps, or out of France – to learn that she loved you, though you had not dared believe it while she was near you, ah, that's the dream!

These real and intangible loves, these loves made up of melancholy and distant regrets, are the only ones that count. Because there is no flesh in them, no earthly leaven.

'To love at a distance and without hope; never to possess; to dream chastely of pale charms and impossible kisses extinguished on the waxen brow of death: ah, that is something like it. A delicious straying away from the world, and never the return. As only the unreal is not ignoble and empty, existence must be admitted to be abominable. Yes, imagination is the only good thing which heaven vouchsafes to the skeptic and pessimist, alarmed by the external abjectness of life.' From this scene he had learned an alarming lesson: that the flesh domineers the soul and refuses to admit any schism. The flesh decisively does not intend that one shall get along without it and indulge in out-of-the-world pleasures which it can partake only on condition that it keep quiet. For the first time, reviewing these turpitudes, he really understood the meaning of that now obsolete word *chastity*, and he savoured it in all its pristine freshness. Just as a man who has drunk too deeply the night before thinks, the morning after, of drinking nothing but mineral water in future, so he dreamed, today, of pure affection far from a bed.

He was still ruminating these thoughts when Des Hermies entered.

They spoke of amorous misadventures. Astonished at once by Durtal's languor and the ascetic tone of his remarks, Des Hermies exclaimed, 'Ah, we had a gay old time last night?'

With the most decisive bad grace Durtal shook his head.

'Then,' replied Des Hermies, 'you are superior and inhuman. To love without hope, immaculately, would be perfect if it did not induct such brainstorms. There is no excuse for chastity, unless one has a pious end in view, or unless the senses are failing, and if they are one had best see a doctor, who will solve the question more or less unsatisfactorily. To tell the truth, everything on earth culminates in the act you reprove.

Octave Mirbeau
(1848–1917)

Fetish Fatigue

The Torture Garden, first published in 1898, is probably known to most people today as the novel which has leant its name to London's currently thriving fetish club, but it's far more than pornographic in intent. Often seen as a disciple of Sade, Mirbeau, the man, was also far more than a pornographer. A successful author, he was, if you like, a champagne anarchist, known in his own lifetime – inaccurately, given the black of the anarchist flag – as the red millionaire. He is also underrated as a writer of extreme conscience. All of Mirbeau's work is concerned with the hypocrisies of everyday life, that there is no such thing as the use of power, only its abuse.

Deeply involved with the Dreyfuss affair, a committed anti-militarist (he was almost fatally depressed by World War I), and a proto-feminist, he shared with Sade a loathing of organised religion. Although far more than a disciple of Sade, and in fact the better writer, he took the latter's dystopic views to a more crystallised, clarified, poignant extreme in which the motivation of all human endeavour is seen as murderous in intent. It's a logical extreme not only of Sade but of the ethics of Baudelaire's *Flowers of Evil*, and *The Torture Garden* remains the best expression of his position. As said, Sade is always open to criticism over the issue that all his sexual concerns are male dom/fem sub, but Mirbeau runs the gamut. 'Blood', says Clara in the novel, 'is the wine of love.'

In the novel, Mirbeau dives effortlessly to a level of cynicism that other writers would shrink from, and swimming in his literary waters presents a wonderfully clear vision of evil. It's not so much a question of Sade's 'beast in man', but that humans are no more than beasts anyway. Its inversion of orthodox morality rings as true and as awfully as the unimaginably tortuous bell in which captives are made to suffer at the denouement of *The Torture Garden*, and the novel excels in its deceptive simplicity. For the established order in all its spheres is based on usury, extortion and the great protection racket that is government. In the words of Woody Guthrie, 'Some rob you with a six-gun, and some with a fountain-pen.'

In Mirbeau's world there is only cruelty, power, lust, slavery, submission, sickness, and beauty. Nothing is 'bad' in this world which increases the feeling of power, and life has no value whatsoever. No man is more important or more 'worthy' or 'better' than any other, no matter what his personal qualities, or what his actions have been. The Garden of the novel's title is a vast collection of plants, flowers, trees, and animals that the Chinese government has constructed and maintained over countless ages: in the very centre of this lush, deliriously beautiful landscape exists a field of torture and execution where all the most painful, ingenious and malevolent devices of cruelty ever invented reside. The flowers are washed with blood, the soil is tilled with the remains of corpses created by the pits of torture, and in this Garden thousands of 'useless' citizens are made to feel the direst extremities of suffering. In the Garden, torture is an art which goes hand in hand with the cultivation of the life. And at the centre of this Garden, the climactic torture device is an enormous bell that peals transporting melodies. Only the most important criminals are placed beneath it, and the vibrations of this divine music rips their sanity and life from them. They die utterly mad, in an intolerable amount of pain. Mirbeau makes it very clear that the Garden is supposed to be considered a symbol of life itself, and that the reserves of beauty, pain, suffering, and pleasure that the world holds for us are so finely intertwined as to be completely inseparable.

Lord knows what Li Yu would have made of the scene in which the Buddhas in the Garden appear to turn at a glance from having beatific smiles to evil leers! There's none of Boccaccio's cheerful stoicism in the face of an adverse nature, but suffused rage and morbid fascination. For, for Mirbeau, nature's not the problem; humankind alone is capable of *injustice* and is therefore the worm in nature's bud.

This short précis of Mirbeau's concerns is presented here all the better to elucidate some of the Divine Marquis's more troublesome attitudes. And as a teaser for a future volume of *Saturnalia*, in which *The Torture Garden* will be extracted at greater length. Sade forever seems to be saying of himself, in the words of the legendary Milwall football chant, that 'no one likes us and we don't care'. Mirbeau, by contrast, has no such chip on his shoulder. His work is crystalline, utterly unconcerned with self-justification, and all the more powerful for it. He was too much of a worldly man to be possessed of an idealism that could be anything other than thwarted, and his work is both pornography and a sincere attempt to make sense of a difficult world. Both writers, however, allow the reader to glory in suffering like a latter-day St Theresa of Avila. Because, for Sade and Mirbeau alike, if the reader finds sexual gratification in their work, it only proves their point. As does the fact that their work has consistently been marketed throughout its publishing history as erotica!

The Torture Garden

'There are tortures wherever there are men. I cannot do anything about it, my baby, and I try to adjust myself to it and enjoy it, for blood is a precious auxiliary of desire. It's the wine of love.' With the tip of her parasol, she traced some naïvely indecent figures in the sand, and said: 'I'm sure you think the Chinese crueller than we. Not at all! We English? Ah, don't mention it! And you French? In your Algeria, in the confines of the desert, I saw this: One day some soldiers captured some Arabs; poor Arabs who had committed no other crime than to try to escape the brutality of their conquerors. The Colonel commanded them to be put to death immediately, without an inquiry, without a trial. And this is what happened: There were thirty of them. They dug thirty holes in the sand, and they buried them up to their necks, naked, with their heads shaved, in the noonday sun. So they wouldn't die too fast they watered them from time to time, like cabbages. At the end of an hour their eyelids were swollen, their eyes bulged from their sockets, their swollen tongues filled their mouths, which gaped frightfully, and their skin cracked and roasted on their skulls. It was unimaginative, I assure you, and even devoid of terror – those thirty dead heads, sticking out of the sand like shapeless rocks! And we! It's still worse!

'I remember the strange sensation I felt when, at Kandy, the gloomy former capital of Ceylon, I went up the steps of the temple where the English had stupidly, without torture, slaughtered the little Modeliar princes who, legends tell us, were so charming . . . Like those skillfully made Chinese icons, with so hieratically calm and pure a grace, and their golden halos and their long hands pressed together. I felt that what had happened there – on those sacred steps, still uncleansed of that blood by eighty years of violent possession – was something more horrible than a human massacre; the destruction of a precious, touching and innocent beauty. The traces of that double European barbarity may be found at every step you take on the ancestral soil of that suffering and always mysterious India. The boulevards of Calcutta, the cool Himalayan villas in Darjeeling, the tribades of Benares and the sumptuous homes of the contractors in Bombay have not been able to efface the impression of mourning and death left everywhere by the atrocity of unskillful massacre, vandalism and senseless destruction. On the contrary, they accentuate it. No matter in what place it appears, civilisation displays that face which bears the double imprint of sterile blood, and ruins forever dead.'

[illegible]

Feeling sexually alive to the tips of one's fingers, however, starts with [illegible] the knowledge that to [illegible] one's [illegible] is to be aware of one's mortality. Sexual union is [illegible] a compromise, a halfway house between life and death (Georges Bataille). It takes a certain moral [illegible] to see such sensibilities as unhealthy in themselves, if they don't make an individual unhappy.

There are inevitably notable omissions in a collection of this kind. All the tales and verses selected here are

Conclusion

Original Sins

If there's anything questionable about being kinky, then we'll be publishing a second volmue of *Saturnalia* in December 2002 to delight those in happy denial.

As we pass beyond another *fin de siècle*, the world seems more absurd than ever, but then it always has. Happily it's seldom necessary to mount a defence of sexual perversity, but it's still worth observing that in the works presented here is a valid, or at least understandable, set of responses to that seeming absurdity. And in the real world, it becomes increasingly untenable to hold surreal, fetishistic or SM sex to be any sort of special case when it's far more dangerous – and counter-intuitive – to parachute out of a perfectly good aeroplane, and yet people who do that with their Sundays – good luck to them – are considered dynamic. Feeling sexually alive to the tips of one's fingers, however, shares with skydiving the knowledge that to enjoy one's carnality is to be aware of one's mortality. 'Sexual union is fundamentally a compromise, a halfway house between life and death.' (Georges Bataille) It takes a certain literal-mindedness to see such sensibilities as unhealthy in themselves if they don't make an individual unhappy.

There are, inevitably, notable omissions in a collection of this kind, but the tales and verses collected here are united in being paradoxically both representative of the mainstream literature of their time, and either self-censored, proscribed or at least sensational, too. Sacher-Masoch, in his day, was – much like Alina Reyes' *The Butcher* or Nicholson Baker's *Vox* – within the envelope of acceptability for the literary classes, whereas Sade, of course, was what Colin Wilson would call an outsider, but he too was published, and read. Some among this handful of writers can be taken to task for their two-dimensional characters and one-track minds, and were less in touch with the world around them than a writer should be, but these are literary criticisms, not moral ones. It's also glib if true to say that lack of self-knowledge was their problem, not being kinky in itself.

If Sade's observation of the presence of 'the beast in [the hu]man' is at all correct, then playing with it is as or more valid a response than putting one's head in the sand and making it go away. Censorship and the attempt to control language – and with it thought – can influence, but seem to fail ultimately because etymology has a life of its own. Without sounding like a party political broadcast for Lindi St Clair (Miss Whiplash, for those Brits that recall), our awareness of issues of abuse and consent has actually been enhanced thanks both to the fetish scene and to the debate which is bound to exist when responsible people make a game of psychological and sexual repression. Innocence is no more than naïvety when it keeps us blind to the abusiveness of particular situations. Of course one has to be cautious in borrowing the semiotics of suffering in a way that at the very least can offend others' tastes, and safe, sane and consensual are valuable watchwords. But never again can we be unaware, with regard to many instances of shame and humiliation – whether it's English public school life as depicted by Swinburne, or in Lindsay Anderson's film *If*, or the treatment meted out to Afghan women who fell foul of the Taliban regime – that something sexual is going on, and that we should often question the legitimacy of the punishers' motives, however much they claim high-mindedness or virtue for themselves.

Without getting further into the politics of over-earnestness, this is the subversive internal morality of fetishism and SM.

Select Bibliography

Adler, Alfred, *Understanding Human Nature* (Ed. Colin Brett), Oneworld, 1998

Aragon, Louis, *Irene's Cunt*, Creation, 1998

B, Dom, *The Lascivious Monk*, various editions

Baker, Nicholson, *Vox*, Granta, 1998

Bataille, Georges, *The Trials of Gilles de Rais*, Amok Books, 1996

Baudelaire, Charles, *The Flowers of Evil*, OUP, 1998

Bloch, Ivan, *Sexual Life in England, Past and Present*, Arco, 1958

Byron, Lord George Gordon, *Don Juan*, Penguin Classics, 1977

Califia, Pat, *Macho Sluts*, Alyson, 1989

Carter, Angela, *The Sadeian Woman*, Virago, 1992.

Dworkin, Andrea, *Pornography: Men Possessing Women*, The Women's Press, 1998

Gibson, Ian, *The English Vice*, Duckworth, 1978

Havelock, Ellis, *Sex and Marriage*, Greenwood Press, 1977

Kraft-Ebbing, Richard von, *Psychopathia Sexualis* Creation, 1997

Nin, Anaïs *Delta of Venus*, Penguin, 1996

Pepys, Samuel, *The Shorter Pepys*, Penguin, 1993

Philips, Anita, *A Defence of Masochism*, Faber and Faber, 1999

Pitt-Kethley, Fiona, *Sky Ray Lolly*, Abacus, 1991

Reyes, Alina, *The Butcher*, Vintage, 1999

Sacher-Masoch, Wanda von, *Confessions*, Juno, 1990

Swift, J., *A Modest Proposal*, Dover, 1996

Voltaire, *Candide*, Oxford Classics, 1998

Wilde, Oscar, *The Picture of Dorian Grey*, Broadview, 1998

Wilson, Colin, *The Misfits*, Grafton, 1988

NEXUS NEW BOOKS

MY SECRET GARDEN SHED
Male Sexual Fantasy in the Twenty-First Century
Edited by Paul Scott
5 September 2002
0 352 33725 7
£7.99

The western world suports a *huge* porn industry (eight million dollars per annum in the US alone, according to one recent estimate), aimed predominantly at men. Many blue-chip media groups are now involved. Since the relaxation of the strictures on selling hardcore pronography in the UK were relaxed in September 2000, the British Board of Film Classification has passed over 250 uncut hardcore videos for sale in licensed sex shops.

And yet no market research is undertaken by this huge global industry. So how true are the porn clichés – sexy French maids, office girls, stockings and suspenders, etc? *My Secret Garden Shed* attempts, unpretentiously, accessibly, with humour and a light touch, to offer an answer to the question of what men want, while accepting, of course, that there are as many individual answers as there are men in the world.

The title takes itself from Nancy Friday's *My Secret Garden*, a collection of women's sexual fantasies which was published in 1979 and which has become a benchmark text of sexual politics *and* women's erotica. Now it's the turn of the chaps! *My Secret Garden Shed* is a compendium of men's sexual fantasies of all kinds, from the sensual to the downright bizarre, and from the sublime to the downright pervy. They have been solicited through ads placed in magazines, both mainstream and pornographic, and on the Internet, and offer a representitive cross-section of men's sexual tastes in a way that is, well, *almost* scientific. This book is a despatch from the deepest recesses of the male psyche. It will follow Nancy Friday's dictum that not every fantasy is necessarily one you'd *really* like to have happen. *My Secret Garden Shed* aims to demystify and reassure. It may even turn you on.

LESBIAN SEX SECRETS FOR MEN
The Ultimate Guide to Pleasing and Satisfying a Woman – from Women who Know
Jamie Goddard and Kurt Brungardt
7 November 2002
0 352 33724 9
£9.99

Lesbian Sex Secrets for Men opens the bedroom doors of gay women to answer your most intimate questions about making love to the woman you love. From the titillating to the taboo, from kisses to climaxes, from G-spots to the Big O, here is the ultimate road map to the hot spots and nether regions of the female body that will help you create new levels of intimacy and sexual pleasure.

Let *Lesbian Sex Secrets for Men* help you discover:

- What women really want in bed
- How to master the Sapphic arts – and enjoy the female body in an entirely new way
- The pleasures of sensual massage
- The ins and outs of erotic love – total surrender and total control
- Your most important sexual tool (a hint – it's between your ears)
- Ways of opening up the channels of sexual communication
- Where fantasies come in
- The joy of toys
- Relationship roadblocks, and how to get past them

Plus; tips, techniques and sex games

Filled with interviews, surveys and the uncensored voices of women speaking honestly about what they want in a lover, *Lesbian Sex Secrets for Men* is more than a manual of gymnastic sexual techniques – it's the ultimate guide to satisfying a woman's sexual needs and desires.

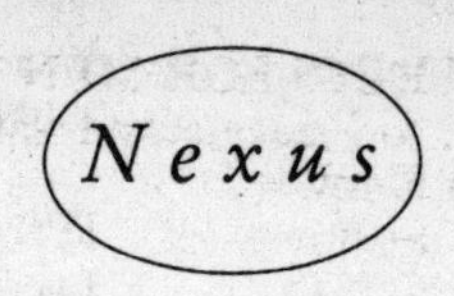

NEXUS BACKLIST

This information is correct at time of printing. For up-to-date information, please visit our website at www.nexus-books.co.uk

All books are priced at £5.99 unless another price is given.

Nexus books with a contemporary setting

ACCIDENTS WILL HAPPEN	Lucy Golden ISBN 0 352 33596 3	☐
ANGEL	Lindsay Gordon ISBN 0 352 33590 4	☐
BEAST	Wendy Swanscombe ISBN 0 352 33649 8	☐
THE BLACK FLAME	Lisette Ashton ISBN 0 352 33668 4	☐
THE BLACK MASQUE	Lisette Ashton ISBN 0 352 33372 3	☐
BROUGHT TO HEEL	Arabella Knight ISBN 0 352 33508 4	☐
CAGED!	Yolanda Celbridge ISBN 0 352 33650 1	☐
CANDY IN CAPTIVITY	Arabella Knight ISBN 0 352 33495 9	☐
CAPTIVES OF THE PRIVATE HOUSE	Esme Ombreux ISBN 0 352 33619 6	☐
DANCE OF SUBMISSION	Lisette Ashton ISBN 0 352 33450 9	☐
DARK DELIGHTS	Maria del Rey ISBN 0 352 33276 X	☐
DIRTY LAUNDRY £6.99	Penny Birch ISBN 0 352 33680 3	☐
DISCIPLES OF SHAME	Stephanie Calvin ISBN 0 352 33343 X	☐

DISCIPLINED SKIN	Wendy Swanscombe ISBN 0 352 33541 6	☐
DISPLAYS OF EXPERIENCE	Lucy Golden ISBN 0 352 33505 X	☐
DISPLAYS OF INNOCENTS £6.99	Lucy Golden ISBN 0 352 33679 X	☐
DISPLAYS OF PENITENCE £6.99	Lucy Golden ISBN 0 352 33646 3	☐
DRAWN TO DISCIPLINE	Tara Black ISBN 0 352 33626 9	☐
AN EDUCATION IN THE PRIVATE HOUSE	Esme Ombreux ISBN 0 352 33525 4	☐
EMMA'S SECRET DOMINATION	Hilary James ISBN 0 352 33226 3	☐
GISELLE	Jean Aveline ISBN 0 352 33440 1	☐
GROOMING LUCY	Yvonne Marshall ISBN 0 352 33529 7	☐
HEART OF DESIRE	Maria del Rey ISBN 0 352 32900 9	☐
HIS MISTRESS'S VOICE	G. C. Scott ISBN 0 352 33425 8	☐
IN FOR A PENNY	Penny Birch ISBN 0 352 33449 5	☐
INTIMATE INSTRUCTION	Arabella Knight ISBN 0 352 33618 8	☐
THE LAST STRAW	Christina Shelly ISBN 0 352 33643 9	☐
LESSONS IN OBEDIENCE	Lucy Golden ISBN 0 352 33550 5	☐
MASTER OF CASTLELEIGH	Jacqueline Bellevois ISBN 0 352 33644 7	☐
NURSES ENSLAVED	Yolanda Celbridge ISBN 0 352 33601 3	☐
ONE WEEK IN THE PRIVATE HOUSE	Esme Ombreux ISBN 0 352 32788 X	☐
THE ORDER	Nadine Somers ISBN 0 352 33460 6	☐

THE PALACE OF EROS £4.99	Delver Maddingley ISBN 0 352 32921 1	☐
PEACHES AND CREAM £6.99	Aishling Morgan ISBN 0 352 33672 2	☐
PEEPING AT PAMELA	Yolanda Celbridge ISBN 0 352 33538 6	☐
PENNY PIECES	Penny Birch ISBN 0 352 33631 5	☐
PET TRAINING IN THE PRIVATE HOUSE	Esme Ombreux ISBN 0 352 33655 2	☐
REGIME £6.99	Penny Birch ISBN 0 352 33666 8	☐
SEE-THROUGH	Lindsay Gordon ISBN 0 352 33656 0	☐
SKIN SLAVE	Yolanda Celbridge ISBN 0 352 33507 6	☐
SLAVE ACTS £6.99	Jennifer Jane Pope ISBN 0 352 33665 X	☐
THE SLAVE AUCTION	Lisette Ashton ISBN 0 352 33481 9	☐
SLAVE EXODUS	Jennifer Jane Pope ISBN 0 352 33551 3	☐
SLAVE GENESIS	Jennifer Jane Pope ISBN 0 352 33503 3	☐
SLAVE MINES OF TORMUNIL £6.99	Aran Ashe ISBN 0 352 33695 1	☐
SLAVE REVELATIONS	Jennifer Jane Pope ISBN 0 352 33627 7	☐
SLAVE SENTENCE	Lisette Ashton ISBN 0 352 33494 0	☐
SOLDIER GIRLS	Yolanda Celbridge ISBN 0 352 33586 6	☐
THE SUBMISSION GALLERY	Lindsay Gordon ISBN 0 352 33370 7	☐
SURRENDER	Laura Bowen ISBN 0 352 33524 6	☐
TAKING PAINS TO PLEASE	Arabella Knight ISBN 0 352 33369 3	☐

THE TAMING OF TRUDI	£6.99	Yolanda Celbridge ISBN 0 352 33673 0	☐
TEASING CHARLOTTE	£6.99	Yvonne Marshall ISBN 0 352 33681 1	☐
TEMPER TANTRUMS		Penny Birch ISBN 0 352 33647 1	☐
TIE AND TEASE		Penny Birch ISBN 0 352 33591 2	☐
TIGHT WHITE COTTON		Penny Birch ISBN 0 352 33537 8	☐
THE TORTURE CHAMBER		Lisette Ashton ISBN 0 352 33530 0	☐
THE YOUNG WIFE		Stephanie Calvin ISBN 0 352 33502 5	☐
WHIP HAND	£6.99	G. C. Scott ISBN 0 352 33694 3	☐
WHIPPING BOY		G. C. Scott ISBN 0 352 33595 5	☐

Nexus books with Ancient and Fantasy settings

CAPTIVE		Aishling Morgan ISBN 0 352 33585 8	☐
DEEP BLUE		Aishling Morgan ISBN 0 352 33600 5	☐
MAIDEN		Aishling Morgan ISBN 0 352 33466 5	☐
NYMPHS OF DIONYSUS	£4.99	Susan Tinoff ISBN 0 352 33150 X	☐
PLEASURE TOY		Aishling Morgan ISBN 0 352 33634 X	☐
THE SLAVE OF LIDIR		Aran Ashe ISBN 0 352 33504 1	☐
TIGER, TIGER		Aishling Morgan ISBN 0 352 33455 X	☐

Period

CONFESSION OF AN ENGLISH SLAVE	Yolanda Celbridge ISBN 0 352 33433 9	☐
THE MASTER OF CASTLELEIGH	Jacqueline Bellevois ISBN 0 352 32644 7	☐
PURITY	Aishling Morgan ISBN 0 352 33510 6	☐

Samplers and collections

NEW EROTICA 3	Various ISBN 0 352 33142 9	☐
NEW EROTICA 5	Various ISBN 0 352 33540 8	☐
EROTICON 1	Various ISBN 0 352 33593 9	☐
EROTICON 2	Various ISBN 0 352 33594 7	☐
EROTICON 3	Various ISBN 0 352 33597 1	☐
EROTICON 4	Various ISBN 0 352 33602 1	☐
THE NEXUS LETTERS	Various ISBN 0 352 33621 8	☐

Nexus Classics

A new imprint dedicated to putting the finest works of erotic fiction back in print.

AGONY AUNT	G.C. Scott ISBN 0 352 33353 7	☐
BAD PENNY	Penny Birch ISBN 0 352 33661 7	☐
BRAT £6.99	Penny Birch ISBN 0 352 33674 9	☐
DARK DELIGHTS £6.99	Maria del Rey ISBN 0 352 33667 6	☐
DARK DESIRES	Maria del Rey ISBN 0 352 33648 X	☐
DIFFERENT STROKES	Sarah Veitch ISBN 0 352 33531 9	☐

EDEN UNVEILED	Maria del Rey ISBN 0 352 33542 4	☐
HIS MISTRESS'S VOICE	G. C. Scott ISBN 0 352 33425 8	☐
THE INDIGNITIES OF ISABELLE £6.99	Penny Birch writing as Cruella ISBN 0 352 33696 X	☐
LETTERS TO CHLOE	Stefan Gerrard ISBN 0 352 33632 3	☐
LINGERING LESSONS	Sarah Veitch ISBN 0 352 33539 4	☐
OBSESSION	Maria del Rey ISBN 0 352 33375 8	☐
PARADISE BAY	Maria del Rey ISBN 0 352 33645 5	☐
PENNY IN HARNESS	Penny Birch ISBN 0 352 33651 X	☐
THE PLEASURE PRINCIPLE	Maria del Rey ISBN 0 352 33482 7	☐
PLEASURE ISLAND	Aran Ashe ISBN 0 352 33628 5	☐
SERVING TIME	Sarah Veitch ISBN 0 352 33509 2	☐
A TASTE OF AMBER	Penny Birch ISBN 0 352 33654 4	☐

- - - - - - ✂ -

Please send me the books I have ticked above.

Name ....

Address ....

....

....

.... Post code....................

Send to: **Cash Sales, Nexus Books, Thames Wharf Studios, Rainville Road, London W6 9HA**

US customers: for prices and details of how to order books for delivery by mail, call 1-800-343-4499.

Please enclose a cheque or postal order, made payable to **Nexus Books Ltd**, to the value of the books you have ordered plus postage and packing costs as follows:

UK and BFPO – £1.00 for the first book, 50p for each subsequent book.

Overseas (including Republic of Ireland) – £2.00 for the first book, £1.00 for each subsequent book.

If you would prefer to pay by VISA, ACCESS/MASTERCARD, AMEX, DINERS CLUB or SWITCH, please write your card number and expiry date here:

....

Please allow up to 28 days for delivery.

Signature ....

Our privacy policy.

We will not disclose information you supply us to any other parties. We will not disclose any information which identifies you personally to any person without your express consent.

From time to time we may send out information about Nexus books and special offers. Please tick here if you do *not* wish to receive Nexus information. ☐

- - - - - - ✂ -